Shadow's Touch

T. M. Hart

S h a d o w S e r i e s : B o o k 2

"The wound is the place where the Light enters you."

~Rumi

4

PROLOGUE

My life was ruined at quite a young age. When I was eight years old I lost something important, something that altered the course of my life. I don't tell you this for pity or sympathy. I just want you to understand why I turned out the way I did.

CHAPTER 1

AT EIGHT YEARS OLD, I never got tired of hearing the story about the princess and the girl, especially at bedtime.

"Tell us, mama," I insisted.

Fresh out of our baths, Zagan and I were wrapped in a thick blanket sharing the rocking chair in his bedroom. My mother was fluffing the pillows on Zagan's bed, as she did every night before we climbed in.

"But you already know it by heart," she pointed out.

"Mama," I whined. I was never one for patience.

Zagan, on the other hand, had mastered patience and courtesy as well as charisma. "Please, Aunt Addie. We like it ever so much when you tell us. When you tell us stories we have pleasant dreams at night." Zagan was directing the full strength of his angelic charm at her.

She sighed. "Well if it will get you two to go to bed, then it seems I have no choice." She folded down a corner of the bedding. "Come. Get in, my little twinkle lights."

Zagan and I jumped out of the rocking chair and into the big bed. The room was dimly lit by two thick candles, one on each of the night tables. As my mother began to speak, she closed her eyes, and her elegant voice filled the room.

"Long ago in a castle far away, a princess slept in her chamber while the full moon rose outside her window. When the clock struck midnight, an angel appeared. The princess awoke and beheld the angel. Her heart soared. The angel was pure light and the most beautiful being the princess had ever seen. The princess could feel love flowing from the angel directly into her chest, filling her until she thought she would burst into a million pieces of happiness.

"When the angel spoke, she had a voice of gentle wind chimes, 'You have been chosen, princess. You will bring unto this world *The Female*. She will be a savior to the race and her union with *The Male* will ensure the strength and safety of all Radiants against the Shadows. You are true of heart and you will lead *The Female* down a virtuous path. This decree is for you alone. You may neither speak of my appearance here tonight, nor of my proclamation. If it be your will, arise and receive your blessing, knowing that you are now and forever more a servant of the race.'

"Without hesitation, the princess knelt before the angel. The angel leaned over, grasping the princess's face between her luminous hands, and gave her a gentle kiss on the lips. The princess felt a lilting euphoria as a small amount of the angel's essence rippled through her. When she rose, the angel was gone.

The princess returned to bed with a full heart, knowing the true gift of the blessing she had received.

"On that very night across the vale in a barn, a poor girl slept on her bed of straw while the same full moon rose. At midnight, an angel appeared before her as well. He too was pure light. When the girl opened her eyes and saw the angel before her, she gasped. His energy filled her, and it was bittersweet. She felt tears fall down her cheeks as her heart both swelled and broke.

"His voice was a warm wind across a valley. 'You have been chosen, girl. You will bring unto the world *The Male*. His union with *The Female* will ensure the strength and safety of all Radiants against the Shadows. However, the power which he shall behold will exceed that of a single individual. Therefore, to give him life, you will sacrifice your own. You are generous of heart and so pity shall be granted unto you. You will know the child for one year. It will be a fleeting gift of happiness, yet it will be a gift beyond any that has been bestowed upon your race. Your short time together will be a gift each unto the other. This decree is for you alone. You may neither speak of my appearance here tonight, nor of my proclamation. If it be your will, arise and receive your blessing, knowing that you are now and forever more a servant of the race.'

"The girl hesitated. She felt such love in her heart unlike any she could have ever known but also, there was such sadness.

"'My heart breaks,' she whispered to the angel.

"He looked at her with sad eyes and simply nodded.

"The girl approached the angel and kneeled before him. He leaned forward and gently kissed her lips. His kiss was a soft rain that washed away the sadness. His essence soothed her as it rippled through her body and the girl was at peace.

"Many years later, on the summer equinox, the princess and the girl gave birth at dawn. It was the longest day of the year, a day very special to those of the Light. As the sun broke over the horizon, the babes born unto the chosen did not cry as they took their first breaths. They were happy and content to greet the world. They looked around with perceptive, wondering eyes. Both the princess and the girl rocked their babes in their arms, and both the princess and the girl felt the same love and happiness which they had during a full moon, years before. There was no sadness, only joy and pure love.

"The princess and her child spent their first year together and many more living a privileged, happy life.

"The girl and her child lived together on a poor farm. Although life was hard, the girl loved and held her child each and every day. She rocked him and sang to him. The girl knew that her child was special, and she could sense the immense love that he had for her.

"When dawn broke on the summer equinox of the following year, the angel of Light came for the poor farm girl. Although it broke the girl's heart to know that she could never hold her child again or watch him grow and discover the world, she was grateful that for a time, he had been hers. She knew that in some small way, she would always be with him, and he with her.

"'Do you regret accepting your chosen role?' the angel asked her.

"'I would give so much more than my life for him, if I had any more to give,' the girl replied.

"The angel smiled at her. 'You do not realize the true magnitude of the gift that you give unto your child, but you will in time.'

"A single tear slid down the girl's cheek. 'What will happen to him?'

"'He will be safe and cared for. And you will be able to check on him now and then from the other side.'

"The girl simply nodded, and as her child slumbered in his basket, the angel wrapped his arms around the girl filling her with peace and took her to the other side."

Although the story had ended, my mother sat there for a moment with her eyes closed, still in the semi-trance she always seemed to enter when telling this story. Zagan and I waited in silence until she opened her eyes and finally spoke again.

"And so you see," my mother concluded, "the beauty of pure love is worth all costs."

Although this story was a favorite of ours, it always made Zagan sad. Like the story, Zagan and I had the same birthday, and like the story, Zagan's mother died on his first birthday.

I could feel the sorrow swirling around him. I reached over and wrapped my hand in his, resting my head on his shoulder. Zagan stared down at his lap for a few moments. Finally, he broke the heavy silence in the dark room.

"I think I would like to sleep now," he said.

My mother gave Zagan a sad smile. "As you like, brightling." She stood and held her hand out to me. "Come, dear. Let us leave our beloved Zagan in peace."

I loved Zagan. When his mother died, he had become a member of our family. I had never known a day without him, and it pained me to know that he was missing such an important part of his life. "Goodnight, Zagan," I said, kissing his cheek.

"We love you more than you could know," my mother said as she leaned over the bed to kiss his forehead.

He nodded once, then pulled the covers up to his chin as he lay down to disappear in the fluffy blankets. My mother blew out the two candles leaving the room bathed in the white moonlight which poured through the windows.

After taking my hand, my mother and I walked through the stone hall in silence. Once we reached my room, I climbed into my own bed.

"Mama?"

"Yes, my dear?"

"Why was Zagan so sad tonight?"

"You and Zagan are growing up. Zagan is realizing what it means to have lost his own mother so long ago. Growing up an orphan is not an easy loss to accept, even if one does have a loving adoptive family."

"That's us, right?"

"Yes, that is us. As much as we might love and cherish him, Zagan will mourn the loss of his own family. It is perfectly natural. All that we can do is show him love and understanding."

"I love him, mama."

"We all do. He is a very special little boy, and he will grow up to be a very special man."

"Yes, but I love him most. I'm going to marry him when I grow up," I said confidently, almost defiantly.

My mother laughed. "I have no doubt that you will do whatever you set your mind to. You are a very determined young lady. I think now, however, you should set your sights on going to sleep. You have a full day of classes tomorrow and you will need your rest."

"Yes, mama," I agreed. The sooner she was convinced that I was going to sleep, the sooner she would leave my room. Although I was quite attached to my mother and loved being in her presence, I did have somewhere I needed to be.

"I love you, my little twinkle light. You are my sun, my moon, and my stars." She squeezed me tight, kissed my forehead, and gracefully exited my room.

After waiting an appropriate amount of time, I climbed out of my bed and crossed through the hallway. I opened the door to Zagan's room as I did every night.

Although my mother went through the process of tucking us into our own beds in our own rooms, she had known that I slept with Zagan each night, as there is where she found me every morning. When I slept next to Zagan, I felt a sense of peace and satisfactory wholeness.

"I want to be alone," he said as I entered the room.

I padded up to his bed and climbed in, snuggling into the thick blankets and yawning. I reached out my hand and let it rest next to him. Sometime later, I drifted off to sleep; but just before I did, I felt a small warm hand grasp mine.

CHAPTER 2

ZAGAN WAS GONE THE NEXT DAY. Sometime in the night while he lay next to me, I had lost him.

Did you hear anything? Did you see anything? Does anything look out of place in the room? Do you have any idea where he might be?

Over and over again, I was asked questions about that night. But I had no answers. No one did.

The window was latched from the inside. The bedroom door was closed. There were no signs of an intruder. Guards had been patrolling the grounds both inside and outside the mansion. Not one had seen anything amiss. There was simply no trail to follow. No clues to piece together.

It was as if he had vanished into thin air.

And it was my fault he was gone. My fault, and mine alone. I didn't even bother to wake up in the night and save him. I would live with the empty pit this knowledge created inside of me for the rest of my life.

Zagan's departure did more than burden me with self-loathing. It left me unwhole. We had a connection. He was my friend. And when I lost that connection, I lost an integral part of myself, of my *soul*.

But the strangest aspect of Zagan's disappearance was the ring. A large glittering diamond ring had been placed on the empty pillow next to me. Zagan's pillow.

When I first spied it, I believed it was a gift from Zagan. An apology for the previous night. The sunlight pouring in through the windows caused the ring to sparkle unlike anything I had ever seen before. In complete awe, I reverently picked it up.

It was too large for any of my fingers. Even when I placed it on my thumb it left a gaping space between the band and my flesh. As a result, the diamond continually rotated inward and down so that it sat in the palm of my hand.

In the aftermath when it was discovered that Zagan was gone, I kept the ring a secret, my little fist closed around it. I believed it was a gift from Zagan and I did not want it taken from me. My intuition told me the only way I would keep my beautiful gift was if I told no one of it. As a small girl who had just lost her best friend, it was a memento to cling to.

Prior to Zagan's loss, I had been instructed in ballet, music, and the equestrian arts—as you might expect any typical princess to be. After he was taken from us, my lessons were replaced with weapons training and physical combat. I learned to wield swords and bows. I was taught various martial arts by the highest grandmasters of the Light, and even street fighting skills by some of the most deplorable and villainous members from society's underground.

By the time I was sixteen, I began training with the elite special forces unit within the Radiant military. My training was kept secret and only those who taught and sparred with me knew of my lethal studies. Not even my parents were aware of my involvement.

And that's how I became immersed in the secret battles that took place at night. The one which no one ever spoke of. The true war that was taking place right under our noses.

***

His hot breath panted in my ear. I could feel his lips against my lobe. He had one arm snaked around my waist and the other around my neck. I was pinned to his body and could feel his erection straining against my backside.

"I'm going to make you scream, little girl. You never should have come out to play with the big boys. I'm going to fuck you for hours."

It was difficult to speak since his forearm was crushing my windpipe, but I was able to gasp a few words out. "There's just one thing I need to do first."

"Oh yeah? What's that?"

"Shove your tiny dick up your ass!"

I realize that wasn't the most lady-like of things to say, especially from a princess who grew up with culture and etiquette standards, but, I mean, come on . . . the guy had it coming.

In that instant I yanked away from the Shadow as hard as I could. He jammed my body against his as I expected, and I changed my momentum to force myself back into him. He flew off balance and we tumbled backwards. I continued to roll until I was able to jack up onto my feet, and I slammed the stiletto heel of my boot into his neck while he was still sprawled on the ground. At the same time, I threw two knives unerringly into each of his palms, pinning his arms against the ground.

Killian and Watts came running up behind me and then slowed as they approached.

"Damn, Violet. You're cold."

"This is how my date, here," I kicked the Shadow in the ribs, "and I like it." I took a step back, removing my boot heel from the Shadow's neck. "Although I did jump the gun a little and skip the love making he promised me."

Killian let out a vicious snarl, bending down and picking up the Shadow by his bleeding neck. The knives impaling his palms were pulled free from the ground as he was hoisted into the air.

"You thought to touch her? I am going to gut you and then play with your insides while you watch!"

The Shadow's eyes rounded in fear and pain, but before Killian could make good on his promise, the Shadow's whole body spasmed. A flare of Light pulsed through him and then he went limp.

Killian let the body drop to the ground. "Fuck, Watts! Why did you do that?"

Watts had used a special kind of knife infused with Light to stab the Shadow in the back while Killian had had him hoisted in the air. It was one of the few ways to kill the enemy race we fought.

"Because you were about to play doctor with the piece of shit and we don't have time for that."

I shoved them both against their chests, first Watts then Killian. "I told you assholes I had him. I don't need you to rush in and save me. If anyone should be watched over it's you two. I'm a better fighter than both of you combined."

I yanked my throwing knives out of the Shadow's hands, wiping the blades against my thighs and began to stalk off down the dark empty street. But as I turned a corner I could hear Watts grumbling, "Oh for fuck's sake! Yes, Kil. Go. I'll take care of all this shit."

A moment later Killian was jogging up behind me. "Violet, wait." He gently grabbed my arm. I didn't stop walking, but I also didn't bat his hand away.

"What is it, Killian?" I was weary. I didn't want to get into with him, but I also didn't want to dismiss him.

"Will you stop walking for just a minute. Please?"

He was my friend. My only friend. If it had been anyone else, I would have knifed him. But for Killian, I stopped.

He stood close to me—*too close*. I had to look up to meet his striking gaze.

"I'm sorry. I don't doubt you or your ability. I know how extremely competent you are. You're right. You don't need us. But I'm your personal guard. I take that seriously. All day long it's my job to protect you and it's not easy to ignore that commitment just because the sun has set."

He paused seeming to be searching for the right words. Grasping my upper arms, he pulled me closer to him until our bodies were almost brushing. "Goddamnit, you know how much I care about you."

His clear green eyes smoldered with intensity. God, he was attractive. More than attractive. He was any woman's dream. His golden-brown hair was a shade women coveted. At well over six feet tall he could make a woman feel feminine and petite. And his incredible body with well packed muscles which would make that same woman feel protected and secure.

His face was boyishly handsome, but what was even more alluring was the open honesty apparent there. He was a good, decent male that you could trust.

I softened towards him. I hated hurting him. Hated that I couldn't meet his intensity and desire. I hated that all I could offer him was friendship.

"Killian." It was a plea.

"No." He moved a hand up to cup my cheek. "I can be good to you. I can make you happy. There's nothing I won't do for you. There's nothing I won't give to you. But you have to give us a chance." His gaze moved to my lips and he spoke as if to himself. "I just have to make you see."

I didn't stop him. I desperately wanted to feel something for him. Maybe he was right. Maybe I had to give it another chance.

His kiss was gentle, coaxing. It was as if he didn't want to frighten me away. I could feel the hunger and ferocity churning just below the surface, but he held back. His lips brushed over mine with the softest pressure while his hand caressed my neck.

He left a sliver of empty space between us instead of crushing my body into his, which was what I knew he longed to do.

When I took that one little step into him and kissed him back, wrapping my arms around his neck, he let out a deep groan. The leash he had on his impulses snapped. He pushed me back against the brick wall of the alley, caging me in with his large body.

He placed his hard thigh between my legs applying deliberate pressure right at my core. The center of my low-cut halter was shoved to one side, freeing my breast to the cool night air. He placed his rough hand over it, rubbing his thumb across the nipple.

With his other hand, he freed my hair from the long braid I wore while fighting, before running his fingers through it. Then he caressed my throat, jaw, and cheek. All the while his hot, wet tongue delved into my mouth over and over again with an insatiable hunger.

Any normal woman would have reached down to rip open his fly and release his straining erection, wanting to stroke him into such a lather that he shoved down her pants and thrust into her mercilessly. Any normal woman . . . but not me.

I felt no building lust. No throbbing ache at my center. No mindless need to have him. Just . . . nothing. Not even the slightest flicker of desire spread through me. I knew it was futile.

I thought about continuing with him anyway. I so badly wanted to give him what he sought. I truly cared for him and wanted to give him the happiness he deserved. Maybe I could just go along with it for his benefit. So what if I didn't feel desire for him on my end? He clearly felt it enough for the both of us.

But I realized that wouldn't be fair to him. I knew him well enough to know he would not want anything less than full and utter surrender. He deserved nothing less than to be worshiped and appreciated. A pity fuck would be the worst kind of insult I could bestow on a strong proud male like him.

I pulled my lips from his and rested my forehead against his chest. Killian slowly removed his hands from me and disentangled his leg. He rested his fists against the brick along either side of my head and bent his head down to bury his face in my hair.

His voice was raw and his breathing short and rapid. "Violet?"

I didn't know what to say. I shook my head against his chest.

I wanted to cry. I knew I wouldn't. I never cried, but I wanted to. The old familiar disappointment and confusion flooded my emotions. My shoulders shuddered from the sob I swallowed.

"Hey." Killian gripped my chin forcing me to look up at him. He searched my eyes with such concern. After a moment, he let go to discreetly adjust my top so that I was no longer exposed before wrapping his arms around me and pulling me into his chest. He rested his cheek on the top of my head. "I'm sorry. I lost control. It won't happen again. I promise we'll go slower next time. I'm . . . I'm so sorry."

I pulled back to look up at him. The guilt and shame on his face was too much to bear. "Killian, no. It wasn't that. You didn't scare me. I—"

I took a deep breath. "I scared myself. There's something wrong with me."

"Violet, there is nothing wrong with you. You are perfect."

"Killian listen to me." I pulled out of his embrace to side step away and lean back against the wall while I stared at the ground. I was embarrassed to meet his eyes. "I am incapable of those feelings. I don't know why, but I can't get . . . *aroused.*"

My cheeks flared with heat at the humiliating confession. After no response from Killian, though, I chanced a glance up at him.

He had a slight smile on his lips and was looking at me like I had said something cutely naive.

"It isn't a joke," I snapped.

His expression turned serious. "Of course not. But Violet I lost control just now and was pawing at you like some feral animal after you were attacked mere moments ago by a filthy night-walker who said vile things to you. It's understandable that you weren't turned on by my advances."

He reached over and tucked a strand of hair behind my ear, his voice softening. "Let me take you home. I'll draw up a warm bath for you in front of a nice fire. I'll have dinner brought in. I need to get you cleaned, warmed, and fed." He took my hand, twining his fingers in mine. "I need to lay you down in my bed and take things slowly. To treat you the way you deserve."

His thumb brushed over the back of my hand in soft strokes. I wished it was that simple. But this was an issue that I had been dealing with for years.

"Killian, that won't change anything. I honestly am not capable of becoming aroused."

"Violet, look at me." He curled his finger under my chin, tilting my head up. "You are capable of it. You just need to have the right circumstances and the right male. Let me take you home. I'll show you."

I turned my head away from him, "No, I'm not. Trust me, I know what I'm talking about. Even when alone, I can't . . ."

Killian straightened. "So maybe you have some intimacy issues. It doesn't mean there's something wrong with you. It just means you need to take things slow with someone you trust." His voice grew gravelly and almost pained. "I want you. You know I want you, but I will wait for however long you need."

I let out a sigh. He would be waiting forever. But I didn't tell him that. Killian was and would always be a knight in shining armor. It was just his way. I knew there was nothing I could tell him that would sway him from his belief that we would end up together. So, I let it drop for the time being.

I cleared my throat. "Thanks, Kil." I gave him a quick hug. It was the awkward kind, where you stick your butt out to make sure that your lower halves don't touch. Killian, however, would have none of that and pressed me flush against him in a tight embrace. When he finally let go, I told him I was leaving.

"Let me drive you home," he said falling into pace with me.

"No, really it's alright. I'm fine."

"Look, you'll be doing me a favor. I drove in with Watts. The last thing I want to do is sit with him while he rails at me for losing my shit over you with that night-walker."

I felt Killian's leather coat drape over my shoulders. It rankled. I hated being coddled. But it was Killian, so I took a deep breath and let it go.

Like I said, though, if it had been anyone else, I would have knifed him.

"Besides, I feel like a complete tool for what just happened. If we leave things the way they are I am going to feel awful all night.

At least let me drive you home. It will make things seem a little more back to rights."

We had arrived to where my black Maserati was parked. I just wanted to be alone. And I wanted to drive my own fucking car. But I wordlessly tossed Killian my keys. He followed me to the passenger door and opened it for me. It took everything I had not to snap at him. Don't get me wrong there is a time and a place for chivalrous acts. But this wasn't what I wanted.

I wanted Killian to accept there never was and never would be an *us*. I wanted to continue being his friend without hurting him. I wanted him to treat me the way he did every other member of our special forces unit. He had to stop treating me like I was his female.

For the time being, I held it all in. I wanted to give him what he needed, and if doting on me would help him cope with the night's events, then I would keep my mouth shut.

Once we had taken off, Killian called Watts. "Don't wait around for me. I'm taking Violet home." He hung up before Watts could respond. His phone began to ring immediately, but he silenced it.

I knew it was Watts. Watts wasn't quite as tall as Killian, but he was wider, bulkier, stacked with hard muscles. With his shaggy white blond hair and broad planes of his face, he looked like some virile Norse god. And I knew if he had the abilities of a Norse god, he would strike me down where I sat. Plain and simple, he didn't like me.

Although he never admitted it to me, he blamed me for Killian's unrequited love. Whether he had an issue with me not returning Killian's feelings or he thought I was leading Killian on,

I didn't know. And really it didn't matter. The point was, in his eyes, I was hurting Killian.

Watts was fiercely loyal to Killian. They were partners in our unit. When we went out to hunt at night, it was always in pairs. I was the one and only exception. I fought alone. It was the only way I agreed to fight. It was yet another reason for Watts (and basically all the men in our unit aside from Killian) to dislike me.

I wasn't technically a member of the unit at all. Our operative leader, Anders, trained and recruited members of our covert fighting squad. Since I had been training with him from the time I was sixteen, he knew very well how capable I was having witnessed my abilities over the last twelve years.

However, as the heir to the throne, my parents and pretty much everyone in the royal court would have lost their shit if they knew I was out battling Shadows at night.

My parents believed that I spent my evenings "working out," which is what I told them. It wasn't a complete lie. I was, in a sense.

Killian glanced over at me. "Is that why you train so much? To relieve pent up tension?"

I couldn't help but let out a laugh. "I don't know. Maybe. I'd never thought about it."

At my laugh, Killian's attractive face broke out into a smile. It was incredibly sexy on him. Even I could recognize that. I sighed, wishing again that I could feel something beyond friendship for him.

"Killian, you should take the day off tomorrow. Go out. Have fun. You need a break. Alexander can fill in for you and babysit me all day."

The charming smile faltered. "Do *you* want me to take the day off? I understand if after what happened tonight, you don't want to see me."

"No, that's not it at all. I just . . . you're by my side every single day all day long and then out chasing Shadows all night. You don't have any time in your life to socialize and meet people." By *people* I meant women, and he knew it.

He reached over and grasped my hand in his big warm one. "I meant what I said before. I'm not going anywhere, Vi."

"Thank you for your support. I appreciate it. I really do. But I can't give you anything more than friendship, Killian. And I honestly don't believe that will ever change. I'm afraid that you're not accepting that."

He gave my hand a squeeze before bringing it up to his mouth for a kiss. "I understand."

I turned away to rest my hand against the window and peer up into the night sky. He clearly didn't.

As we approached the front of the mansion, where my family resided, firelight was ablaze in the first floor sitting room. It was odd that a formal room intended for the visitation of guests was occupied in the middle of the night. Everyone should be sleeping.

Killian and I exchanged a glance. Instead of continuing to my private wing around the side of the estate, he parked the car at the grand entrance and got out with me.

"I just want to make sure everything is all right," he said by way of explanation.

I didn't expect anything less from ever dutiful Killian. As my personal guard, he was as involved with my family as anyone could be. So, we walked inside together.

Had I known what was waiting for me, though . . . I would have run.

CHAPTER 3

WE ENTERED TO FIND MY PARENTS, the P.R. representative for the royal court, my mother's personal advisor, and the ambassador for the Council of Elders all meeting with *a Shadow*.

Killian immediately put his arm across my chest, halting my steps.

The stranger was well dressed in an expensive tailored suit. He was impeccably groomed and sat with graceful manners, balancing a teacup and saucer on one knee. Although he was not dressed for fighting and did not have the stink of aggression wafting around him the way those we usually fought in the night did, he was still a Shadow. He could not hide the telling signs of his fair skin, black hair and grey eyes behind an air of refinement.

As all conversation ceased, he looked up at Killian and me with a genial smile.

"Violet," my mother said with surprise, "you're home early."

My father stepped up behind her to place his hand on her shoulder. "It's all right, Adriel. She should be here for this."

"Davis, I don't think—"

"She should be allowed to make up her own mind, love." He gestured to the open couch. "Violet, Killian, won't you please sit?"

When my mother opened her mouth to object once more, my father said, "He's her personal guard. He should be aware of the situation at hand. And he is trustworthy. Killian will not repeat what he hears tonight."

My mother's eyes widened as she looked at me, and I realized I hadn't changed my clothes. Usually when I returned home from my nightly activities, I went straight into my own private wing of the manor without being observed. Fortunately for me, she decided not to say anything about my skin-tight leather in front of all her guests. At least I had had the good sense to quickly secure my tousled hair into a simple braid before we had entered.

Once we had all settled in, my father introduced the Shadow. "Violet, Killian, this is Barrister Corbett. He is here on behalf of the Shadow Court. We have been discussing how to find an accord between our two races. It seems that both the Radiant and the Shadow Court wish for peace."

I let out a disbelieving snort at that.

"Violet!" My mother's tone was mixed with embarrassment and censure.

I turned to the Shadow. "Barrister Corbett, I apologize for my outburst."

He inclined his head. "No need to apologize, your highness. I understand that such a declaration might sound disingenuous. It is hard to overlook the long standing . . . *history* between our two courts. I am also aware that certain splinter cell organizations have terrorized your lands and aggressed your people as of late with a renewed fervor. Part of the reason for my visit is to alert the Radiant Court of our desire to work together in disassembling and eradicating these rogue factions."

Killian leaned forward. "Rogue factions? They aren't operating under the instruction and support of the Shadow Court?"

"No. For some time, the Shadow Court has been without a ruler, and parliament officials have been running the Dark Nation, or rather letting the Dark Nation run itself. Our society was crumbling under the absence of a monarch. That is part of the reason for my visit here this night. As I have informed my gracious hosts earlier," he inclined his head towards my parents, "the one true heir has been found. The Shadow Prince is finally seated at the Dark Throne."

"It was my understanding that the bloodline was lost eons ago. How could your people be certain of a rightful heir after so much time?" Killian interjected.

"He bears *The Mark*. It is certain." Barrister Corbett's tone was grave.

I was somewhat aware of that which the barrister spoke. It was believed in Shadow lore that their true prince would one day return to lead their people from the darkness. He would be identified by *The Mark*, although I didn't know specifically what that was supposed to be. I was tempted to ask the barrister, but his grey eyes found mine and his already serious air grew more intense.

I fought the urge to shiver. Something was going on. There was a nervous tension permeating the room. Whatever it was, my parents and the others already knew, and I had a feeling I was about to find out.

The barrister placed his saucer and teacup on the coffee table before capturing my gaze once more. "Your grace, The Shadow Prince proposes a union between the Light and Dark Courts. A gesture to the people of both races. One of goodwill and unity. A conclusion to the unending strife between our peoples. And through this union, he desires to enter into a new era of peace and prosperity for both our lands." He paused, looking at me expectantly.

When I didn't respond, Killian asked in halting words, "What exactly are you saying, barrister?"

My heart had begun to beat rapidly, and my palms had turned clammy. I was afraid I knew precisely what he was saying, and it terrified me.

Barrister Corbett reached into his jacket pocket and pulled out a small black box. He pulled back the lid and set it on the coffee table in front of me.

"You can't be serious!" Killian lost his composure, whipping up from the couch and turning to my parents. "As Violet's personal guard and head of her security, I request permission to remove this Shadow from the manor grounds at once."

My father was the one to respond. "As Violet's personal guard and head of her security, you will act as such—with detached logic and reasoning, leaving any personal feelings and bias out of this. The barrister is our guest and you will treat him as one."

35

My eyes had not left the box in front of me. I was horrified and transfixed by what I saw. Nestled in the black velvet was what I knew to be an engagement ring.

An oversized black cushion cut diamond sparkled and reflected the firelight from its many facets. Although the stone was obsidian, it seemed to have an inner luminescence, creating a mesmerizing shimmer. It was surrounded by white diamonds and mounted on a thin simple band.

"You cannot seriously be considering this," Killian insisted.

My father placed his hand on my shoulder from where he stood to the side of the couch. "You are correct. We are not considering this proposal, as it is not our decision to make. Violet is an adult. She will be the one to consider and then accept or reject the offer."

When I was finally able to tear my gaze away from the hypnotic black diamond, I looked around the room at all the individuals gathered there. Everyone was motionless, staring at me.

I turned back to the barrister. "Why?" It was all I could manage.

"Officially speaking as a representative for the Dark Throne, we wish for peace and unity." He leaned forward. "However, if I may speak candidly and off the record for a moment, our society is in turmoil. The Dark Prince must take bold actions to rally allegiance and cooperation. If you agree to this accord, many will see their prince as one who is powerful and bold. If he is able to make the Princess of Light, his consort—a feat seemingly impossible—there will be little he cannot do in the eyes of our people."

"This could all be a trap. A way for the Shadows to get a hold of our princess," Killian bit out.

Barrister Corbett inclined his head. "Yes. That is true. I doubt there is anything I could say or do to convince you of the sincerity of this offer. It is, if you will, a leap of faith on your part. However, the Princess of Light will be allowed to bring whatever and whomever she likes, whether it be a chest full of weapons or a brigade of soldiers. The only stipulation the Shadow Prince has placed is that she is to reside at the Dark Manor. Though, she will have her own, private quarters there."

I turned to the Elder Council representative, "And what do the Elders have to say of this?"

He replied in an ancient, hollow voice. "They are in support of this union."

Killian made a frustrated groan.

I finally looked at him. "It's all right, Kil. I can handle this."

He stabbed a hand through his hair and stood. "If it pleases your grace, I will wait in the hall to accompany you to your chambers when your meeting is through."

He needed a minute. I think we all did. I nodded to him and he exited the sitting room.

I turned back to Barrister Corbett. "I accept."

My mother let out a gasp. "Violet, I believe it would be wise for you to take your time in considering this offer."

"Mother, if there is even the slightest chance this proposal is legitimate, I have to accept. I have seen firsthand the hardships, injuries, and loss of life our people have endured because of the ongoing contention with the Shadows. If I can do something to help bring an end to this warfare, I must."

The firelight in the room flickered, betraying her emotions, but in a calm voice, she said, "I understand. You wear your crown well, my dear." She looked around the room, "Now if you will all excuse me, I wish to check upon the princess's guard." As the queen of the kingdom, she did not wait for a dismissal. She simply strode out with her head held high.

Killian was like family and it didn't surprise me in the least that my mother was concerned for him. I think on some level she knew of his feelings for me. While she was dignified and austere in her day to day countenance, she was loving and caring with her family behind closed doors.

All eyes in the room went back to the barrister once my mother exited the room. When no one else uttered an objection, the barrister stood. "Then it is done. I will return to the Shadow Court at once to relay the good news." He bowed to me. "Congratulations your grace. I believe you have made a wise and goodly decision. I will have the marriage papers drawn up and sent to you."

And just like that, he left.

The room was silent. No one moved. My eyes traveled back to the coffee table. That luminous diamond sat glittering in its case like a silent black heart.

***

Killian was tense and silent as he walked with me to my quarters. When we finally reached the entry way he held the door open for me and allowed me to pass through first. I sensed his intention just an instant too late. Because before I had time to react . . . *Killian snapped my neck.*

CHAPTER 4

"YOU SON OF A BITCH!"

I sat in the middle of Killian's bed rubbing my mending neck. Although I had never been in his bedroom, let alone his residence, his scent was all over the unmade bed, which told me it was his. "I'm going to nail your balls to the wall."

"I needed to get you out of there and I knew you wouldn't cooperate. Temporarily subduing you was my only option." The bastard didn't have an ounce of remorse in his words. He didn't even bother to glance at me. He just went about his business stuffing items into a military backpack.

"So you snapped my neck and *killed* me?!"

"Don't be so dramatic Violet. You're immortal. It was a little nap."

"Okay. Who are you and what have you done with my friend?" Just a couple hours earlier he had been guilt-ridden when he thought he had overstepped his bounds. Yet here he was, completely unrepentant and even borderline callous.

"I'm acting under orders. This is for your own good, Vi. You get very stubborn when you make a decision and you would have made a huge mistake if we didn't intervene."

"*We*? Who's *we*?"

Killian didn't answer, but he didn't need to.

"My mother," I muttered.

"She's right, Vi. We need to keep you safe until we can take out this *prince*."

"Okay. First of all, I am an adult and I do not need my mommy siccing her lapdog on me to hole me up in his dog house."

Speaking of the lapdog's house, I took a good look around the space realizing how skewed our relationship was. Although Killian was my personal guard in an official capacity, he was also my best friend. He had spent countless hours over the years in my home, my personal quarters, and even my bedroom. The fact that I was now in his personal space for the first time in the history of our relationship was startling.

Clearly, I had passed the night healing from my neck injury as the late morning sunlight poured through the bay window. Since the sun was the direct energy source for our powers, all Radiant dwellings had oversized windows, French doors, and glass walls wherever architecturally possible and Killian's room was no different.

It was a decent size and fairly in order, apart from the unmade bed and a few clothes thrown over a chair. The furniture was modern and nice without being fancy. It basically looked like it could have been featured in the pages of a home store catalog, except for one corner of the room.

An art table was littered with charcoal sticks and drawing papers. Some papers were blank, some depicted unfinished works, some completed drawings. There were portraits, landscapes, and even floral subjects. Each one was so realistic that if not for the drawing tools I would have sworn they were black and white photographs.

One particular portrait made me hitch in a breath. On the floor, next to the drawing table, a sketch sat propped in the corner of the room isolated from all the others. A woman had her face tilted up and to the side. Her delicate, feminine features highlighted. Long ribbons of her dark hair danced around her shoulders and face, swept by the wind. The corners of her lips were slightly upturned in an unassuming smile. She seemed to be basking in some basic glory.

Even with her eyes closed, I knew who it was. I knew beneath those lids were violet eyes. I was stunned silent for a moment. All I could do was try and process the feelings the portrait stirred in my chest.

When I was finally able to tear my gaze away from the drawing and look at Killian, I was surprised at the fire I found. I was expecting him to be contrite or embarrassed, maybe even a little wounded. Instead what I found was a resolved male who would not deny his feelings or apologize to anyone for them.

"Is that how you see me?"

"Yes. Always."

Something slipped down my cheek. When I patted my hand to my face, it came back wet. A tear. I had shed a tear. "Thank you."

I know it might seem like an odd or even awkward response, but when you receive a glimpse of the way someone sees you and it is so truly beautiful in spirit, in a way in which you could never see yourself, what can you do but make an offering of gratitude.

He nodded once. "I didn't mean to upset you."

"I'm not. I'm ... honored. And although mere words are an insignificant gesture in comparison, I think you are a male rare in your value of worth."

Killian gave one more nod and then let out a heavy breath before resuming his packing. "You didn't think so a moment ago, Vi."

"You. Broke. My. Neck."

"Yeah well, I believe you just referred to me as your mother's *lapdog*, so how about we call it even."

"Fine. But really, Killian, this is ridiculous. How exactly is kidnapping me going to solve things."

"Number one, this isn't my plan. It's your mother's. I'm just following orders. And if I happen to wholeheartedly agree, well that's just a bonus. And two, I am not kidnapping you. I am simply taking you to a secure location out of reach of any Shadows."

"And if I refuse?"

Killian threw the bag he was packing to the ground and gave me a look I had never seen before. "You'll die, Violet. You'll fucking die. Do I really need to spell this out for you? This ... *marriage proposal*," he spat. "It's a trap. It's so obvious. Do you really not see that? Are you really that blind?"

"Is it, Killian? Is it a trap? Or is it an *opportunity*?"

Killian looked around the room as if to find who I was talking to. "What are you talking about?!"

I stood up and crossed to him. "Think about it. This is our chance to finally put an end to this war."

Killian grabbed my arms. "Are you listening to me? It's a ploy, Vi. They will kill you."

"Not if I kill them first."

He pointed a finger at me. "You're certifiable." He looked around. "Let me find a recording device. That right there is probably enough to have you committed."

"Killian, listen to me. They think they're getting a privileged, little princess. They don't know what I do. What I'm capable of. Once the marriage is official, I take out the Dark Prince and this war is over."

Killian didn't bother with a reply. He simply went back to packing. "I grabbed a few things from your room last night. There are fresh clothes in your bag as well as some toiletries. The bathroom is in the hall, if you'd like to take a moment before we leave."

There was no point in arguing with him. I picked up my bag and headed out of the room. I walked straight down the hallway and opened the front door. A blast of energy came hurtling behind me, slamming the door shut.

"You passed the bathroom," Killian said.

I turned around. "I'm leaving," I told him.

"I'm afraid I can't let you do that, Vi."

I laughed. "What are you going to do? Fight me?"

He stalked towards me. His green eyes bored into mine. "There is nothing I won't do to keep you safe."

45

"You don't get to make these decisions for me, Kil."

"I'm not. I am following orders from the ruler of the Radiant Court."

I looked around his place. It was nice. I knew he had been orphaned as a child, and I knew he had worked hard for everything he possessed. The last thing I wanted was to destroy his home, which is what would happen if we got into it here.

Killian was an excellent fighter. One of the best. But I was better. The only reason he had gotten the upper hand on me the previous night was because I trusted him implicitly. I hadn't been expecting an attack.

I played out what would happen in my head. I'd insist I was leaving. Killian would try to stop me. We would spar. His place would be wrecked, and in the end, he would lose. Then he would have to report his failure to my mother.

I didn't want to do that to him.

I dropped my bag by the front door and went to peruse the living room.

Nice. Neat. Flooded with sunlight.

I made my way into the kitchen and stopped when I saw the bar top counter. A decadent stack of strawberry pancakes sat atop a neatly arrange table setting.

The son of a bitch had made me pancakes.

I veered over to the freezer, and my hunch paid off. I found a chilled bottle of vodka. After grabbing the bottle and shutting the door, I rummaged around and found a couple shot glasses. Then I plunked myself down onto the bar stool and poured two shots.

"It's eleven o'clock in the morning, Vi. What are you doing?"

I downed one of the shots and gave the other a nudge. "It's practically the afternoon," I told him.

"We need to leave," Killian pushed.

I gave the shot glass a second nudge. "I know. We will." I poured another shot for myself and downed it.

"Violet. Now is not the time for this."

I slowly rolled my head from one side to the other, testing just how tender it was. I even closed my eyes and stroked my collar bone while my hair swished across my back. "My neck is still in a lot of pain," I sighed.

He swore and crossed to sit on the adjacent bar stool, downing the shot I had poured for him and placing his head in his hands. "I'm so sorry. I feel awful for hurting you."

I felt bad for playing on his guilt, but I needed him to listen to me.

I put my hand on his shoulder, making sure to avoid his back. Killian had two long scars running down each side of his spine. And no matter how much time passed, they were always sensitive.

I had questioned him once on how they had come to be, but he didn't know. He said he had had them for as long as he could remember. And being orphaned, he didn't have anyone he could ask.

"Hey. You were protecting me," I told him. "I appreciate the lengths you go to. I'm incredibly lucky to have you watching out for me." I held my breath, afraid I was laying it on too thick. But Killian turned his head to me and flashed a tight smile.

I sighed—genuinely sighed.

That golden-brown hair. Those piercing green eyes. My god, even with a ghost of a smile his dimples were apparent. But more than anything was his genuine character—he was such a good person.

What was wrong with me?

I tried desperately, for what seemed like the thousandth time, to feel something for him then. I willed myself to want him, to feel some kind of attraction. But all I had for Killian was a sisterly type of love and appreciation. And I knew it would never be anything more.

I poured another shot for each of us and clinked my glass to his, downing the shot. No longer trying to butter him up, I was sincere with what I told him next.

"Killian, you are the noblest, most decent male I know."

He ran a hand through his hair and shook his head. "Vi, I'm not."

I held my hand up to silence him, but he took it in his own and brought it to his heart. "If you had any idea how close I've been to . . . how many times I've almost tried to force you to love me. This plan of your mother's . . . I was more than happy to follow it through. It was what I've always wanted to do, and now I've been given permission to carry it out."

He let out a heavy exhale. "But it's not the way I want to begin something with you. And Violet, you have to understand—we all love and care about you. There's no way we can send you off to the Shadow Court."

"Killian, I have a plan."

"No—"

"I'm not going to just bust in there, guns blazing. I'm going to learn, observe. I'm going to know everything about this guy—where he goes, what he does, who he trusts. I'll bide my time.

And once I know everything there is, I'll know what I need to do."

Killian ran his hand through his hair again. Clearly frustrated. The muscles in his arm and shoulder bunched and flexed with the movement. "Even if you are successful, and that's a big *if*, it will be too obvious. They'll know it was you. They're not going to let you get away with it."

"So I won't let them know it was me."

Killian threw his hands up in the air. "We're immortals, Vi! It's not like you can make it look like an accident."

"I'll frame someone else. There are tons of other groups who are fearful of this guy or afraid of what his rise to power will mean. I take him out and then it looks like it was the dragons, or the shifters—heck, maybe I can get a banshee to sing for him. Whatever. Once I know more, I'll figure it out.

"Then, as his widow, and the ruler of the Shadow Court, I pardon the offense. I make some big statement about how the fighting and killing must stop. How I am choosing not to retaliate in an attempt to finally put a rest to the warfare between immortals. I'll call upon other leaders for peace and finality.

"His death will be mourned and respected. His people will see that he gave the ultimate sacrifice for them and their well-being . . . Like I said, I'll figure out the details, but you get the idea."

"There are so many things that could go wrong with that plan. No. Just, no."

"Killian, why do you fight every night? Why do you guard me every day? You care about your race. You care about others. You feel that you are capable of defending those who cannot defend themselves."

I took his hand in mine, once again. "You are noble and courageous. Please. Allow me to try to be the same."

He eyed me for a long moment before squeezing my hand in his big warm one. "I go with you, and I go first. I'll take a team with me and we will scope out the Dark Manor, as well as the route there."

I tried to play on his sense of honor and duty. "The Radiant Court needs you, as well as every other team member the squadron has. Your people *need* you. It doesn't make sense to risk others. I need to do this alone."

He began to shake his head.

"Look. Killian. I get it. It's very possible—actually likely—that I won't make it through this. But I *have* to try. We will never have a chance like this again."

Killian didn't acknowledge my plea. Instead he made one last ditch attempt to change my mind, his words desperate. "Come away with me. Not because of any of this. But for us. Let me be enough for you. We can leave right now. I have a penthouse in New York. We can get lost in a sea of mortals for a while. Or we can go to the Caribbean and lounge on the beach for a few weeks. I will forsake everyone else for you."

I looked at him then. Really looked at him. And I hated myself for what I was doing to him. But for whatever reason, I knew my destiny was not with him. And I also suspected that somewhere deep inside, he knew that his was not with me.

I leaned forward and gently grasped his face in my hands, placing a light kiss on his lips. And knowing I was breaking his heart, I sadly whispered, "No, Killian . . . you won't."

CHAPTER 5

TRUE TO HIS WORD, Barrister Corbett returned with papers the next evening. I signed them, and that was it. One night I had been out fighting Shadows, and the next, I was married to their prince.

We arranged to have a transitional meeting, wherein a contingent of guards from the Radiant Court would escort me to a neutral location. I would then be entrusted to a contingent of guards from the Shadow Court who would take me to the Dark Manor.

We scheduled the meeting for two nights later. I wanted enough time to get some things packed, while limiting the window of opportunity for Killian and my mother to lecture, guilt, badger, and potentially kidnap me again.

And that was how I found myself in a field at dusk. Killian, Watts, and I had been *pulsed* there by three archangels. One moment we had been in the great courtyard outside the Radiant mansion, and the next we found ourselves in this field.

A woman approached us as soon as we arrived. She was tall and toned in skintight black leather and spike heeled boots. Her dark hair was pulled off her face in a braid, highlighting her sharp features and piercing jade eyes.

I was aware we were meeting an outsider. Apparently, she knew these lands and could be trusted. But if I'm being honest . . . she was one scary bitch.

And I was jealous. *I* wanted to be the scary bitch in skintight leather, looking like I was about to lay some serious smackdown. But instead I had tried my best to look like a sweet innocent princess—chestnut hair in loose waves flowing down my back; white virginal dress that was demure yet curve hugging; and innocent doe-eyed makeup.

All stone-cold business, she said, "The location of the hand-off is fifty miles east of here. I have a vehicle which will arrive in," she glanced down at her watch, "exactly twelve point five minutes."

As if bored, the female angel replied, "Excellent. Thank you, Evelyn."

It had been decided that we would drive the last portion of the journey. If there was an ambush waiting for us, pulsing to the exact spot would be a death sentence. If we drove, we could see what we were getting into, and pulse out if necessary.

I looked around, expecting a continued discussion, but no one spoke. Killian and Watts kept twisting their necks and rolling their shoulders while checking their weapons—they were clearly expecting a fight. The blonde female angel, Daphne, was inspecting her nails with disinterest. And the brown-haired male, Cord, was standing at attention, unblinking and unmoving.

Giddeon, the leader of the archangels, kept leaning back on his heels and arching his neck, trying to check out Evelyn's leather clad butt. I couldn't understand how he had been appointed his position by the Council of Elders. I had briefly seen him around court on official business from time to time but did not know him personally. He was always forgoing the traditional white robe for casual attire.

And today was no different. Instead of wearing the ceremonial robe, the way the brown-haired angel did, or fighting attire, the way Killian and Watts did, Giddeon was wearing jeans and a t-shirt which read *JENIUS*. It didn't detract from his incredible good looks in any way, I just had a hard time taking him seriously.

As if on cue, Giddeon broke the silence. "I feel like we should all drink a special potion that makes us look like Dumbledore."

There was a palpable shift in the group dynamic. Everyone turned to look at him. He scanned our little crowd and his look of surprise turned to disbelief. "Okay. You're going to tell me that none of you have read *Harry Potter*?"

I raised my eyebrows. "You have?"

"Of course. It's only the greatest story ever told."

I shrugged. "I thought it was for kids."

G squinted his eyes at me. "You're joking, right?"

I just shrugged again.

"Wow. Ignorant. It's an incredible adventure for all ages. And by the way—you *are* a kid."

"No one turns into Dumbledore," Killian groused.

"You mean Harry," Daphne corrected.

"No," Killian insisted. "*Dumbledore*. No one drinks a special portion to look like Dumbledore."

"Not you. Giddeon. Giddeon means Harry."

"I mean Dumbledore. You know that scene where they all meet to escort—"

"It's Harry, *Jenius*!"

"You don't even know what I'm referencing!"

"Of course we do, and you've got it all wrong!"

"Shut-up, *Thor*. Go find your hammer."

"This is ridiculous. Someone pulse to get a copy of the book so we can put an end to this."

"What does it matter?"

"Oh, it matters."

"Forget the book. There are like twenty in the series. We'd have to figure out which book it's in and then find the right page. Someone pulse the author here. She'll settle this."

"With great power, comes great responsibility. We cannot simply pulse mortals at will to settle an inane—"

"Oh god, Cord. Shut it."

"Huh. I guess he can speak."

"I believe it was, in fact, Harry," said a deep voice with a cultured English accent.

Everyone turned to the speaker. Without anyone noticing, a Shadow had joined our group.

"Oh shit!" G exclaimed before drawing his sword of fire and lighting up in a brilliant flare. He pointed the tip of the sword at the Shadow's neck. "How the *fuck* did no one notice this guy?!"

G shook his head and spared a quick glance at the rest of us. "You bozos have really done it now. Oh man. When I report this to Adriel, she is not going to be happy. You poor losers are going to be on KP duty for the next thousand years. The whole reason you were all assigned this mission was to guard the princess from any and all threats. And you just let a freakin' Shadow mosey on up to her. *Pfff.* The 'best the Radiant Court has to offer,' my ass."

With his free hand, he gestured to his sword at the Shadow's neck. "You're welcome, by the way."

Daphne rolled her eyes. "Enough, Giddeon. Take his head already and let's be done with it."

"No, wait." I spoke up. "I believe this may be my escort."

"Indeed, your highness," the Shadow answered calmly. "Maxim Steel, Master-at-arms for the Dark Court, here to humbly assist you."

Without moving, he looked at the sword pointed at his neck. "It would be my custom to bow when addressing the new Princess of Shadows, but I do wish to keep my head, your highness. My sincerest apologies."

"G, put the sword down," I told him. And then I had to fight not to laugh at the exaggerated incredulity on his face.

"Are you kidding me, woman?! What the hell is this guy doing here?"

"I arranged to have him meet me here," I answered.

Killian looked furious. "That was not part of the plan."

"What the fuck kind of name is Maxim Steel? Sounds like an alias, if you ask me." Watts added.

"It is a family name with a long-standing history of honor and prestige among my people. Thank you for your interest, *Watts.*"

G's eyebrows rose even higher (which I wouldn't have thought possible) and his voice went up an octave. "Now he knows our names?"

With slightly less boredom, Daphne said, "Hmm, things just got a little more interesting."

Cord stepped forward. His broad frame was undeniable beneath the ceremonial robe. Although he was physically present, his mind seemed to be somewhere else for most of the meeting. With his size and strength, I could understand why he did not feel the need to be on high alert. He was probably a lethal weapon in his own right. And I couldn't imagine anyone being able to strike him down.

His deep voice was even and assertive. "I agree with the attractive boy," he said glancing at Killian. "This was not discussed. We shall take the Shadow's head and then continue as originally planned."

Watts slapped his big palm on Killian's shoulder. "Yeah, I also agree with the *attractive boy*." He nodded at Cord. "And the emotionally dead angel."

Killian shot him an annoyed look. Cord, on the other hand, simply nodded in a kind of satisfied agreement.

"I don't think any of that will be necessary," I told them. "G, please. The sword?"

"Nah-uh, babydoll. This is the very reason we're all here. To prevent any random attacks."

I tried a different approach. "I just told you *numb-nuts*, I arranged to have him meet me here."

"Dude! I'm going to get so much shit if he kills you. There's no way."

"G. We didn't notice him approach. He could have killed me already if he wanted to."

G finally shrugged. "It's your funeral." He extinguished the fiery sword, and the brilliant Light radiating from him dimmed.

Everyone was tense for a moment, watching for any sign of an attack from Maxim, but he simply turned towards me and gave a bow. "Your highness."

Killian put his hand on my lower back. "Okay. That's it. We tried this. It didn't work out. We're leaving."

"I will kindly ask you to remove your hand from the Princess of Shadows." Although politely delivered, Maxim's request was clearly a threat of consequence.

With a high-pitched swish of steel against leather, Killian withdrew his fighting knives in a flash . . . which caused Watts to withdraw his . . . which caused G to draw his fiery sword. And since G was the commander of the archangels, Daphne and Cord followed suit. In the end, Maxim was basically facing a small army.

To his credit, his calm demeanor was unruffled. Maxim stood his ground, back straight and head high. "Your highness. Whenever you are ready. It will be my honor to escort you to your new home."

"She's not going anywhere with you," Killian growled. "You'll probably lead her straight to her death."

"I can assure you that I have no intention of harming our new princess. In fact, I will be defending her with my life."

"He speaks the truth."

Everyone turned to look at Evelyn. Until that point, she had been silent. Now her jade eyes glowed. I shivered at the eerie sight. There was something unsettling about her.

Killian didn't seem to be bothered, though. "Even if that's true," he countered, "you could be leading her into certain death without knowing it. Any one of your people could be planning an attack against her."

"The Shadow Court has made no announcement of this union. We want the princess safely established within the Dark Manor before her new position is to be publicized. There are a scant few, whom I have selected personally, that are aware of her arrival. She will be safe. There is no threat against her."

Again, Evelyn's authoritative voice rang out. "He speaks the truth." And again, everyone turned to look at her with those jade eyes aglow.

Maxim seemed to weary of the pettiness. "And all of this should have been outlined prior to this evening."

"Yes," I spoke up. "It was." I turned to the group. "And I thought it would be better for everyone involved if Maxim and I met and traveled the rest of the way alone." I gave a pointed look at all the weapons drawn. "I thought tensions might run high if the Radiant and Shadow contingents were to meet."

Killian didn't take his eyes off Maxim. "Violet, this isn't safe."

Watts sheathed his knives and placed his palm on Killian's shoulder once more. "Come on, man. It's time to let her go," he said quietly. After no response from Killian, he darted a look at Evelyn and added, "The creepy lady says it's okay."

He took the knives from Killian and stashed them away. Then standing behind Killian, Watts took hold of his upper arm. He was keeping Killian from coming after me, and he was offering strength and support, knowing how hard this was.

I squeezed Killian's hand and gave him a kiss on the cheek. "You'll always have my love," I told him. I met his eyes and said, "I *will* see you soon."

I gave Watts a tight nod in thanks, and he nodded back.

Finally, I approached Maxim. "I'm ready. Thank you."

He gestured beyond the clearing. "I have transportation just over this hill. If you will please stay right beside me, your highness. I did surveil this area, and there are no others present. But it is best to be safe."

As Maxim and I walked away from the group, I forced myself not to look back. I knew it was what Killian was waiting for. One look from me, and he would pick me up and lock me away somewhere for the next thousand years.

My time was up.

But the last thing I heard, just before we passed over the hill, was Giddeon grumbling. "Well that was anticlimactic."

And I couldn't help but smile.

CHAPTER 6

WE DROVE FOR SOME TIME through the countryside, and I tried to mentally prepare myself for what I was about to face.

From what I knew about Shadows, they dwelled in black holes. The Dark Manor was allegedly no different. I had heard it described as a subterranean horror house.

After fighting them for years, I had yet to actually step foot in a residence of theirs. The Radiant Court was located in the Allagash, a wilderness area in Maine. Yet the Shadow Court was located south of London in the English countryside.

The Shadows we encountered were those who aggressed upon our lands. They would hunt innocent Radiants and feed from our Light.

The defense unit in which I fought was a ghost operation. Unofficial and off the books. It didn't even have a name. We simply referred to it as *The Unit*.

Our goal was simple. We would keep our people safe and protected, eradicating any guerrilla attacks before they occurred. We were so busy defending our domain that we never bothered, or much cared, to travel to their territory.

But what I truly dreaded was not the appalling abode in which I would soon reside. What I truly dreaded were the Shadows themselves. Depictions of them from our archives were seared into my mind. As a people, they were tall and thin—almost emaciated. They had ashen skin, lifeless gray eyes, and dark hair.

It was said that the Shadows would capture witches and torture them. They did this to force glamour spells from the wicca. That was why Barrister Corbett, Maxim, and those we fought appeared as attractive men. I squirmed in my seat, hoping Maxim's glamour would not fade before we arrived at our destination.

At the moment, he appeared to be in his early thirties with quite an attractive face. His features were sharp and handsomely defined. He also filled out the suit he wore, seeming to carry a good deal of muscle beneath the fabric. His dark hair and features were not unusual, but the tan tone of his skin was certainly not typical of a Shadow.

The glamour would probably hold, I reassured myself. Even after their deaths, the Shadows we hunted did not lose theirs.

Oh, god. Will I have to watch any of them eat?

I also remembered from our court reference sources that the Shadows preferred raw meat and had no problem consuming another of their kind when the opportunity arose. I turned to look out my window—revolted.

Worst of all was the Shadow Prince, himself. In the few short days since we learned of his rise to power, there had been all kinds of murmurings about the lore surrounding him. He was said to have not just ashen skin but rotting flesh and a putrid stench. In some accounts, he had horns. In others, fangs. Sometimes both.

And while he too enjoyed the flesh of his people, his favorite was babies. He liked to dine on the tender meat, and he experienced a perverse joy at desecrating such innocence.

I was admittedly horrified at the idea of residing in the Dark Manor—even if there was a personal wing provided for me. The idea of being in the same residence as such evil was sickening. And I could only imagine the hole in the ground I would be provided as living quarters.

But I meant what I had said to Killian. This was an opportunity. And I was going to take it. I wanted a chance to do something good. Something worthwhile. It was all I had in this life.

Although I was mentally steeling myself for what was to come, I had not let down my guard. I was aware of Maxim's every move, every breath, every blink. I had a dagger of Light strapped to my thigh, under my dress. One wrong move from Maxim, and I would not hesitate to end him.

I was sitting in the back seat directly behind him. It was the most advantageous spot in the SUV. My hand was clutched around the hilt of the dagger. And that was why the instant the attack happened, I was more than ready.

Our vehicle jerked violently.

I didn't hesitate. I unsheathed the dagger and flung open my door. Diving out of the car and hitting dirt, I began to roll. I had been tracking the tree line along our path. I sprang out from the tumble and began sprinting for the cover of the trees.

I knew chance was on my side. I doubted they would have expected me to make such a fast break. I would disappear into the tree line, climb one of the oak trees, and take an assessment of the situation. Again, they would probably think I was running, and not expect a counter attack as they entered the woods.

I was going to send their dark souls back to hell.

I had hoped I would at least reach the Dark Manor before they made an attempt on me. If I had made it that far, I might have had a chance of taking down the Shadow Prince. I had thought they would perhaps keep me for ransom at first. But these assholes were going straight for the kill.

I would take out whoever or whatever they had sent. It couldn't be many. They had no idea what I was capable of.

I heard Maxim shout something, probably a directive. I tried to make out his words. It would be useful to know how they were proceeding.

"Begging your pardon, your highness! If you've changed your mind, I will be happy to escort you back to the Radiant Domain!"

I scoffed. What kind of idiot did he think he was playing with?

I chanced a glance over my shoulder to survey the situation. Maxim was standing calmly beside the SUV, his hands clasped in front of him. I didn't see any other Shadows in view. I let my senses roam. I was unable to detect anyone else surrounding us. Perhaps Maxim was making the attack on his own?

Chancing a second glance over my shoulder, I saw that the paved road had ended, and our vehicle had just entered rough, rocky terrain.

The kind of terrain that would make a vehicle jerk and bounce . . .

I glanced over my shoulder again, watching Maxim. I slowed. When I saw he was not moving from his post by the driver's door, I eventually came to a stop.

Stall, I thought. I needed a minute to assess exactly what was going on. "I, ah . . . have to pee!" I called over my shoulder.

I walked the rest of the way to the tree line and slipped behind one of the large oaks. I chanced a peek around the trunk. Maxim continued to wait patiently by the SUV.

After watching him for a couple minutes, my chest began to feel tight and my cheeks hot. I realized it was possible there might not be an attack. It was possible I had overreacted. I was so on edge, so ready for a fight, that I *might* have mistaken a bump in the road for an attempt on my life.

I took a few deep breaths and began to make my way back to the vehicle, picking leaves and twigs out of my hair and trying to brush all the dirt off my dress. When Maxim saw me approaching, he opened the back door without a word.

"Small bladder," I mumbled as I climbed in.

Maxim raised his brows. "Ah," was his polite reply.

We started down the rocky path once again. Luckily, I hadn't entirely blown my cover. I had not demonstrated my fighting skills. I had only run.

But now Maxim knew I was quick and on the defensive. That wasn't good. I needed to play up the innocent princess persona. I thought about pretending to cry, but I wasn't sure I could do so convincingly.

Instead, we rode along in silence, the countryside cloaked in darkness.

It seemed that the only thing trying to creep upon us were the trees. The farther we went, the closer the tree line got. Until finally we came to a point where they had encroached upon either side of the path, creating a tree tunnel. Hundreds of oak trees grew shoulder to shoulder on each side of us, arching overhead and twining into a canopy above, effectively blocking out any light from the night sky.

They were silent sentinels in the dark. And I knew that once we passed through, there would be no turning back.

I reached for my cloak and wrapped it tight around my shoulders, slipping the dagger of Light into the pocket, but maintaining a firm hold on the hilt. We crept through the dark passageway, and as we passed tree by towering tree, I couldn't help but feel that I was being watched.

We finally reached the end of the tunnel and came to a stop. An intricate wrought iron gate, as tall and wide as the oak trees, blocked our path. Maxim waved a hand through the air and murmured something in the *Dark Tongue*—the Shadows' ancient language. The imposing gate seamlessly obeyed, slowly swinging open without disrupting the silence of the night air. An ominous welcome.

We emerged from the oak tunnel into a rolling valley surrounded by stark cliffs. On a hill, directly ahead of us, sat a dark manor with ancient stones that had blackened over time. Not even the tiniest flare of light flickered from behind the cobwebbed windows.

Yet, hanging low in the sky was a red harvest moon, looming behind the manor like an unholy halo.

We pulled up to the front door. I looked around, but I could neither see nor sense anyone on the manor grounds. If anything, the surrounding space reeked of abandonment.

Spaces that are active, that host the living, have a certain residual energy—regardless of what type of being has been there, be they Radiants or Shadows or anyone else.

This space lacked evidence of any life. There had been no activity here in . . . *ages.*

I couldn't fathom what this place was or why I had been brought here. "Where are we?" I breathed.

Maxim looked at me through the rear-view mirror, his gray eyes shimmering in the darkness. "Welcome to your new home, your highness. Welcome to the Dark Manor."

"But this is aboveground," I countered.

"Yes," he agreed, sounding confused.

"It's deserted."

Glossing over my comment, Maxim parked the vehicle and replied, "Please allow me to assist you," as he exited the SUV.

I didn't wait for Maxim. I got out on my own and stood next to the vehicle, looking up to take in the entirety of the manor. It was a dark shell which housed no life within. The grounds surrounding the front were overgrown and unkempt.

"Are you locking me away here?"

Maxim looked horrified. "Not at all. You are free to leave whenever you like. If there is somewhere you request to visit, I will take you. You need only ask."

"Does anyone live here?"

69

Maxim looked uneasy. "The prince and the Crone."

"Who?"

"Our prince," he cleared his throat, "that is to say, your groom. And the Crone. She tends to the manor." He crossed to the front entrance and opened one side of the large double doors. The ancient wood creaked on its hinges. Maxim tried to discreetly wipe away a cobweb from the casing, but it was in vain. There was no hiding the webs and grime that coated this place.

When I hesitated to enter, Maxim shook his head. "Your highness—"

I held up my hand, weary of the night's events. I had had adrenaline constantly pumping through every twist and turn of the evening. I was tapped out.

I had been expecting to arrive at the heart of the Shadow Court—some hole in the ground swarming with ghoulish looking Shadows who would try to torture me in the most gruesome of ways. I had not been expecting to arrive at an abandoned, haunted mansion in the middle of nowhere.

"Please, just call me Violet," I told Maxim.

"I don't believe that would be appropriate, your highness," he countered.

"Okay, well what if I command you to?" I asked, desperate for this night to come to an end.

Although his jaw clenched, he nodded. "Very well . . . *Violet*."

I immediately had to stop myself from laughing. Simply calling me by name seemed a certain kind of torture for him, but Maxim managed to persevere. "I understand the Dark Manor is in an unacceptable state. I did request that you be escorted to the Shadow Court instead of the manor. However, Barrister Corbett insisted the terms of the marriage agreement state you are to reside here."

"The Dark Manor is not the seat of the Shadow Court?"

"No, it has not been for many years. The court moved to London some time ago. It is where our parliament currently takes office."

"Among the mortals?" I asked in surprise.

"Yes," Maxim confirmed.

"Have you outed yourselves to them?" I was suddenly panicked. It had been agreed long ago by a council of various immortal factions that our *differences* would remain clandestine.

"No," he reassured me. "Our government operates under the guise of a private corporation."

He looked up at the façade of the manor. "I did manage to have your quarters prepared for your arrival. If you would like to follow me? It is a tad more pleasant than the exterior suggests."

I looked up at the soulless structure that was now my new home and let out a slow breath. I didn't care what Maxim said. This was clearly a grave. It was above ground, but it was somewhere to bury me away, alone and forgotten.

If he spoke the truth, though, if the Shadow Prince did in fact reside here, well that was all that mattered.

I turned to Maxim. "Please, lead the way."

The interior was dark, lit only by the moonlight which poured in through the open door.

"Maxim, may we have some light?" I asked.

"Yes, of course, your . . . *Violet*. Allow me to—"

"I'll take care of it," I told him. I sent a pulse of energy to the chandelier overhead. Two dozen candles flared to life.

71

Chandeliers lined the long foyer in each direction. One after the other sprang to life until the space was bathed in the warm glow of light from above.

I was startled at what I found. The interior was quite opulent. Marble, mahogany, and crystal filled the space. It was all buried under dust and cobwebs, but this had once been a grand setting.

"Your quarters are this way." Maxim took me up several flights of stairs until we reached the fifth floor. I lit chandelier after chandelier along the way and found more of the same—dust and cobwebs covering abandoned, forgotten luxury.

We arrived at a set of interior doors. Maxim opened the doors and stood back to allow me to enter.

The wing opened into a sitting room. An oversized fireplace sat on each end of the room. Flicking my wrists in opposite directions, two large fires roared to life . . . and, again, I was startled at what I found.

It was lovely.

I sent another pulse of energy overhead and the large crystal chandelier shimmered with candlelight. A Persian rug covered the wood floor. Sitting atop it was a white antique settee, covered with soft throws and pillows. There were also two wingback chairs arranged for a cozy sitting area. And two towering bookcases lined the graceful archway which led to a welcoming dining room and main hallway. The space was clean and clear of the dust and grime found around the rest of the manor.

"Your bags have been unpacked. All your items are in the master bedroom. There is a bathroom, as well," Maxim gave a surreptitious glance at my hair, "if you would like to bathe."

I fought the urge to touch my hair. I had a feeling there were still a few leaves stuck in there.

He withdrew a card from his suit pocket and handed it to me. "This is my number. You need only to call and I will be available to assist you in whatever you request." Then he gave a bow. "Welcome to your new home, your highness. I hope you will be comfortable. Good night."

"Wait," I demanded. "That's it?"

Maxim looked uncomfortable. "Yes, I am afraid so, your— Violet. I did inquire as to a staff to tend to your needs, but again, Barrister Corbett insisted that his instructions had explicitly counseled against the placement of any individuals within the manor. My deepest apologies. It is rather uncouth, but I have been assured that your meals will be delivered to your dining quarters."

It was silly and childish, but I had a moment of panic. I didn't want Maxim to abandon me in this place. I would have so much rather been attacked.

Yet, I threw my shoulders back and notched my chin. "Thank you, Maxim. That will be fine."

And with another bow, he left.

I stood there, uncertain what to do. Before I was able to make a decision, though, I heard something shuffling out in the hall.

I turned to the suite doors. Ready.

A hunched, robed figure hobbled into the room. The individual had the hood of the tattered robe drawn, and I could not make out a face beneath. Ancient, gnarled hands carried a covered tray.

Without so much as a glance in my direction, the figure shuffled through the sitting area and into the dining room.

The Crone.

I was horrified that someone so old was waiting on me.

"I can take that." I began to cross to her, but she stopped where she was. Her cloaked head swiveled in my direction, and I halted in my attempt to help. I could not see beneath the brown hood, but I knew better than to take another step towards her.

There was an air of authority. It was weak and flickering, almost as if traveling from a great distance, but there just the same.

She resumed her course to the dining table and, with great difficulty, set down the tray. Without looking at me, she began to make her way to the door.

"Thank you," I tried. "This really isn't necessary. I can fetch my own meals."

But there was no acknowledgment from the Crone. She shuffled away as if I wasn't there, closing the door of the suite behind her.

I went over and collapsed on the settee, utterly confused. There had been no formal welcome. No ghoulish court members awaiting my arrival. No Shadow Prince hosting a banquet of raw flesh in my honor. No ghastly introductions.

And there had been no attempt to kill me. No attack. No threat.

It was just . . . well . . . it was *fucking rude,* is what it was. I could guarantee that at the Radiant Court, we would have at least done one or the other—*we* had some manners.

Sitting there, stewing over my current situation, I stared into the fire.

I hadn't meant to fall asleep. It was foolish to think I was safe. But I was lulled by faraway whispers. They circled around me, flitting in and out of my hair. Murmuring. Murmuring. They told me to sleep. To dream.

There were no problems. No worries. No need to be on guard.

Little by little my eyes drooped, heavy anchors I could no longer hold open. I became swept up in an undertow . . . and I drifted away.

CHAPTER 7

I ARCHED MY BACK *and my shoulders dug deeper into the mattress. My feet slid over the softest cotton as I rubbed my thighs together. I spread my arms wide just to feel the cool downy material against my burning skin.*

When I opened my eyes, I saw from the light of a bedside candle that I lay on black sheets in a massive bed. A damp chill hung in the air and despite my skin being ablaze, the cool air made my nipples pucker under the gauzy lace bra I wore.

My blood was on fire, tearing through my veins like an inferno. My breasts ached in the scant lingerie that barely covered them. But what was most torturous was the throbbing need at my very core. The lacy panties I wore were soaked, and my center felt hot and swollen. I rubbed my thighs together again and cried out.

I stilled. Someone else was in the room with me. I turned my head, feeling my hair caress my shoulder, and looked to the entryway of the dark bedroom.

A man stood there. He was cloaked in the shadows, but I could see his broad shoulders heaving up and down with each rapid breath he took. His hands were stretched out to either side of the doorframe and he was clutching the wood there.

I sat up and moved onto my hands and knees. I began crawling across the bed towards the man. "I need you." My voice was raw and desperate.

The wood on either side of the doorframe splintered where the man crushed it in his big hands. I needed those hands on me. I needed him to come to the bed. But he just stood there.

When I reached the edge of the bed, I rolled onto my back with my head hanging off the side. I arched my back again. This time it was with purposeful invitation.

I trailed my finger up from my navel, between my breasts, up my neck, to my mouth. Then I sucked on it before drawing it out with deliberate slowness. All the while my gaze burned at where I knew his eyes were.

"It's so simple. It's so easy. Just come to me," I begged.

He took one halting step forward before jerking himself to a stop.

I sat myself up and continued forward until I was on my hands and knees again. This time I was facing away from him. I let my chest and head fall onto the bed, propping my hips up in the air.

My knees were spread far apart and just a scrap of lace fabric stood between him and his view of me. I knew the sight I was displaying for him was ratcheting him even higher as he let out a low hiss. It was as if he had been burned.

With my head angled to the side as it was, I still had a view of him. His hand traveled down to his own aching shaft, but he clenched it into a fist just before he was about to palm himself over his pants.

I rubbed my cheek against the cool cotton. "Just put your hands on me," I whispered.

As his sexual fervor had been escalating so too had something else. Something dark and dangerous. I had felt it pulsing in time with his lust. It was . . . anger.

I could feel a snap in the air when it hit a breaking point. He threw his head back, bellowing to the ceiling, before vanishing away in a swirl of inky shadows.

***

The moment he disappeared I awoke. I snapped up, panting. I had to look around and it took me a moment to realize where I was and what had happened. I was lying on the settee in the sitting room of the Dark Manor.

A dream. It had been the most intense and realistic dream I had ever had, but still, it was just a dream.

Sweat covered my body causing my dress to cling to my skin. I was breathing fast and heavy, but what was most disturbing was the throbbing ache I felt at my core.

I was slightly panicked, never having experienced this feeling before. My body felt alien and wrong. Unsure what to do, I slipped my hand into my panties.

As in my dream, the fabric was drenched. I was hot and swollen and I had to stifle a cry when my fingers grazed my sensitive skin. With a start, I realized what was happening.

After so long. After thinking I was broken. Thinking I would never experience base desires as others did so readily. I was aroused.

My body was sexually responsive. With an eager greed I stroked again, and again I was forced to stifle a cry. Two more strokes and the need, the build, the throb, the ache culminated in a flooding crescendo of unimaginable pleasure. Wave after pulsing wave battered through me until I was left sweaty and breathless.

I lay there stunned. I was unsure what to think or even feel.

I thought of the man in my dream. He had been so *real.* And I had experienced sexual desire for someone for the first time in my life.

In the darkness of the room, with the embers smoldering in the fireplace, my lips curled into a slow smile.

***

I had survived my first night in the Dark Manor. I wasn't gagged and bound. I hadn't been tortured and raped. No one had killed me in my sleep. Quite the contrary, my quarters had been flooded with light as soon as the sun rose, and breakfast had been set on the dining table for me.

It was . . . *weird.*

Unsure what to do, I poked around the quarters, inspecting the various rooms. Nothing seemed amiss. And all in all, it was a lovely suite. Additionally, I had to admit that my personal bedroom wasn't too bad. In fact, it was striking.

The room was large with high vaulted ceilings. Along the east facing wall were three, floor to ceiling windows. Each one must have been eight feet wide.

Substantial drapes made from heavy fabrics were tucked into discreet casings, completely hidden from view. They casings allowed the windows to stand unobstructed, without any frills.

However, the drapes could be pulled free to effectively block out the copious light filtering in.

The exposed bricks along the eastern and southern walls had been painted white. But the paint had faded and peeled in many spots, allowing some black to show here and there. And from the age darkened mahogany beams running across the ceiling, a large crystal chandelier hung. Even the diffused light from a cloudy sky was enough to make it sparkle and shine.

The bed was sizable but sat on a wood frame which was low to the ground. There was no headboard or footboard. The frame had the same black-brown color as the exposed beams overhead and extended just beyond the mattress. Paired with the fluffy white bedding, the effect somehow reminded me of a nest or cozy pallet.

And best of all, directly across from the foot of the bed was the immense fireplace. While the walls running along the windows and the bed were the painted white brick, the southern and western walls were a smooth plaster. Jutting from the white wall was the oversized mantle. The light gray stone created an incredible square arch, running up and across the length of the fireplace.

However, the beauty of the room aside, I didn't want to be there. Maxim had said that the Shadow Prince and the Crone lived in the manor. I wasn't about to waste any more time than necessary in this place, even if things were off to a better start than I had hoped for. I immediately began reconnaissance.

I tried to spend the day learning all I could about the manor, the prince, and the Crone. Only, there was nothing to learn.

Room after room of the imposing structure was uninhabited. Each and every one stale, dusty, and unused in far too long.

There was absolutely no evidence that a crone or a prince lived here. I seemed to be the only soul present.

The one and only room not covered in cobwebs, other than my suite, was the kitchen. I had stumbled upon it mid-morning. It was spotless with not one single item out of place. The surprising part, aside from the lack of grime, was that there was food in the refrigerator and pantry. It made sense since I had been served dinner as well as breakfast, but it was still an unexpected discovery.

By the afternoon, I had checked every room in the manor with nothing to show for it. Returning to my room, I retrieved the card Maxim had given me and called him. I wasn't expecting an answer, but he picked up after the first ring.

"Yes, your highness. How may I be of service to you?"

"There's no one here," I accused.

"Begging your pardon, your highness?"

"This place is an empty tomb. No one lives here. I get it. This is my prison. I haven't tried, but I'm guessing I won't be able to leave. Also, I don't understand why you're bothering to feed me. Although if you're planning on eating me, I guess it makes sense."

Maxim began to splutter on the other end of the line. He was very convincing at sounding aghast. "Your highness, I can guarantee that absolutely no one is planning to *eat* you—"

"It's Violet, bozo." I was stealing the term from Giddeon, but he wasn't around to know. And I was pissed. More so at myself than Maxim, but again, another detail that another person didn't need to know.

If I was being honest, my feelings were hurt. I had thought, one way or another, that I was going to be some big deal within the Shadow Court. Instead, I had been tossed aside like yesterday's garbage.

"Begging your pardon, Violet. You have my sincerest apologies for the less than ideal circumstances. It has been a rather uncouth welcome, I understand. I am at the mercy of my orders. Please believe me when I tell you it is for your safety alone that you have been placed in a secure location. It is by no means a prison.

"And as for those in residence with you . . . The prince is somewhat of a recluse. I do not know what I can do other than apologize on his behalf."

"Yeah, well, you'll be hearing from me again," I threatened. And then I abruptly hung up.

I tapped my phone, happy about how that conversation had gone. If Maxim was to be trusted—no one was planning on eating me. That was a plus. And he was clearly under the impression that the Shadow Prince lived here. I sighed. But he could have very well been lying. There was no way of knowing.

He was also keeping up with the whole loyal subject act, which for the life of me, I couldn't figure out why. I was exactly where he had wanted me. I hadn't objected or put up a fight. Why continue with the charade?

However, aside from my self-imposed mission and my self-preservation, there was another reason I wanted to get closer to Maxim. And it had to do with that dream.

After so many years of never experiencing the barest hint of sexual excitement, I had suddenly been plunged into a deep, dark well of arousal only hours after meeting him . . . It was hard to believe that was mere coincidence.

I had wanted to hear his voice again, had wanted some sort of connection to him. I'd had my first taste of raw lust. It had been heady and addicting. I wanted more.

And just to be clear, it wasn't that I wanted to *do* anything with Maxim. I was simply after more of the experience—the desire itself. After all, I was well aware of how he actually looked. Believe me, the thought of being physical with a Shadow was revolting. But I was so desperate to experience basic desire again that I firmly pushed the image of Maxim's true form aside. The glamour he wore was quite appealing, and I focused on that.

Unfortunately, there had been no spark upon hearing his voice. Maybe I needed to see him in person. I dialed his number again.

"Yes, Violet. How may I be of service to you?"

"I want to see you tonight," I blurted.

"Begging your pardon?"

My face heated at my lack of finesse. "I mean I want to go out tonight."

"Would you be so kind as to clarify what you mean by *out?*"

"A bar. I would like to go out to a bar tonight."

"I am sorry, but that will not be possible. It is best you remain at the Dark Manor, during this initial transition, where it is safest. If it is liquor you desire, I will have some brought to you."

"You just said I'm not a prisoner here, but it sure seems like it," I countered. "And it's not like there's anyone here to miss my presence."

"Again, you have my sincerest apologies, but I must follow my orders."

I tried to sweeten my tone. I had to remember that I wanted everyone I encountered to see me as an innocent, naive girl. "Maxim? May I ask who issued your orders?"

"My apologies, Violet. I am not a liberty to say."

I swore under my breath. If he apologized one more time, I was convinced it would be impossible for me to get hard-up over him ever again.

"No problem," I replied. "But Maxim?"

"Yes, Violet?"

"You did refer to me as the new Princess of Shadows yesterday, didn't you?"

"Yes, of course."

"So if I'm not a prisoner here, and if I—well—I *command* it, then don't you need to follow *my* orders?"

"Please understand, it is for your safety—"

I rolled my eyes. This guy was insufferable. I took a deep breath, trying to hang on to my patience. "And besides, it's like you said yesterday," I interrupted. "No one knows I'm here or even of this new . . . *union*. It's not like anyone will know who I am. I have my cape. I can wear it and keep the hood drawn the whole evening. Or you can even have your witch spell up a glamour for me, if you like."

Again with the spluttering, Maxim began to say something, but I'd had enough.

"Okay, gotta go!" I told Maxim. "I'll see you here tonight!" Then I hung up on him again, which, if I'm being honest, I thoroughly enjoyed.

I spent the rest of the day continuing my search of the manor, going over the rooms with more care. I should have known I was wasting my time. I should have known it was not the open rooms that held secrets, but the ones locked and buried away deep in the earth. I should have known it was not a room I needed to find at all, but a door. An old, rotted door.

CHAPTER 8

I CLASPED THE RED CLOAK around my neck and drew the hood. However, instead of a basket of fruit, I carried a couture clutch filled with weapons, and I made my way down the overgrown drive.

Looking back, the red riding hood complex was a bit obvious, but I can assure you I was oblivious at the time.

The darkness of night was swiftly falling, and a blanket of fog was encroaching upon the manor. The eerie atmosphere caused goosebumps to brush across my neck.

As I made my way through the unkempt grasses and bramble, I heard a howl from the surrounding woods. I turned to check for an approaching beast. But it wasn't an animal I found.

There was a figure standing on the cliff high above. At least, I had thought there was. I squinted, trying to make out the person in the twilight, but when I adjusted my focus, there was no one up there, just a lone oak tree.

I looked back towards the tree tunnel as the enormous wrought iron gate began to open and that same black SUV from the previous night started its ascent up the drive. I took a deep breath, trying to measure my excitement. Unable to see through the blacked-out windows, I hoped Maxim wore his glamour.

The vehicle came to a stop in front of me, the driver's door swinging open. And I held my breath.

Maxim rushed to my side. Thank the Light, he looked like the strong, attractive male from the previous night. His dark hair was combed back, slash of brows emphasizing the gray eyes that seemed to shimmer in the evening light, and his chiseled masculine features looked exactly as I remembered. Even the suit he wore was filled out with packed muscles underneath. I had been afraid that if the glamour held, perhaps it would shift or alter from one encounter to the next. Luckily, he looked exactly the same.

"Your highness, what are you doing out here? You should await my arrival in your quarters. I will always escort you from within the manor. It is not safe for you to be out here alone."

"Ugh, Maxim. This is not an attractive quality of yours," I informed him.

He looked confused. "Begging your pardon?"

"Never mind. Let's go!" I made my way for the passenger door.

He jumped in front of me to open the vehicle door and attempted to give me a hand.

"Your—Violet, I have brought many bottles of varying kinds of alcohol with me. Perhaps you would like to remain here. I have also procured a cocktail recipe book and will be happy to serve you in your quarters if you like."

"Wow. That sounds like a total blast," I told him. "You really know how to entice a girl, Maxim. But I would rather go out, thanks." I pushed him back and shut the door.

I wanted to get out of the creepy manor. Twenty-four hours was enough in that place, especially since I hadn't come across anything worthwhile to stay for. Plus, I wanted to get a feel for the surrounding area and people. I needed to know everything about this new place to determine my best course of action.

Maxim's shoulders looked tense as he crossed in front of the SUV and over to the driver's side. I couldn't help it. I giggled. He was such a tight-ass. Upon initially seeing him, I had felt zero chemistry. But I wondered how much of that was due to him being an immediate buzz-kill.

To my surprise, he didn't argue further, and we began our departure. I spent the entire drive surreptitiously glancing at him, searching for that blazing attraction I had experienced in my dream. I also noticed a second black SUV begin to tail us once we made our way to the main road.

Maxim would catch me staring at him and look at me with uncertain questioning. He finally broke the silence. "There are not any high-end establishments in the vicinity. The closest bar is one I fear that will be lacking for your standards."

"I've been busy, a lot," I told him. "But on the rare occasion when I did go out, my favorite place was a casual little hole-in-the-wall."

Maxim didn't seem convinced, but he also didn't argue.

After about forty-five minutes, we finally came upon a little town with a small main street where Maxim slowed and eventually parked the SUV on the side of the road. Our vehicle, and the one that had tailed us, were the only ones in sight.

"What the heck is this?" I asked him.

Buildings composed of wattle and daub with thatched roofs lined the street. A few carts containing fruits and vegetables were present and random chickens milled about. There were gas street lamps lining the thoroughfare, aglow with flickering light.

The few people strolling along were dressed in an odd manner. I decided to refer to their attire as *neo-medieval*. While the men mostly wore tunics with trousers and the woman were in long dresses with tight bodices, the garments had an undeniable modern look.

I wore a sheath dress and cloak so I kind of fit right in. I looked over at Maxim with a smirk. I was just another gal out for the evening.

If anyone stood out, and was going to call attention to themselves, it was Maxim and the two goons who were getting out of the SUV next to us. All three were wearing expensive dark suits.

I directed my chin towards one of the men passing by. "Did you not get the memo on the dress code?"

Maxim wasn't amused by my teasing. "I am working in an official capacity for our government. A suit is standard attire for my position. This is well known among the Shadow villages. My attire alone is no cause for notice. However, the fact that a beautiful, young, affluent woman is being chaperoned by three elite government officials from our security branch ... well you can imagine how that may cause some questions as well as invite gossip and speculation."

I ignored Maxim's veiled censure. "Why is everything so . . . *antiquated?*"

Maxim shifted as if uncomfortable. "While the Shadow Court has relocated to London, and many of our people now reside there, there are a few villages and areas where our people still live life as they once did. Not much has changed throughout the years. They are somewhat isolated and stuck, in a sense, in the old ways."

I wasn't ready to commit to an opinion on this, so I refrained from a reply.

Maxim turned in his seat to face me more directly. "There is nothing here to entice you. Allow me to escort you back to the manor. I will make any drink you like there."

I tried to read the swinging wood sign on the building in front of us. "Why don't you and your buddies head back. I'm going to check out," I squinted to make out the faded lettering, "*The Screaming Banshee.*" Then I opened my door to head inside.

Maxim immediately sprang out from his door, streaking across the front of the car, and crossed to my side. With my elbow in his hand he pulled me back. "We must first assess the location." He gave a nod to the two goons at the other vehicle, and they entered the pub.

"Killian would love you," I muttered.

After we got the all clear, Maxim and I entered the quaint establishment. It was old and dim inside, with wood everything, and small gas lanterns placed throughout. Some kind of fragrant tobacco permeated the air, and a big lug of a man stood behind the bar.

From a brief glimpse of the handful of patrons drinking in the pub, and the folks that had been strolling about outside, it seemed they all wore glamours. I couldn't, for the life of me, understand why. I had assumed that when upon their own lands and among their own people the Shadows would maintain their true form. Yet every single individual looked completely *normal*.

Although, truth be told, the bartender could have used a few improvements. Maybe he was forcing an inexperienced witch to cast his glamour.

Without waiting for Maxim, I headed straight for the bar. "Good evening." I directed the pleasantry to the beefy bartender. He flicked his beady eyes over me before grunting and returning to the glass he had been polishing.

"Is this lovely establishment yours?"

Another grunt was my only reply. I slipped a hundred-dollar bill onto the bar top, and the sweaty oaf stopped his polishing, eyeing the bill before setting down the glass. He placed two burly hands onto the bar counter and leaned in towards me. "What can I do for you?" His voice was like gravel being ground.

"Do you happen to have the *Green Fairy*?" I asked him.

He eyed my dress under the front of my cloak and sneered. "Do I look like a man who can afford that rubbish?"

I inclined my head. What I really wanted to do was tell him he was being a jackass, but years of practice at the Radiant Court had me holding my tongue and offering my warmest smile. "What is the most potent libation you offer?"

"I've got some kerosene in the back you're welcome to."

I nodded at a whiskey jug. "Perhaps two of your finest whiskey, if it isn't a bother."

He grabbed the jug without looking away from me and brought the cork stopper to his mouth. Using what teeth he had left, he removed the cork and filled two tumblers before shoving them towards me.

Instead of cringing, I smiled and thanked him. Giving a pointed look at the bill on the countertop I told him, "There's more if you keep them coming."

I set the drinks down on one of the small wooden tables and took a seat after Maxim pulled a chair out for me. However, instead of taking the other seat at the table, Maxim continued to stand behind my shoulder—*hovering*.

"Now, Maxim," I chastised. "I know your refined manners will not allow for me to sit here and drink alone." I gestured to the opposite seat. "Please."

Although clearly unhappy about it, Maxim took a seat at the table. And with all the enthusiasm of a man facing the gallows, he raised his glass, and drank.

***

Stiff, formal, mannerly Maxim . . . was *lit*. I had no idea how it had happened. I had thought getting him drunk was going to be a monumental undertaking requiring the highest level of chicanery. But god ol' Maxim continued to down drink after drink as they were delivered to our table. And little by little he had loosened up until he was downright affable.

I had begun with mild, unassuming conversation. Asking Maxim about the weather in the area, scenic places to visit, and what holidays the Shadows celebrated.

He was definitely more fun to be around, but as far as my libido went, there was nothing. I was not feeling the slightest attraction to him.

I also couldn't stop thinking about his true form. The idea of what he truly looked like was haunting me. I reasoned that I needed to see him without his glamour, a kind of immersion therapy. I needed the ordeal over with.

I began to direct the conversation towards Shadow-life. And while he was wrapped up in his happy yammering, I casually brought up the glamours.

"So do you ever take the glamour off?" I asked.

Maxim snorted in his whiskey. "Pardon?"

"Like what about when you go to sleep? And where do you keep your witch? Do you really have to keep her captive? Isn't there any way the Shadows and Wicca could come to some sort of arrangement? I mean, I'm sure you could strike a deal with the witches. They could continue to spell glamours for you in exchange for freeing all those you keep captive."

Maxim squinted his eyes, slowly nodding. "Ah, yes. The glamours... us Shadows wear... and the witches we hold captive." He gave a final nod as if coming to some sort of understanding, and I was hopeful that my suggestion would be seriously considered.

Feeling adventurous, I leaned forward in my seat. "Would you ever consider showing me your true form?" I asked.

Maxim seemed to be mulling something over.

"I'm sorry. Is it rude for me to ask that?"

"Not at all," Maxim reassured. "If anything, it is rude of me not to have offered. After all, what if my witch escapes? Then I will be forced to interact with you without the aid of a glamour. You would not recognize me in such a situation. It is best I do show you my true face, so that you may know me in all instances."

I pulled my cloak tighter around my shoulders. "When? Here, now?"

"Yes, absolutely. Prepare yourself."

Maxim closed his eyes and cleared his throat. He began to hum. I shifted in my seat, unsure if I really wanted to see him change.

The humming got louder and louder, building to a crescendo. Then he whipped to his feet, shouting, "Behold the glory of true Shadow form!" before ripping his shirt open and flinging his head back. "RAWWR!"

Only . . . there was no change. He looked exactly the same as he collapsed back into his chair. The only difference was that now his highly muscled torso was on display. And it looked like prim and proper Maxim had some kind of tattoo on one side of his chest.

"What happened? Are you okay? It didn't work." I reached my hand across the table to touch his arm, concerned for him.

Maxim's face contorted, and he began to . . . *laugh.*

A cocktail waitress walked past, and he tried to flip up the hem of her skirt. "Let's see under that glamour. Give us a peek, love!"

She glowered and batted his hand away as she continued delivering drinks. Maxim broke out into boisterous laughter once more.

I sat back in my chair, folding my arms across my chest. "You're mocking me."

"Can you blame me?" he questioned through his laughter. "You just accused me—of us all," he amended, spreading his arms wide, "of holding witches captive in exchange for glamours."

"You don't?"

He scowled. "No. Sorry to disappoint you, Violet, but this is what we look like. What monstrous idea of us do you have?"

"Let me get this straight. You don't wear glamours?"

He pinched the bridge of nose. "No."

"You're not planning on eating me?"

"*No!*"

"But you are cannibals in general." I stated it as a fact.

He let out an exasperated breath. "By and large, we are mostly vegetarians. But any who do eat meat consume *animals*, not fellow Shadows."

"Your homes?" I persisted. "Are they underground?" Having now been to the Dark Manor as well as this little town, I had a feeling I already knew the answer.

Maxim simply shook his head.

"Is any of what I've heard true?"

Maxim downed the drink in front of him before looking around as if about to conspire. Leaning in, he crooked his finger, indicating he wanted me to come close. With our heads bowed, he whispered. "I'm afraid there is one rumor which is undoubtedly true."

I nodded, encouraging him to go on.

Then he glanced down, whispering with agony. "We are tragically well endowed." He threw his head back and raised his arms to the ceiling shouting, "Why, gods, have you cursed us so?!"

This time I couldn't help but smile. I reached up and grabbed his arm, pulling it down. "Alright, point taken."

He looked at his empty tumbler on the table. "I say, you do not seem phased by all this alcohol consumption." He squinted his eyes at me. "Have you been spitting your drinks out?"

I patted his hand. "No, big guy." I downed the whiskey in front of me. "I can just handle my drink."

I stood up. "And now, if you will excuse me, I must visit the restroom."

"How odd. This is very unlike you, Violet. Shouldn't you dive from your chair rolling through the pub and sprinting for the facilities with the small bladder aliment you tragically possess?"

I raised an eyebrow at Maxim, thoroughly enjoying this side of him, before turning for the bar and inquiring as to the whereabouts of the loo. The bartender thrust his head towards the back hall and grunted. "Outhouse. Alley."

I stifled a wince at having to use an outhouse and headed back. But before I exited through the rear door, a bright red flyer hanging on a bulletin board caught my eye. It had only three words printed on it, and an odd little symbol which looked like three crescent moons intertwined.

JOIN THE REVOLUTION

Not knowing what it was, not knowing what it would one day lead to... I snatched the flyer from the bulletin board and tucked it into the depths of my clutch, where it joined my arsenal of shiny weapons.

CHAPTER 9

THE LITTLE OUTHOUSE WASN'T THAT BAD. The air inside the structure was fresh and the toilet flushed. There was a charming spigot emerging from the stone wall with a basin below. There was even a mirror hanging in one corner in which I gave myself a once over before leaving.

After seeing the inside of the pub as well as this little outhouse, I began to suspect that although the town appeared to be very much left in medieval times, amenities had been added to the structures in an attempt to modernize the facilities and make the overall living arrangements more comfortable.

As I emerged from the outhouse into the alleyway, I was feeling somewhat positive about the night's events. But the moment I crossed the threshold of the wooden door, a big, beefy hand clamped down on my wrist.

I looked up into the sweaty face of the bartender.

"You haven't settled your tab," he drawled.

I tried to twist my wrist from his grasp. "Alright," I snapped. "We'll settle it inside. Now get your hand off me."

He squeezed tighter, pulling me into him. "I think I'll take my payment out here."

When I realized what this miserable excuse for a being meant, a hot fury began to well inside my chest. "I see," I replied. "And if I refuse?"

He laughed, and spittle escaped his lips. "I'll be taking my payment with or without your consent." He leaned his red face down to mine. "I prefer it if you struggle, chit."

I let a slow evil smile spread across my lips. "Oh, you're in for a treat then."

He looked confused at my response. But confusion quickly gave way to anger. He pushed me against the outer wall of the pub and held me by my neck with one hand. With his other hand he shoved the waist of his pants down before grabbing my dress to yank it up.

I held up a finger. Although my airway was cut off, I rasped out a few words. "Just one question."

His anger over my lack of submission intensified. His face became enraged and his hold on my neck tightened. Still I persisted in a barely audible wheeze. "How many women . . . ?"

Although I lacked the ability to finish my question, he understood. A cold gleam shinned in his beady little eyes and a perverse smile spread across his mouth. "No bloody idea. Sorry, love," He leaned in, placing his face next to mine. "There's absolutely nothing special about you."

I turned my face and bit off his ear.

His scream tore through the quiet night air, echoing in the little alley. He stumbled back from me, pressing his hand to the bloody hole on the side of his head. "You fucking bitch! I was going to let you live! Now I'm going to kill you when I'm done!"

He made a grab for me, but I ducked him and spun out from the wall. When he turned around, I introduced my foot to his face.

There was a loud crack and blood gushed from his nose. He didn't go down but staggered back into the wall. He blinked. Wild-eyed. Angry and confused.

I let out a shrill laugh. A soft glow lit the space of the alleyway between us, and I knew my eyes were alight. A light breeze stirred then, lifting my hair and cloak. I could feel the bastard's blood around my mouth and chin. And I knew this deplorable man held an eerie sight before him.

The look of anger on his face turned to terror, and he began to inch along the wall towards the door.

Wanting him to suffer, to know unadulterated fear, I slowly lifted the hem of my dress up my leg and grasped the dagger of Light I had strapped to my thigh.

He turned to make a run for it, but I grabbed him by the neck and shoved him against the wall, even though he had a good eight inches on me. He didn't struggle. Fear had made him weak and compliant.

"Please . . ." he tried. "Mercy."

I cackled. "Did you show mercy to all those women? Do you honestly believe you deserve *mercy*?"

I raised the dagger. "And yet, mercy you shall receive. You deserve the same done to you for every single woman you've harmed. Instead, you shall receive the gift of death . . . There is your *mercy*."

But, I didn't kill him. I wanted to. I was going to. However, just as I was about impale his heart, I heard a drunken voice splutter, "What the fuck?!"

I turned towards the door and saw Maxim standing there with the two assisting agents.

I let my arm drop and muttered. "Well, shit."

***

Maxim paced back and forth over the Persian rug in my sitting room while his two goons flanked the suite doors. Maxim had sobered up in quite a hurry, silently fuming the entire drive home. At the moment he was grumbling to himself in the Dark Tongue. I didn't know what he was saying, but it didn't sound good.

I tried to sit quietly. I tried to be patient. I really did. But after a certain point, I just wanted to get things over with.

"Look, Maxim, about what you saw—"

His head jerked up and he stared at me with black eyes. "About what I saw?" he asked. "About what I *saw*?!"

He gestured behind him. "May I introduce you to Rheneas and Stefan who also *saw*. May I remind you of the pub owner who *saw*. And may I inform you that the inn on the other side of the alley was full of people watching the commotion from the windows above.

"Had it only been me who'd witnessed your little display, things may not be so dire. But as it is, an entire village is now aware of not only your presence but fearful of you! I can guarantee that you became the topic of conversation this evening. I doubt there will be anyone in town who has not heard of the evening's events. They will be talking about the Radiant female within our midst who is *eating* Shadows!"

The irony of his comment was not lost on me, but I balked at his words. He raised his brows and held his breath, as if daring me to argue. When I remained silent, he continued.

"Do you know what happens to people who are fearful? They become angry and violent. They focus on annihilating that which is causing them fear. You have just become our resident monster. You have—unequivocally—made your presence known."

"So what?" I countered. "That guy was about to rape me. And he admitted to raping countless others. Was I supposed to just let him? I demand he be punished for his crimes!

"And why the hell is my presence a secret anyway? None of this makes any sense! You guys came to me with this proposal, and there were two possible outcomes.

"There was the very minuscule possibility that the proposition was sincere, or there was the very likely possibility that it was a ploy to assassinate me. There was no third possibility where I become the secret, secluded charge of the Shadow Court's Master-at-arms."

Maxim raised a hand to stop me. "I told you, we want to be sure that your safety is secured before revealing that you have become the Shadow Court's new princess. The general reaction to this announcement promises to be extremely volatile."

I was tired. Any wish to argue my point left me. I shook my head and looked at Maxim. I barely knew him, but I believed he was honorable . . . a word I never would have thought to use when describing a Shadow.

"Something else is going on, Maxim. Whether you know it or not, something else is at play here."

He didn't look away, but his jaw ticked. And I knew that he had had a similar suspicion. "I carry out orders. That is what I do. Right now, my orders are to keep your presence unknown and to keep you safe. How do you suggest I do so when you are out picking a fight with someone three times your size?"

"Are you kidding me?! If anyone needed protecting it was *him* from *me*! You have no idea what I could have done to that asshole."

I bit my lip. *Check yourself, Vi.*

"Oh please, I am well aware of your penchant for brawling."

"What?"

"I was notified that the proposal would be extended to you. I was told you would most likely accept. And I was told that I would promptly be removed from all current duties to guard you. I immediately traveled to the Radiant Court in order to observe and learn all I could about you. The very first night I was there, you were out picking fights."

"*Picking fights?!*" I screeched. I had no idea when Maxim had watched me, but the only time I was ever outside of the court grounds fighting was when I was working with our unit.

"Try, protecting my people—*innocent people*—from Shadow attacks!" I narrowed my eyes. "And if you were out there watching, why didn't you do anything to stop it? Barrister Corbett claims they're a rogue faction, yet the Shadow Court's very own Master-at-arms does nothing to stop them."

I marched up to Maxim and stuck my finger in his chest. With my voice measured I told him, "I don't know what is going on here. But I can promise you that I am going to find out. And I can guarantee you that I will not be *kept*. I will leave this place as I please, and you can be damn sure that I will defend myself whenever necessary. I don't care who's watching."

I took a step back from Maxim and crossed my arms over my chest. He looked like he was going to say something but then decided against it. Instead, with his jaw tightened he gave a formal bow. "If it be your will, I shall excuse myself now, *your majesty*."

"Before you go, answer me one question," I insisted.

Maxim gave a tight nod.

"Are you the Shadow Prince?"

"Violet! Is there no end to your absurd assumptions?!" He pinched the bridge of his nose. "What cockamamie, hair-brained conspiracy theory will you come up with next?"

"So you deny it?"

"With a resounding and emphatic yes!"

I gave a shrug before gesturing to the door. "Then by all means, enjoy your evening, *Master-at-arms*."

If Maxim had been the type of person to roll his eyes, I think he would have at that point. Instead, he turned and left with Rheneas and Stefan silently following behind.

I stood there for a moment, not knowing what I was going to do next. But before I had a chance to retreat to my room, I heard those shuffling footsteps outside my suite doors.

The Crone entered without knocking. She hobbled in, the hood of her ragged robe drawn once again, cloaking her face.

Limping and carrying that heavy dinner tray, she headed straight for the dining room.

"Hello, good evening," I greeted. Although I cringed at watching her struggle with the tray, I refrained from offering to help. I didn't want to piss her off again.

"I'm terribly sorry. I failed to introduce myself last night. I was a little overwhelmed. I apologize for forgetting my manners. My name is Violet. It is a pleasure to make your acquaintance."

She shuffled by without acknowledging me. After she set the tray down on the dining table, she began to make her way to the door.

"And you are . . . ?" I prompted.

She hobbled out the door, closing it behind her.

"Great! Nice to meet you," I called after her before muttering, "you old bat."

I flopped down onto the settee, annoyed and confused. I really didn't know where to go from here. I looked around as if I could find some answers. There were none to be found.

The only sound in the room was the crackling fire, but after a moment of sitting there, I thought I heard something else. I closed my eyes and held my breath.

I thought I could hear . . . *music*. But it was so faint, I couldn't be sure. I strained to listen, not moving for several moments.

I wasn't entirely certain if it was coming from somewhere in the manor or if it was merely a figment of my imagination—some bleak and dreary soundtrack my mind was providing to underscore my haunted surroundings.

However, as I sat there, still as the dead, it was not the imperceptible music which crept into my mind but something else. Something less melodious and more rhythmic. Delicate, wispy threads.

Whispers.

They called to me from the fire, murmuring my name over and over again. Urging me to slumber. To dream. Soft and fragile, but insistent. *Whispering . . . whispering . . .* Entering my mind and then dissolving into thin air, not to be captured by memory, gone and forgotten the moment they were heard.

Hundreds of whispers snaking around my mind in airy tendrils, until I entered that plane of existence where thoughts coalesce. And I had no choice but to dream.

CHAPTER 10

I SET ABOUT EXPLORING.

Again, I had awakened during the night, hot and sweaty having dreamt of a dark figure. And again, I believed Maxim must have been the cause for my dreams . . . which was infuriating.

Adding to my frustration was the fact that there was nothing to find in this god forsaken place. I spent the entire day searching the manor a second time. Each room, each closet, every bookshelf was inspected with nothing to find but dusty old furniture and layers of cobwebs.

Under all the grime, however, it seemed that the manor was a place of pristine opulence. If someone simply took the time for a thorough cleaning and opened all the shutters to let in some air and sunshine, this place would be luxuriant. Aside from a boarded-up area in the foyer, the manor was overall in excellent condition.

After finding nothing of significance inside, I turned my attention to the surrounding landscape. I went over the grounds, gardens, stable, and utility structures. But my efforts were in vain.

It had all been forgotten. All abandoned. No one had set foot upon this land in ages. Vines and bramble grew over every path and each framework. Thorns and burs were getting stuck in the running sneakers and workout pants I wore. And because of all this, I searched halfheartedly, knowing it was a waste of time.

The last building to search was the stable. I had to give the old wood door a few kicks to get it to budge. When I was finally able to get the door open, I couldn't help but think what a shame it was.

Although overgrown with weeds, it was clear this had once been a grand setting. Beautiful wood stalls lined the space with a towering ceiling that arched above, and tall windows ran down each side of the structure. The glass panes were now covered with layers of dirt, but I could imagine how they would have let the sunlight pour through once upon a time.

However, the stable was dark now, and I felt as though in a tomb. I didn't stay long, and I knew there was no need to. Just like everything else, this place had been forgotten long ago.

As I exited the building, I looked towards the woods which surrounded the property. For a moment, I thought about exploring those as well, but the sun was setting. And with the onset of dusk, I began to feel ill at ease.

I felt a need to return to my suite.

Although void of life, there was evil here. It lurked somewhere in this manor, calling the abandoned mansion its home.

It seemed to slumber during the day, hiding from the light. I felt protected during the daylight. But as night approached and shadows fell, I felt that protection begin to wane in the darkness.

I had been there for such a negligible amount of time, but I already felt as if my appointed rooms were a sort of bastion. They were somehow safe and secured from the darkness which surrounded them. And so I called an end to the day's search.

Returning to my suite, I stoked to life large fires in every room and set the chandeliers ablaze. Once the entire space was flickering with light, I found myself back in the sitting room. Uncertain. Uneasy.

It seemed even with the warmth of the fires, I couldn't shake the chill from outside. I grabbed a blanket from the settee and wrapped it around myself. Although my quarters glowed with light, I couldn't help but think of all the empty darkness which surrounded me.

I decided to check in with Killian.

He had provided me with a satellite phone. I retrieved it and standing in front of the fire in the sitting room, I punched in Killian's number.

He answered on the first ring. "Violet—"

"Hey, Kil."

There was a moment of silence, and I thought perhaps the call had dropped. But before I had the chance to hang up, Killian finally replied.

"ARE YOU KIDDING ME?!" he exploded. "You were supposed to check in with us two nights ago, after your arrival! We have not heard from you! We've been trying to call you every hour—for two days! We thought you were dead! And you finally pick up as if we're twelve-year-old girlfriends chatting after school?! How selfish are you, Violet? Do you *ever* stop to think about anyone else? Do you have any idea what a wreck your mother is?"

I paused, caught off guard. I didn't know how to react or respond. After I remained silent, I heard Killian take a ragged breath. "Are you okay?" His voice was raw.

"Yes," I told him. "I am." I took a few steps to stand closer to the fire. "Killian. I am so sorry. I didn't get any of the calls. I . . . You're right. You're absolutely right. I should have checked in—"

"What is your status?" His voice had turned militant, and I sighed. I wanted to do my best to make amends, so I answered in kind.

"I am at the Dark Manor. I was brought directly here and have remained here since. There have been no threats against me and I have been made comfortable."

"Will I be able to contact you on this line again?"

"It is working for my use, but I did not receive any of your calls."

"Do you need to be extracted?"

"No."

"Are you rested?"

Killian was now speaking code. We had agreed upon this question before I left. If the answer was 'yes' or 'no,' he would know that I could not speak freely—that my answers were being coerced.

"My answers are not being forced or manipulated in any way. I am speaking to you alone."

Killian let out a heavy breath. "Are you sure?" he persisted.

"I'm safe, Killian. I'm not being compelled to give answers. Something weird is going on here, but I'm not in danger."

"What do you mean *weird*?"

"The Dark Manor has been abandoned. It's empty. Apparently, the Shadows moved their court to London a long time ago. They have been operating amidst the mortals under the guise of a private corporation. The Dark Manor is no longer the seat of the court."

Just talking about the dark, lifeless mansion made me shiver and I pulled the blanket tighter around my shoulders.

"I seem to be the only occupant here. There is an old crone who brings my meals. She allegedly resides here, but I have yet to find evidence of that. I have also been told the Dark Prince inhabits this place, but again, I have yet to find any proof of that. I have yet to even meet him."

I could hear Killian pacing across hardwood. I could picture him in his office at the Radiant Court. "I don't like this, Violet."

"Look, Killian. I'm here. I'm doing this. I need you to trust me. I will let you know if anything goes wrong. I need you to focus on The Unit. How are operations going?"

"Everything's fine." There was an edge to his voice.

"What happened?" I asked, not believing him.

"Violet, it doesn't matter. You left. It's not your concern anymore."

"That's not fair," I snapped. "Stop trying to punish me. What happened?"

"Two citizens were killed."

I let out a breath. This had been happening more and more as of late.

Killian didn't continue. "There's more, isn't there," I demanded.

"I wish I didn't have to tell you this, Vi." Killian's voice softened. "It was Gwen and Daniel."

I gripped the phone tighter, mentally warning myself not to squeeze so hard that it broke. I reminded myself to hold on to my energy. If I let my power flare in a fit of emotion, I would short the electronics in the phone.

Gwen was a young woman around twenty. She was taking university courses at court where she also interned for the Office of Public Affairs. I would sometimes work with her there in an official capacity and had liked her from the start. She was kind and soft spoken, but also intelligent and determined. She'd had a bright future ahead of her.

Since Killian was with me every day acting as my personal guard, he too had come to be well acquainted with her. But it was Gwen's little brother, Daniel, who he had grown quite fond of.

Only twelve, Daniel would wait for Gwen after school. He would sit in the office doing homework. Occasionally Killian would sneak him outside and they would throw a football or kick around a soccer ball. Not having a family of his own, I think Killian felt that Daniel was like a little brother.

"I'm so sorry." I managed to murmur.

And although I was sorry for what had happened to Gwen and Daniel, and I was sorry for the loss of two innocent lives—what I was really sorry for was the fact that I had not been there to prevent their deaths.

I didn't know the details of what had happened, but I was sure if I had been there, doing my duty, I would have stopped those responsible. I was the best in our unit and I had abandoned them.

And for what? I was wasting time rummaging about in a haunted house chasing ghosts. *This* was probably what they wanted all along—to send me on a wild goose chase, effectively removing me from the Radiant Court and allowing these rogue attacks on innocent civilians.

With guilt crawling over every inch of me, I told Killian, "I should have been there."

I could hear the faint creak of wood on Killian's end of the line, and I imagined him sitting down. "You wouldn't have been able to stop this, Vi. You can't be everywhere at once. There was no way to predict where this would have happened, when, or to whom."

"I never should have come here, Killian. You were right. I'm coming home."

"I think you should stay." The words were begrudging but not hesitant.

"What? Killian—"

"We captured the Shadows responsible. We interrogated them through the night. Before they . . . *expired*, they admitted that it is the Shadow Prince who leads them."

Killian let out a breath. "Violet, if you think you can get some information on him *without any risk to yourself* . . . it could help."

"I think I'm wasting time here, Kil. It's like I said, this place is abandoned. I need to be in London where the Shadows are actually holding court. I'll give it another day or two here, but I'm pretty sure it's a dead end."

Already mentally gathering my belongings, I concluded, "I'll pack up and come home in a couple days. We can re-group and then make our way to London, we'll see what we can find there."

"Wait. There's something else." The weariness in his voice was evident and I doubted Killian had been sleeping lately. "I went to see Wayland. There's an . . . *illness*. Right now there are only a few people affected by it and it's only on the periphery of the Radiant Domain, but immortals are getting sick.

"Wayland said he has never seen anything like it. There's no explanation. I am going to talk to your mother about it tomorrow, and it's not an issue that is affecting life here at court. But I think you should stay away until this is resolved. Just to be safe.

"I'm going to send you the encrypted coordinates and security code for the penthouse I have in New York. I think you should go there. Just until we get this cleared up. I'll have your mother arrange for an angel to pulse you there. But you'll need to get somewhere they can reach you. Wherever you are now, it is inaccessible to them."

I shivered and sent a pulse of energy towards the fire, stoking it higher. "How do you know that?"

Killian huffed. "When you didn't answer any of our calls, I tried to have you extracted immediately. You were impossible to find. Giddeon tried but couldn't get a read on you. So you'll need to get outside the boundaries of wherever you are for pickup. Giddeon will be able to pulse you to New York."

I wasn't going to any goddamn penthouse in New York, but I also didn't want to get into it with Killian. Although I had heard about Wayland, I had never met him. Apparently, he had been somewhat of a mentor to Killian for a time.

And I was sure he was a nice old man, but I was also sure he didn't know everything having spent most of his life living out in the desolate areas away from court life. Just because Wayland was confused about something, didn't mean there was cause for panic.

Instead of committing to his plan, I simply said, "I'll take note of the info. I'll be in touch. And Killian?"

"Yes, Violet?"

"Get some rest." With that, I ended the call and tucked the phone in my pocket. I took a step towards the fire, feeling very cold. I wrapped my arms around myself, trying to hold everything in, but it felt like I was failing.

And that was when I felt him, there in the shadows behind me. The sitting room was large, and the firelight did not reach the very depths along the edge of the chamber. The perimeter was cast in darkness, but I could sense him in that darkness.

I didn't turn towards him as I spoke. I wanted to keep my back to him, embarrassed that I had been caught in a vulnerable state, and I was not prepared to meet a gruesome face. Still, I braced myself for what might happen.

"How long have you been watching me?" I asked the fire.

His voice drifted over to me, silky and deep. "From the beginning."

"Why haven't you introduced yourself?"

"I apologize if I have been rude." He still did not approach. I could feel him along the fringe of the room, safe from the illumination of the firelight.

I dug for courage and turned in his direction. As I did, the candles in the chandelier overhead were extinguished and the fires in each hearth dwindled. He was simply a dark shape in the shadows. I couldn't make out any distinguishing characteristics.

Neither of us spoke just then and I began to feel unnerved. I realized that while I could not see him, he was able to see me. Although the room was now only lit with the dying fires, I stood amid that light and knew that my features were certainly definable. I fought the urge to hide and instead raised my chin a notch and straightened my spine. I would not let him see me as weak or insecure.

"I am sorry," he said.

"For what?" I asked.

"I am making you uncomfortable. I will go." I could see his dark form begin to move, however instead of walking in a straight line for the door, he stayed to the periphery of the room, to the shadows.

"Wait." I realized too late that it had been a plea rather than a command, and I regretted the show of weakness.

Yet he stilled. I didn't know what I wanted from him, what I wanted to say or ask.

I took a step towards him and then a second and a third. I didn't get any closer though. I could see, or maybe just sense him stiffen, and I knew our introduction was over. He completely faded into the darkness at that point and a moment later I heard the snick of the door as he closed it behind him.

I was left alone in the room with the dying fire and the expanding darkness.

And the Dark Prince had made his first mistake. Because by that simple visit, I was somehow able to get a lock on him. To *sense* him. Because of that innocent meeting . . . he would not be able to hide for long.

I would come to find that deep dark hole, where he had buried himself away.

CHAPTER 11

I FLUNG MY HANDS OUT towards the oversized fireplaces at each end of the sitting room. Flames leapt from the hearths, clawing and crackling at the open air. I wanted light in the entire suite. I wanted to chase away any shadows.

After setting the chandelier ablaze as well, I headed straight for the master bathroom. On my way through the adjoining bedroom, I kicked off my sneakers and grabbed my music player. Although the fire was already roaring in the room, I flicked my wrist in its direction stoking the flames for good measure.

Wanting an escape from the silence of my quarters, I turned on the speakers for my music player. Hozier's *It Will Come Back* began to echo through the bathroom. Before the opening guitar chords were over, I had steaming water filling the claw foot tub.

I stripped out of my workout clothes and zip up jacket, pulling my hair free from the ponytail it had been secured in. I found a couple burs stuck in some strands and I was reminded of how futile my pursuit had been. I had spent the day searching for *him* . . . and he had been in my very quarters.

I had encountered the Dark Prince. One feared by many. One I had thought would showcase his gruesomeness in a display of power and aggression.

But he had been so . . . *hollow*. He had no presence. I understood now why I hadn't initially picked up on his energy. He had none. No will of spirit. No crackling power. No uninhibited aggression. He was just another haunted shadow floating, untethered, in this forgotten place.

And now that I understood what his presence felt like, I could feel it everywhere. The moment he had slipped from my quarters, I realized his essence was all over my sitting room. He had also been in the dining room and spare bedrooms. I could feel the remnants of his presence out in the hallway to the suite as well. It wasn't from just this evening either. He had been here over the past few days.

For whatever reason, he had not been in the master bedroom or bathroom. It was why I had retreated here. Why I felt comfortable enough to strip down for the bath. He had not trespassed upon this area.

But I had fallen asleep the first two nights in the sitting room. He could have been there. Watching me. I would not make the mistake of falling asleep there again.

After promising myself I would sleep in the bedroom, I settled into the tub. And I went on with my evening as if nothing had happened.

What else was I supposed to do? What *could* I do?

Had I been attacked, I would have known what to do. I would have fought. I would have kicked ass. I didn't believe there was any Shadow I couldn't take on, be he the freakin' prince of them all or not.

But instead I had been left alone once again. So I soaked in the hot water and reassessed.

At least now I knew that he was here. That he had *been* here. Perhaps this wasn't a total waste of time. Perhaps I still had a shot with my original plan.

It was like I told Killian. If there wasn't an immediate threat, I didn't need to rush things. If I could have this marriage officially announced, I would be one step closer to taking control of the Shadow government.

But there *was* an immediate threat. Perhaps not to myself, but how many more innocent people like Gwen and Daniel would die before I was successful? I needed to make this happen.

However, I had one go at it. I couldn't be foolish. I couldn't rush into any actions or decisions. I would have to learn as much as I could before deciding on a final course.

God, if I could pull this off, I could stop the needless violence and senseless deaths.

When the water began to cool, I stood from the bath. I could see my reflection in the bathroom mirror and while there was nothing surprising about the rosy hue to my fair skin from all the heat or the darkened wet color of my hair, what was unexpected was the violet glow from my eyes.

Try as I might to tell myself I wasn't affected by my run in with the Shadow Prince, my eyes betrayed my true emotions. Instead of admitting the unease, I shut my eyes and turned away, grabbing a towel to wrap around my torso.

I picked up my brush and began to run it through my hair. Performing a routine activity was calming, and I focused on the smooth swoosh of the bristles gliding over the wet strands.

The brush was my favorite possession. It had been a gift from my parents when I was thirteen. It was chased silver with an intricate floral pattern as well as my initials delicately scripted across the back. I had felt like such a grown-up whenever I had used it. And through the years, the timeless beauty of it hadn't faded.

I also believed it had been spelled somehow. I wasn't sure what the exact intent had been, but I always felt calm and confident after using it.

I had considered not packing it, in the event I didn't make the transition to the manor or if I had to make a quick escape. But now I was glad I had my own things. Things that grounded me. That were a part of my life. And feeling even better, I slipped on a robe.

I picked up some dossier files I had been reading and sat on the downy bed. As soon as I did, I heard shuffling. I could imagine the Crone limping along with that heavy tray out in the dining area. I felt bad for not going out to help or thank her, but really, she probably didn't want to see me just as much as I didn't want to leave the security of the bedroom.

So I leaned back in the bed, knowing that I would not sleep that night. Knowing that no matter how hard I tried I was not going to relax enough to completely let go.

But I was wrong.

As I sat there, the fire began to whisper to me. Those wispy little tendrils floating around my hair like a crown. Whispering my name over and over again, those far away voices told me to sleep. They told me I was safe. That I could drift and be protected. I was gently lulled and swept away. I had no choice but to believe them . . . and I dreamed.

***

Instead of searching the manor the next day, I remained within my room. I spent the day on my satellite laptop, researching private corporations in London. I tried to find anything that might be a potential clue in uncovering the Shadow Court.

I wanted to call Maxim. I thought he could provide some useful information. But I didn't pick up my phone. It was immature, but I didn't want to face him after the way he had chastised me. At least, not just yet.

And I didn't attempt to unveil any more about the manor or the Shadow Prince. I knew that he was there . . . somewhere. And I knew that I could bide my time. I didn't believe he was a threat. I hadn't sensed any great power from him. I could kill him if and when it became necessary.

First, I needed to learn more about the Shadow Court, about those involved with it, and how to gain entry. I needed my new role officially recognized and announced if I was to lead the Dark Nation under Radiant rule after the prince was removed.

Aw, screw it, I told myself. I called Maxim.

Just thinking about him made me recall the dreams I had been having. Every night they were so vivid. They affected me physically. I was waking up writhing and orgasming. It was all so new to me, but I was beginning to understand why people acted so foolishly when it came to sex. I could see how these feelings were addictive.

And having learned that Maxim's appearance was his true form had made me disappointed that I was not experiencing this attraction for him in person. He was tall, muscular, and certainly handsome with his dark features, chiseled jaw, and intense eyes. Learning that he wasn't a cannibal had been a huge plus also. Not to mention he could actually be *fun* when he loosened up.

I began to feel nervous at the thought of speaking to him, though. I decided to end the call. And that was when Maxim answered.

"Yes, Violet. How may I assist you?"

"Oh, uh . . . wrong number," I blurted before hanging up.

My cheeks became hot. I was certain I could never face him again. But then I remembered why I had called him in the first place.

I needed access to the Shadow Court and Maxim was my best source. My *only* source. Humiliated, I picked the phone back up.

Maxim answered again. "You have dialed the same number as before. If you require guidance operating your mobile device, I can send Rheneas to assist you. He is quite adept with technology."

"I'm sorry about that," I told Maxim. "I did mean to call you, I had just momentarily forgotten the reason."

"How lucky for me that you have remembered."

By his dry tone, it was clear I was on his shit list. His voice also had a gravel sound to it as though he had been sleeping, which made sense since most Shadows slept during the day. I'm sure other women would find it sexy, but it didn't do anything for me the way the dreams had. I did feel bad, however, for waking him.

"Look, Maxim, about the other night . . . I apologize for losing my composure. I appreciate everything you have done for me, and I want to make that clear. I'm sure it can't be easy to have been pulled from whatever important work you were doing to babysit me. So, thank you for all your help, and I'm sorry."

There was a pause and then Maxim was clearing his throat. He began fumbling around for words and I cut him off. It was clear he was uncomfortable, and I really didn't want to drag this out for any longer than necessary.

"I would like to just move on now if we may," I told him.

He cleared his throat again. "Certainly. What is it that I may help you with?"

I was going to dive right in, prepared to fight the good fight. "I would like to visit the Shadow Court." I braced myself for the rebuttal I was sure to hear.

Maxim's reply was quick and succinct. "I will contact Barrister Corbett and arrange a visit on your behalf. Is there anything else?"

I was taken aback, not expecting him to so readily agree. I was certain I would have to argue my point. I had been prepared to have the door shut in my face.

"Ah, no. That was all." It was ridiculous, but I floundered for something else to talk to him about.

"Oh, and I'm sorry for thinking you were the Shadow Prince. Obviously, you're not. I met him last night, in a way."

There was a pause on Maxim's end of the line. Finally, he responded. He was very quiet as if not wanting to scare away a small animal. "Are you unharmed?"

"Yes, I'm fine," I reassured him.

"I can come by to collect you if you would like to leave the manor. I will be there in twenty minutes." His words were rushed as if he was already grabbing his things to be on his way.

"No," I told him, "That's not necessary." I wasn't going *anywhere*. Now that I knew the prince was here, I was carrying out my plan.

Maxim's voice dropped. "Is he there with you now?"

"No!" I cried. I was starting to get annoyed. "Maxim, what's going on?"

Maxim seemed to snap out of the fearful concern he had slipped into. "Nothing is going on, Violet. Not everything is a conspiracy. Sometimes one individual simply inquires as to another's well-being. And despite your pigheadedness, you seem like a nice enough young woman. I have been charged with your care. I am taking that responsibility seriously. I have followed my orders to place you within the Dark Manor. However, that does not mean that I agree with your temporary residence. Had it been up to me, you would not be staying there!"

Before I could respond, Maxim took a breath and seemed to calm. "I am glad you are well. Please contact me should you need anything further. I apologize, but if there is nothing more, I will excuse myself from this call."

I was thrown. I didn't know what to do other than comply. "Sure. No problem, Maxim."

"Violet, wait," he said before I could hang up.

"Yes?"

"Stay to your quarters. And . . . should you like to go out, please call me."

"Okay." He was being so weird, to make up for it I was overly cheery. "Bye!"

"Good night," he murmured before ending the call.

What the hell had that been? Was I the only sane person left these days?

It seemed everyone around me was fucking nuts.

CHAPTER 12

HOBBLING AND SHUFFLING, the Crone entered my quarters while carrying the heavy dinner tray. Of course, she wore her ragged brown robe with the cowl drawn. There was nothing to see beneath the hood but blackness. The only part of her body that was visible were her gnarled, arthritic hands.

She wasn't the same as the Shadow Prince had been. I couldn't get a read from her. It was almost as though whatever energy she possessed existed far away. I know that doesn't make much sense, but it's the best way I could describe her. Every once in a while, there would be a flicker from her, but nothing significant, nothing with lasting presence. I had never encountered someone like her before.

If I was being honest, I had been hiding in my bedroom all day. After a certain point, I decided I had to get over myself and get back on track. I was here for a reason after all. I had encountered much more violent and aggressive individuals than the prince and the Crone. I could handle some creepy freaks . . . at least I tried to convince myself I could.

After all, I had thought coming to the Dark Manor meant I was to be thrown into a gruesome, cannibalistic setting with morbid and maniacal *animals*. Instead I was in a dusty mansion with a little old lady and a weak and skittish prince. If anyone should be afraid, it was them . . . of me.

Although Maxim had admitted he was aware of my fighting capabilities, I didn't know if he had shared that information or not. Regardless of what the Dark Prince knew about me, I wanted to try and portray myself in a certain light. I wanted him to think I was sweet, demure, and innocent. I wanted him to see me as nonthreatening.

I was going to continue to dress the part wearing all the flouncy and flowy dresses I had sent over. It didn't matter if I saw him or not. I now knew he lurked about and I would continue to keep in mind that he could be concealed in the very shadows of the same room I occupied.

That included the nightgown I was currently wearing. Normally when I was going to bed, I preferred some basic cotton bikini underwear and a fitted tank. My mother was always slipping stuffy formal nightgowns into my closet, though. Although they sat untouched at home, I had sent them along with my other things to the Dark Manor. They were ideal for the character I was hoping to create. And I wore one this night.

I had been sitting in the anteroom of my quarters reading, hoping that if I made myself available, I might make some progress with my goals. I had opened myself up for another visit from the Dark Prince. Only, his presence was nowhere to be found. In and around my suite, his essence was fading. He had not been back since the previous night.

So when the Crone entered, I was feeling just a tad foolish having dressed in the long gossamer nightgown. It was white vintage chiffon and I felt like I was wearing a costume. But I resented feeling that way, and I ended up overcompensating for it.

I stood but didn't cross to her. "I'm sorry. I still don't know your name," I told her as she made her way to the table.

No reply.

"Thank you ever so much for the meals," I tried.

The dinner tray rattled and thunked as the Crone set it down. She turned and began towards the door.

"Would you care to join me? I would be much obliged for the company."

She made absolutely no acknowledgment of me. I began to get annoyed. I wondered if perhaps she was hard of hearing. Raising my voice my questions took on a frustrated tone. "So, you got a boyfriend?" I asked. "Want me to paint your nails? Maybe we could have a girls' night sometime."

She reached the suite door and began to close it behind her. "We could play scrabble," I called after her. "If you happen to have it handy," I amended. The door seemed to shut a bit harder than the previous nights.

I have never liked a door slammer. It's one of my pet peeves. I decided to have the last word. Marching over and opening the suite door, I stuck my head out to call after her. "Same time tomorrow?"

Of course, she didn't acknowledge my comment, she just shuffled down the dark empty hall. But watching her limp through the dust covered elegance made me wonder . . .

Where is she going?

I decided to follow her. I slipped out of the suite and paused. After the Crone turned the corner for the stairs, I silently began after her. Peeking around the corner, I saw her begin to descend.

It was clear that each step was a monumental hurdle for her to overcome. Grasping the banister, she painstakingly lowered each foot, inch by inch, one at a time.

I pulled back from the corner to wait, pressing myself against the wall there. I couldn't for the life of me understand what she was doing here. Why, of all people, was it her task to *tend* to the manor?

I waited, glancing around the corner to check on her progress from time to time. When the sounds of her labored descent finally ceased, I waited another moment and then took the stairs myself.

However, when I got to the bottom level the Crone was gone. There was no sign of her anywhere. I couldn't tell which direction she had gone, and the darkness of the manor seemed to sit heaviest on the ground floor.

I didn't dare attempt to light any candles as I did not want to call attention to the fact that I had followed her. But creeping through the dark hall, I began to hear that music again. It was still faint, almost imperceptible, but I was more certain of it down here, and I no longer wondered if it was my imagination.

Inch by inch, I crept down the west wing of the foyer. The music was coming from somewhere down there. And coming from the same direction was a dark energy. A presence I had been exposed to recently. I stopped as a chill passed down my spine. But I did not turn back. I took a deep breath and continued on.

Yet, I had been down this section of the hall before. It did not lead anywhere. The only thing down here was that old rotted part of the wall.

When I finally stood before it though, I realized what a fool I had been. The festering wood plank was not a boarded-up portion of the wall . . . It was a *door*.

I only recognized it as such now because I *knew* something lay beyond it.

I held up my hand to try and push the plank open but immediately withdrew it, clutching my fist to my chest. Just having my skin near the wood had been painful. Instinctually my energy had flared, and a glow of warm Light bathed my hand, relieving the pain like a protective balm.

Allowing a small glow of energy to escape my hands, I tried again placing both palms against the door. I could feel cold dark forces within. And the instant my Light made contact with them, it was as though tortured screams that had been buried within the wood were released deep inside. I yanked back my hands as my heart began to pump faster and my breathing deepened.

Summoning more power, more energy, Light burst from my palms as I pressed against the door again. I fought against the cold, the dark, the buried screams that tried to seep into my skin, sending more warm Light coursing through my hands. I gritted my teeth and struggled to budge the door. A crack formed between the wood and the surrounding stone.

I leaned my shoulder into the plank continuing to push. A larger section of the wood separated from the stone, and I stepped back extinguishing my Light. Over my heavy breathing was the faint music. I glanced down the long foyer, making sure I was alone, and then I slipped through the doorway.

I held my palm out in front of me and released a soft glow of Light. I was standing at the top of a narrow, spiraling staircase made completely from old blackened stone.

I began to descend.

It was icy cold. The darkness grew, expanding, becoming heavier, until it pressed down on me like a heavy weight upon my back that I could not carry much longer. And once I reached the bottom of the stairs, I found an abandoned wing of the manor.

The music was coming from somewhere down here—a lonely piano. It called to me. The desolation and abandonment of hope soaked into my bones. Up ahead in the long-forgotten hallway, a dim orange glow of light seeped out from the only door which sat ajar. Despair saturated the damp, dank air of the decrepit corridor. The haunting music ebbed and flowed through the darkness like a desperate beacon.

I knew I should turn away. I knew my presence was an invasion upon some private grief, and I had no right to bear witness to it. But I also knew who I would find. The music he bled was all encompassing. As I neared the room, I felt something drip from my chin and I realized a tear had slid down my cheek.

I reached the door, resting my hand and forehead against the ancient wood, collecting the strength necessary to walk into such sadness. The notes dipped and slowed, and I realized that if I did not move right then, I never would. If I let the melancholy wash over me any longer, it would bury me where I stood. My skin would harden until it became stone and I would forever remain a soul lost to dolor, a forgotten statue.

I pushed the door. It opened without a sound, not daring to disrupt the bleak sonata. And there he sat, at a beautiful piano in a dreary room with nothing but the glow of embers warding off the all-consuming darkness.

His dark head was bowed as strong yet graceful hands moved over the keys. His back was to me, and as a result his mourning went uninterrupted. I stood there watching him as he bled raw emotion with each stroke of the keys and with each pause between notes. The tears I shed would not end. In that moment, I did not think they ever would.

I do not know how long I stood watching him, but eventually the last note was exorcised. I do not know what gave me the strength to speak. Perhaps it was that same fear of becoming stuck, but finally I did. "What ghosts haunt you?"

He did not move, other than the slightest cock of his head, bending an ear in my direction. When he finally responded his low voice was hollow. "They are my own."

There was a significant silence between us before he continued, "You found my wing."

"Yes."

"You should not be here."

"No."

"Most would not be strong enough to bear it."

"No."

"Yet you are."

I didn't feel right agreeing to his assessment of me. If he only knew how close I had come to never opening the door, to becoming lost to the despair and icing over, he wouldn't think me so strong. I wrapped my arms around my waist, even now battling the ice of the shadows.

The embers in the sunken fireplace flared to life and a small fire chased away a little of the dark and cold. "Thank you," I whispered.

He bowed his head in acquiescence.

I took a step towards him.

"You can't save me," he said.

"I'm not here to save you," I responded.

"You can't defeat me either." He was not warning me, he was simply stating a fact.

"It seems that someone has already done that," I told him.

He let his head drop and released a breath.

When he said nothing, I took another step towards him. "Don't you think it's about time you met your wife?"

He stood then in a slow and deliberate manner drawing up to his full towering height. "I don't want you here." Whereas his words had been hollow and devoid of emotion before, now they turned cold.

I laughed. "Well I'm here. And I have to say, you've been a rather rude husband. Wouldn't you say, *Prince of Shadows*?"

He slammed his fists down on the keys and the piano gave an angry shout. "Do not call me that." Each word was carefully spoken in a quite controlled voice, like a knife slice.

I laughed again, purposefully trying to taunt him. "What's the matter? You don't care to be the seat of evil, your highness?"

I didn't see him turn around, nor did I see him approach me. He was too fast, and the room was too dark. Before I knew it, he was in front of me. His hands remained just a fraction away from my arms as though he was going to grab me but had stopped himself at the last second. I found myself looking up into his face and I gasped.

The descriptions I had heard of the Prince of Shadows had been ones of horror. He had been described as a beast with horns, a monster with rotting flesh, a psychotic lunatic, the ultimate personification of evil.

What I saw before me was much worse, much more frightening, than any of the nightmarish pictures which had been painted of him. What I saw in front of me took my breath away and made me question my ability to carry out my plans. I gasped in horror.

He was gorgeous. Even with the combination of despair and rage contorting his face, he was the most beautiful being I had ever beheld. His marble skin was flawless. His eyes were haunted, yes, but they were an incredible electric blue, accentuated by the dark slash of his brows.

His patrician features were an artist's dream. Even the grim set of his lips could not disguise their fullness. The front of the black shirt he wore was unbuttoned revealing a sculpted chest that was highly defined. Ridges of granite muscle traveled down his midsection.

I took a step back, and this time he did clamp his hands down on my arms, holding me in place. "You do not get to force your unwelcome company upon me and then leave at will," he hissed.

I cried out, unable to stop myself. The sensations from his touch were all consuming. The despair, the desolation, the fear and anger, the need, the want, the desire; it all came pouring into me.

The control began to slip from his words and he spoke with a growl of anger. "You want a proper welcome from your husband? You will be sorry. Perhaps you will learn a valuable lesson." And then he crushed his lips over mine.

The brutal assault of his emotions came slamming into me, and my knees buckled. His arms wrapped around me, caging me against the hard ridges of his body, keeping me upright. It was too much, I was suffocating from the onslaught. There were too many warring emotions and yet they were all leading to one outcome. The fear, desolation, lust, and desire were all culminating into an unbearable need. I experienced his emotions as if they were my own, and I needed touch, acceptance, and love so desperately I would do anything to possess them.

My fists which had been pounding against his chest moved up to clasp the back of his neck. But the moment I tried to pull myself into him, he reached back to remove my hands and shove me away. I drew my fingers up to my mouth in shock and embarrassment. I had wanted him. I would have done anything with him if he had not pushed me away. The emotions had been too forceful to fight, and I had surrendered.

Yet he had rejected me.

He stood there, chest heaving. Black veins had begun to thread through the beautiful blue of his eyes. "Leave," he commanded. When I didn't move immediately he shouted, "Now!"

With his roar, the small fire extinguished casting the room into complete darkness. Instinctually my energy flared, creating a new source of light in the room. However, the Prince of Shadows was nowhere to be seen.

I didn't wait around to find out what happened to him. There was dark evil in the room. Although my Light protected me, I had a feeling it was not as much of a bastion as the prince himself had been.

I turned and ran.

CHAPTER 13

WEAK.

I had thought him weak. I couldn't stop shaking after being exposed to his power. How he had held it all back—how he could hold it all *within*—I couldn't fathom.

It was difficult for me to understand what I had felt from him, what I had experienced. But one thing that was clear was that I had wildly underestimated my objective here. This was not going to be simple.

The Dark Prince hadn't even unleashed his power upon me, I had merely been a tourist—taking a peek inside. Exposed to a mild fraction of it. But that was all I needed to see to know he would not be easy to kill.

However, although I was wary, I was not fearful. Something strange was certainly going on, but I did not feel I was in immediate danger. Maxim, the prince, the Crone . . . they could have made any number of attempts on me, but I had been left alone.

That was why when I saw something strange the next evening, I went to see what it was.

I spent the day trying my best to research info on the Shadow Court's private company again. I also called Maxim to get an update on my introduction to the court. He made some excuse as to why a visit had yet to be scheduled, assuring me that he would continue to work on it. And I had a suspicion that he was jerking me along.

I also continued to search the Manor. I wanted to know it from top to bottom, like the back of my hand. That way if I found myself in a compromising position, I would know the tools, hiding spaces, and exits around me.

But when evening fell, I returned to my suite figuring I would wait for the Crone. I still wanted to follow her and find out where she went at night. However, first I went through each room of my quarters to make sure I was alone. I decided I should be doing this every time I re-entered the suite.

I was just about to exit one of the spare rooms, when I noticed something from the window. From the woods behind the manor grounds, I saw two pinpricks of light slicing through the dark night.

I couldn't imagine what it was. Anytime the two thin beams moved, it was in synchronization. The beams were too small in diameter to be from a vehicle, and they moved together so it was hard to imagine that two flashlights were being wielded in perfect unison. Even if they were, the beams were too thin, they did not widen the way a flashlight beam would.

My quarters were on the fifth floor of the manor. From that height, I could see the light through the tops of the trees and arcing across the night sky. Whatever was causing the illumination was down on the forest floor.

Despite my encounter with the Dark Prince the previous night, I still believed myself to be incredibly capable. I believed that I had the upper hand in this entire situation . . . It's funny how our views of ourselves do not change quickly.

But more importantly, I was used to slinking through the darkness of night while hunting monsters. I had yet to develop a healthy fear of the dark. Of the unknown. I had yet to learn the rules. I had yet to learn of the evil things that the darkness can bring.

So you can understand why I made my way outside. I possessed a false sense of security. And with that, a person can do reckless things.

Another factor which made me bolder was a shift in my perspective. I had felt an evil presence in and around the manor. However, after finding the abandoned wing buried underground—the prince's wing—I knew that space was the dark, lifeless heart of this manor. It was where the evil upon these grounds nested. The rest of the manor now seemed almost tame in comparison.

Closing my suite doors without a sound, I made my way down to the large foyer and out the back entrance. Through the weeds and bramble, I passed by the overgrown gardens and the empty stables. I headed straight for the forest.

After stepping on a thorn, I realized I hadn't bothered to put any shoes on. I thought it odd, that I had rushed straight out in the flimsy dress I wore and bare feet. With the sting of my torn flesh, I became confused about my hurried actions. I slowed for a moment, deciding I should return to my quarters, but then those pinpricks of light sliced through the blackness of the night sky again, and I couldn't help but direct my focus upon them.

I made my way towards the tree line to get a closer look. As I approached, I studied the beams of light. There did not seem to be any predictable pattern to them. They would shift around, wink off for a moment, remain steady, and then disappear for several seconds.

Once I felt I was close enough, I silently scaled a tree. If I'm being completely honest, before I began to climb, I tucked the hem of my dress into my panties. I'm sure it looked ridiculous, but I didn't expect anyone would see me. I grumbled to myself, annoyed that I was in this useless garment and irritated at the loose hair tumbling around my face and shoulders. *This* was why I always wore leathers and a braid.

Despite my attire, I deftly climbed towards the top of the tree and reached a sturdy branch. I crouched there against the trunk and surveyed the forest around me searching for the source of those beams. What I saw in a small clearing below, surrounded by trees and darkness, gave me chills.

It was a little girl.

She had white-blonde hair and was wearing a tattered dress. She seemed to be playing some sort of game while muttering to herself. Rows of stones and pebbles were lined up in front of her, and she kept shifting them around.

Mutterings of her child's voice were drifting through the night air. " . . . not right . . . won't work . . . maybe . . . no, no . . ."

A lantern sat in the center of the clearing providing a small glow of light. Next to the little girl was a massive black wolf. He was lying down with his head on his paws, watching her.

And those two bright pinpricks of light . . . were coming from her *eyes*. She would pause every now and then to stare up into the night sky, seeming to search for something, before returning her attention back to the stones on the ground.

I had not been expecting anything like this. I sucked in a startled breath. The little girl picked up her head, and the two beams of bright light landed on my face.

Out of reflex, I threw my arm up to shield my eyes, and I went falling backwards.

Had I been in a fighting state of mind, I would have righted myself and landed on my feet in a crouch. But the eerie tableau I had just witnessed had me confused and disoriented. I landed with a thud on my back—the breath knocked from me.

Before I had a chance to sit up, the little girl was above me. She peered at me, not saying a word.

I couldn't take her blinding stare. Trying to push myself away from her, I sat up. "What are you?" I breathed.

"That is a rude question," she replied, her voice void of emotion.

"I'm sorry," I told her. I stood, adjusting my dress. "What are you doing out here? Where are your parents? Shouldn't you be at home?"

"I'm playing a game. I like games." She turned around and made her way back to her rows of stones. Sitting down in front of them, she picked one up and held it out to me. "Would you like to play?"

I took a step towards her, wanting to get her out of the woods immediately. But the large black wolf rose to its feet then. Hunching its back, it bared it fangs and growled at me.

I lifted the hem of my dress, wrapping my hand around the hilt of the dagger strapped to my thigh. Not wanting to frighten the little girl or startle the wolf, I kept my voice low. Keeping my eyes on the wolf, I said, "Very slowly, I want you to cross to me. Okay, honey?"

Instead, the little girl stood and went beside the wolf. She placed her tiny hand on the wolf's head and began to pet it.

"He won't hurt me," she said. "You should be nice to him. He knows you don't like him. He could be your friend if you're nice to him. Just because he's big and scary, doesn't make him bad."

The little girl blinked her large beaming eyes up at me, seeming to wait for a response. It was impossible to meet her blinding gaze. I assessed the wolf instead. The dark beast had turned his head up to the girl's touch and was now nuzzling her hand.

Regardless of the fact that the wolf seemed to tame at her touch, I knew I needed to get her away from it.

"Honey, where do you live? I'll help you get home." I told her.

"Not yet," she replied. "I'm still playing." She went to sit in front of her stones once more. The black wolf resumed his spot, lying next to her on the forest floor.

The little girl picked up one of the rocks and held it out to me. "This one can be yours."

"Okay," I told her. "But how about we take a few of the rocks inside and we can play until your parents are able to come get you?" I tried.

The little girl sighed, cradling the rock she was holding. "It's too bad I have to break it," she murmured.

"It's okay. You don't need to break it. Just bring it inside."

She looked up at me again, those beams of light blinding me. "If I don't break it open, I can't show you what's inside."

"I've seen rocks before. You don't need to break it just to show me."

There was something about the timbre of her voice that made goosebumps break out across my skin next. "This isn't an ordinary." She held it up, twisting it this way and that while staring at it. "You would never know there was more inside . . . unless you break it open."

At that, she squeezed the rock. With a loud crack, it split down the center just as a strong wind swept through the forest clearing. The fallen leaves went flying and arcing around us in a fluttered frenzy. The small flame in the lantern extinguished and at the same moment, the little girl closed her eyes. The clearing was plunged into blackness.

"Why keep such beauty hidden away from anyone to see?" the little girl whispered in the dark.

When she opened her eyes, those beams of light fell upon the rock in her hands.

It was true. It had not been an ordinary rock she was holding, but a geode. Clear quartz and purple amethyst sparkled within the center.

The little girl tried to piece the two halves back together and set the geode on the ground. However the moment she let go, it tumbled open. She canted her head while staring at the sparkling centers and her voice was sad. "It can never be as it was."

After a moment of silence, I felt a need to comfort her. "Does it matter that it's broken? It's quite interesting and lovely. And you can still use it in your game, can't you?"

She held her delicate and dirty hand over the two broken pieces. With a wave of her fingers, the two halves fused together and were made whole once again. Yet, a thin white scar was left where the crack had been.

She shook her head with deep regret. "No," she breathed. "I'll always know . . . it was broken."

I gestured to all the other rocks in front of her. "You have so many others."

The little girl shrugged. "I suppose." Her gaze swept across all the little stones and pebbles lying before her causing those beams of light to arc across the ground. "But how will I know which are special and which are ordinary. I will have to break them all to find out."

"I quite like them broken open," I told her. "Regardless of how you find them, they are all still rocks and stones whether they're whole or not. They are just taking on a new shape and size. And through the process you get to explore and discover. I think it's rather exciting to uncover new facets about things. Don't you?"

But before the little girl could respond, a howl pierced the air of the quiet night. The black wolf sprang to its feet again arching its back and baring its fangs with a growl.

The little girl also stood and turned her head. "It's coming closer," she whispered.

I had had enough. "Look, we need to get you home," I demanded. "Where do you live?"

She pointed behind me. "On the other side," she said simply.

I glanced over my shoulder. I tried to look through the trees to see if there was a house or building, but there was nothing in eye sight. "I can walk you back," I told her.

But when I turned around . . . she was gone.

CHAPTER 14

I KICKED IN THE BACK DOOR. I was so angry. I couldn't handle any more ridiculous bullshit. And on top of it all I looked like an idiot. I was barefoot and in a flimsy dress with my hair loose, all down my shoulders and back.

I needed to kick someone's ass. I would have given anything to be out hunting Shadows. I began to storm up the stairs on my way to my suite when I realized I could—and should—be hunting *the* Shadow.

I was going to head straight for my closet. I was going to dig out the one pair of fighting leathers I had tucked away along with my black halter top and boots. I would secure my hair in a long braid, check all my weapons and do what I fucking came here to do. I was going to assassinate the Dark Prince.

I had had enough of the theatrics.

A small voice protested. *It's not the right time. Your position hasn't been announced. You don't have enough information. Just wait a minute and calm down!*

But I stuffed the objections away. The details didn't really matter. A dead prince was a dead prince.

Reaching my quarters, I flung the suite door open and slammed it behind me. Then I stopped in my tracks. He was here.

Although I had left fires burning in each hearth on both sides of the room, they now smoldered with embers. The candles in the chandelier overhead had also died down, and only two remained.

And without a moment's hesitation, I struck.

With one hand I sent a blast of energy hurtling through the room, igniting each fireplace with an explosive start. At the same time, my other hand grasped the dagger from under the hem of my dress and launched it unerringly for the prince's heart.

That should have been the end of it. The speed and precision of my deadly throw along with the distraction of light filling the room, should have killed him. In any of the circumstances I had ever found myself in, this attack would have been fatal.

But instead of the satisfying thunk of metal into flesh I was expecting, I heard a cold ping reverberate through the room. And just as fast as I had lit the room into bright light, it was plunged into darkness. Before the knife had even made it to the wall where it was lodged, I was trapped.

One sinewy arm was snaked around my waist while I was jerked against the granite wall of his torso. My chin was grabbed and yanked to the side. Cold lips pressed against my ear.

His silky dark voice was agitated. "I warned you. Do not be foolish. You cannot defeat me."

And at his touch I shuddered. Just as before, I was somehow immersed into that darkness he carried. There was such coldness. Such emptiness. Such misery. Bottomless. The torment and despair culminating into that unbearable need. God, he made me ache.

It was naive of me, but I had written off our last encounter as an initial error. Something I had not been expecting. He had gotten the better of me. I had told myself it would not happen a second time. Yet here I was immersed in him once again.

However, this time there almost seemed to be a faint spark of *something* . . . something different, buried under it all. Something I hadn't noticed the last time. The flicker was so brief, though, that it was impossible to focus on it.

It didn't matter. The overwhelming need and desire eclipsed all else. And in bearing witness to it, it became my own. I cried out, the assault of longing crippling.

He tightened his grip on my chin and squeezed his arm around my waist. My back was crushed against him. Then he ground his lips against my cheek as he spoke. "I do not know what witchery you play at. But it will not work. You waste your energy."

I grappled for strength. For some semblance of control. For power. "I will kill you," I gritted between my teeth.

A humorless laugh was my reply. He spun me around grabbing my upper arms in a bruising grip and shook me. "Then do it," he challenged.

The ice blue of his eyes sparked in the darkness. The air around us vibrated. Again, he wore a black shirt, open in the front. Trying to escape the hold he had on me, I shifted my gaze to his chest. He was perfect. His skin was flawless, and each muscle was highly defined. There was something like a black tattoo over his left pectoral though. His shirt was covering most of it and I only saw a brief glance.

I desperately needed to get away from him. To put some distance between us. I could not control my impulses. I remembered how he had vanished after kissing me before. How he had rejected me. I prayed that he would again. Because I knew I would lack the strength to break away from whatever this was.

Looking back up into his perfect features, I broke free from his grasp. I grabbed the back of his neck with one hand, clawing my nails into his skin just below his dark hair. With my other hand, I fisted the front of his shirt and pulled him down to me.

Only this time, he didn't push me away. This time, he kissed me back. Over and over again I parted my lips for him, unable to get enough of his kiss. I moaned in despair. I was lost. It was over. There was nothing to me. I was want and need. That was all I was. All I would ever be. And he was it. In that moment he was everything. There was nothing else. Only him.

In that moment, I would do *anything* for him.

And that realization was enough to shatter the spell I was under. From somewhere I didn't know existed, I pulled. I gathered this unknown strength I had–this unknown strength I never thought I'd need—and I wrenched myself away from him with an agonized moan, driving my fist into his face.

The blow barely affected him. He stood there. Chest billowing—hands flexing and clenching at his sides. But the blue of his eyes was completely consumed by black.

He grabbed my face with one hand, digging his fingers into each side of my jaw. A dark angel. That was what he was. What he must be. He was too perfect. He was shaking. His jaw clenched so tightly I thought it would shatter.

"Leave. If you stay, I will bury you here. You will know only a pit of darkness for the rest of your existence." Each word had been a monumental task.

He stared at me for a moment with what looked like contempt. At my lips. My hair. My skin. My eyes. He drew in a deep breath and with a determination I had never witnessed from another, he let go of my face.

Moving his hand away inch by agonizing inch. It was as though each fraction of a retreat was pure torture. Then he turned his back and walked away from me towards the suite doors, fading away into the shadows of the room as he left.

Along with the undeniable lust, I felt raw anger. I was infuriated that he had made me *feel* this way. That he of all people, could affect me as no one else had.

I had wished and prayed to be able to experience desire and lust. And now I had . . . at the hands of a monster. It only proved all the more that something was wrong with me. And I vowed I would kill him for it.

"I'm not going anywhere," I hissed after him.

Just before the slamming of the door I heard a low growl. "You will leave. Tomorrow."

I took a shuddering breath trying, in vain, to compose myself. Then I flung my hands out towards both fireplaces lighting warm crackling fires before stumbling my way to one of the bookshelves in the room.

I had seen a section of books dealing with various beings from folklore and mythology. Running my hand over the old leathery spines, I found one on demons. I flipped through the brittle pages praying to find what I was looking for. And finally, towards the back of the book, I did.

I studied the sketched image at the top of the page, searching for some connection, some type of confirmation.

A woman lay haphazardly on a bed. One arm above her head. Hair splayed about. She was completely open. Vulnerable. Exposed. The thin nightgown she wore displayed every curve and valley of her body. Although she was supposed to be sleeping, she looked more as though under a spell.

Looming above her was a dark figure. He was shirtless with arms and wings outstretched. There was a sinister air to his presence, but it was difficult to discern specific feature. He was hazy, dreamlike, seeming to blend in with the background. And under the sketch in Gothic script was printed: INCUBUS

According to the tome, an incubus was a male demon who visited sleeping women. The incubus would seduce a woman in her sleep and engage in sexual activity with her. Although there was not a specific quality that attracted them, they tended to focus their attentions upon one mate at a time preferring to revisit her alone until her vitality was drained which would result in death for mortals and any manner of psychosis for immortals.

There was no mention of the effect incubi had on a woman while awake. But perhaps they possessed the same seductive qualities.

I had never met one nor seen one. I was vaguely aware of their existence, and I did not know anything about them. The tome did not provide much information. There was no mention of how to stop an incubus. But I believed a witch might be able to conjure up a protective spell.

That had to be what he was—why I felt so powerless against these feelings.

I retreated to my bedroom, surveying the space for any signs of *his* presence. But as far as I could sense, he had not invaded the privacy of this room. Grabbing my phone, I forced myself to calm down.

When I heard the click on the other end of the line, I didn't wait for a greeting. "I need a vehicle," I demanded.

"I will be there in twenty minutes," came Maxim's smooth reply.

"I don't need a *ride*," I ground out. "I need my *own* vehicle."

"I will be there in twenty minutes," Maxim repeated. And then he hung up . . . The son of a bitch hung up on me.

***

I glared. I blazed. I seethed.

Maxim wasn't bothered in the slightest. Or at least, he acted like he wasn't. He just continued to drive ahead, eyes and attention focused on the bumpy dirt path.

"You're really going to try and tell me that there are no other vehicles for use in the area."

Maxim nodded. "That's correct."

"Are Tweedledee and Tweedledum going to be tailing us once we reach the main road again?"

"Yes."

"Then I can take their car and they can ride with you."

"I'm afraid that's not possible."

"You *know* you're incredibly irritating. You know that, right?"

Instead of replying, Maxim simply shrugged.

"When can you supply a vehicle for me? I will need one for my personal use which remains at the manor."

"I have been informed by Barrister Corbett that there are none available for use at this time."

I wasn't stupid. I knew what was going on. I knew that I was purposefully being denied access to a vehicle. Just like Maxim was purposefully stalling in arranging a visit to the Shadow Court.

It didn't matter, though. Maxim had agreed to take me back into town, and that was all I needed at the moment. One way or another I would lose him once we arrived. I would kick his legs out from under him if I had to.

I turned to look out my window, watching the dark forms of the oak trees as we drove past. From somewhere out there in the darkness, I felt like I was being watched. The feeling crawled across my skin, and I pulled my cloak tighter around my shoulders.

We reached the main street and it was just as it had been the other night. Gas lamps aglow, a few pedestrians strolling in and out of shops along the cobblestone street, and some random chickens milling about. Except this evening, the front door of the Screaming Banshee was boarded up and the wooden sign that had hung above the door had been removed.

Apparently, Maxim had smoothed things over with the witnesses from my little ... *encounter*. What he had said or done, he hadn't shared. And I didn't ask about the fate of the pub owner. I couldn't. Maxim was already helping me out of our vehicle and I was rattling my brain for a way to lose him. I still hadn't come up with a plan.

I didn't want to resort to violence. Maxim had been decent to me, and I needed an ally. I didn't think he would be too happy if I kicked his ass in the middle of this little village. And then there were his goons I would have to deal with as well. Rheneas and Stefan had parked just behind us and were standing in front of their vehicle scanning the street.

Maxim already sounded irritated as he shut the door behind me. He had thought I called this evening because I wanted to leave the Dark Manor and return to the Radiant Court. At least that had clearly been his hope.

Whether it was because he was purely concerned about my safety at the manor or because he didn't want to babysit me any longer, I didn't know. But he had obviously been surprised this evening—and then disappointed—when he found out I had merely wanted to return to town and was not fleeing the Shadow countryside.

"If you have come here with a pub visit in mind, there is the inn just behind the alley. They serve mead and wine. However, please be aware now that despite the impoliteness of it, you will indeed be drinking alone."

"Actually, I just want to visit that vegetable stand," I replied gesturing across the street to the small cart with twinkling lights.

A little of the tension in Maxim's shoulders eased, and without another word he began to escort me towards it. My eyes darted around searching for a way to stall, desperately seeking an excuse to leave him behind.

We were halfway across the little thoroughfare when I decided I would need to take another approach. Maybe if I got Maxim and the goons settled at the inn, I could ditch them there. "Um, never mind," I began, "I, ah, don't think they have what I'm looking for. You were right, I'd rather—"

But I didn't finish my sentence because at that moment everything around me froze. Maxim paused mid step, becoming still as a statue. The few other pedestrians who had been ambling about halted as well. The flames flickering in the gas lamps which lined the street all stilled. And even the light breeze sweeping through the night became inert.

From the old trailer parked behind the vegetable stand, a young woman emerged. She waved me over, clearly beckoning me to hurry. "C'mon, I can't hold them for long," she admonished. Her Bronx accent threw me for a moment, but I scurried over to her just the same and darted through the camper entry.

Although the trailer was clearly old, the exterior was freshly painted in color blocks of white, gray, and teal. I had expected the interior to be a little less retro chic and a little more dark and ominous—based on who she was. However, I was surprised to find more bright cheery colors inside. There was a new laminate floor, newly upholstered furniture, and even a sparkly little chandelier hanging from the ceiling which lit the space with a cozy glow.

"I'm damn powerful when it comes to time. But I can't hold an entire street frozen for long. We got to make this quick." She pointed at the compact dining table. "First payment. And let me tell you. Power like this ain't cheap."

From my clutch I procured five hundred pounds and laid it on the table.

The witch pursed her lips together and snatched up the bills. "Okurrrp," she said as she tucked the bills into her bra. It was like she was saying okay while using a funny little chirping sound.

With a flick of her fingers she procured a business card out of thin air. Then she placed it on the table in front of me. I picked it up and felt the buzz of fresh magic on it. It read:

Belcalis
Time Mage and general practitioner for all your Wiccan needs.

"It's pronounced BELL-ka-leez," she said with a pop of her hip, and I could feel a tremor of magic in her name alone.

I looked over at her. She was average height with black shoulder length hair that was parted on the side in big waves. She had flawless caramel skin, large brown eyes, and full lips that were glossy. An array of studs lined her one visible ear, and she wore a short white dress that had multiple straps crossing over her shoulders and around her neck.

"So why are you here?" she asked.

"How did you know I needed to see you?" I replied.

She smacked her lips together making a tsking sound. "Gurl, you reeked of desperation. It stunk up my camper so fast, I had to stop time just to get a chance to air it out." Her face was scrunched up at the recollection.

"Sorry about that," I tried, feeling as though it was too little too late.

When Maxim had brought me into town the other evening, I had noticed the small pentagram carved above her camper door. It was why I had wanted to patronize her vegetable stand. I needed a witch's help.

"Look. What I got goin' on out there ain't no small feat. So you better start explaining what you need. Otherwise your investment will go to waste," she said gesturing to her bra where she had stored the cash.

"I need a spell to ward off an incubus," I told her.

Her eyebrows rose. "You got one visiting you?"

I eyed the floor. "Yes."

"I hate to tell you," she replied, "but if that's the case. Gurl, you could be pregnant." She eyed my abdomen. "You want me to do a scan?"

I nodded.

"It's an extra hundred," she warned.

I opened my clutch and placed another bill on the table.

Without warning, the witch waved her hand across my hips. I braced myself for the worst.

But a look of confusion crossed her face. "You ain't got no incubus troubles! If you'd been with one of em, you'd have some—ah—*evidence* in you, if you understand my meaning. You as dry as the Mojave Desert in those terms. In fact," she waved her hand across my hips again. Her eyes widened before squinting almost shut and pursing her lips. "Gurl, please. You a virgin!"

I could feel the heat begin to flame across my face. But Belcalis lifted her hands up as if trying to not cast judgement. "Hey, it don't matter that you are, but I can tell you that you ain't been compromised by no incubus."

166

I fought the urge to cross my arms over my waist. "Well I'm living with one," I told her. "And I think it's just a matter of time. I want something to stop the dreams. And I need something that will prevent any influence from him during waking hours as well."

Belcalis pursed her lips. "Honey, what you describing don't sound like no incubus. If you been living with one, trust me, you'd been compromised."

"I think he might be trying to avoid me."

Belcalis eyed me from head to toe. "I find that hard to believe. Ain't nothin wrong wit' you. No reason for an incubus not to knock boots wit' you."

"Regardless, can you give me something?"

She tilted her head. "You sure? Is this incubus hot? They usually are. Seems like you could use a little, uh, *fun*. No need to cock-block when you're desperate for cock," she said with a shrug. "Know what I mean?"

The impulse to tell her that I was not *desperate for cock* flared, but I shoved it aside. "I'm sure," I told her.

She gave another purse of her lips and a shrug. "I can give you something to ward off this incubus, but I ain't ever heard of their powers having any impact during waking hours. From what I know, they only get down when their mate is asleep."

She leaned in closer. "I mean don't get me wrong, those boys can be sexy as hell when you meet them, but the seduction they throw off ain't nothing like when they visit in dreams."

"I think this one is incredibly powerful. And he may have gone a long time without feeding on someone. I need something to block his powers day and night."

Belcalis turned over her shoulder in a huff of irritation. "I know she's a damn fool!" she snapped. "But she's paying cash, so she'll get what she's asking for." Then she turned fully around to face the shelves behind her. "You think I can keep that street frozen much longer? I need to get her fool ass outta here!"

Belcalis turned back to me with a pleasant smile plastered on her face. "Sorry about that. Don't mind my granny. She likes to butt in from time to time. One extra strong ward for an incubus, coming right up."

She turned to the shelves and began rummaging around through various jars, containers, baskets, and drawers. I couldn't see or sense anyone else in the camper with us, so I assumed Belcalis was able to commune with spirits.

After pulverizing a few different items in a mortar and pestle, she said an incantation over the black powder and it turned white. Then she poured the mixture into a little cloth bag and pulled the string closed. When she turned to hand me the small bag I noticed blood was trickling out of her nose.

She saw me staring at the blood and waved her hand in dismissal. "Hittin' my limit," she said, words slowing. "Frozen street. Strong spell. Sucking me dry."

She gestured to the cloth bag I now held. "This will keep any incubus away. Pour a circle of it around your bed where you sleep. He will not be able to enter your dreams."

She paused to swallow and leaned her hands on the dining table for support. "Carry the rest in your pocket and he will not be able to seduce you when awake either." The blood began to gush from her nose faster. "Go now. Time is up."

168

I wanted to ask her what she was doing here. Why she was in a little Shadow village in the south of England. I wanted to ask her if it was true that the Shadows were not holding witches captive for glamours. But I could see she was reaching a breaking point.

"Thank you," I told her. Instead of asking any questions, I turned to leave. As I reached for the door, I noticed a bulletin board on the back of it. Tacked there was a red flyer.

The paper had that black symbol of the three crescents intertwined. The same as the flyer I snatched from the pub. In addition to the *JOIN THE REVOLUTION* text, this one had an additional message included on it. The paper was scorched as if it had been held too close to a flame.

I glanced back at Belcalis. She was still leaning over the table with her back to me except now she had begun to shake. I snatched the flyer and shoved it into my bag as I flew out the door and into the street to resume my spot next to Maxim.

In a snap, the street came back to life. Maxim completed his step, the gas lamps flickered, and the breeze stirred the night air as if it had never been interrupted.

The whole experience was jarring for me, but no one milling about the street seemed to notice anything amiss. I tried to hop back into step with Maxim, but it was rather awkward, so I pretended to stumble.

Maxim grabbed my elbow and tried to steady me. "Are you alright?" he asked.

"Yes, fine," I reassured him. "But as I was saying, I can see this stand doesn't have what I was looking for. I am ready to return to the manor."

169

Before we left, Maxim gave me an odd look . . . And I couldn't tell if he glanced at the clutch by my side or not.

CHAPTER 15

THE LOUD CRASH WRENCHED ME FROM SLEEP. It was followed by shattering and the splintering of wood. An enraged roar ripped through my quarters louder than all the other sounds of destruction.

I bolted up in bed and looked around. I was confused and disoriented. There was no sunlight pouring in through the windows, and it took me a moment to understand that it was dusk. I reminded myself that it had been just before sunrise when Maxim had dropped me off, and the sun had been shining brightly by the time I had gone to sleep. It seemed I had slept the entire day.

Somewhere nearby a frenzied pounding began, and with each stomp was the crunch of delicate materials.

I realized I was waging a war within myself. There was a need and want so deep, I thought I would implode from lack of fulfillment. But it was a desire I did not wish to possess. One I refused to give in to. I had been through much greater tests than this. I would not succumb.

But that was a deeper battle. What drove me now was the resentment and fury which blanketed all else. I needed to lash out. I needed recompense. My demons were leashed, but by no means tame. They rattled the bars of their cage, demanding to be fed.

I tried to breathe, to focus. To calm the chaotic cyclone of energy whirling through me. With each inhale came a gradual clarity . . . These were not my thoughts and emotions.

I grabbed the small bag from next to my pillow and jumped out of the bed. The thin line of white powder I had poured that morning still encircled the bed in an unbroken circumference.

With the bag clutched to my chest, I dashed to the suite doorway. I pressed my body against the door, listening. He was out there in the hall. But I had the spelled mixture this time. I would have the upper hand.

I opened the door.

There was no reason to. No need to. I could have stayed within the protected circle of the bed. Or at least within the bedroom which had become a safe haven of sorts. But there was a pull. Each time I sensed him, there was an inexplicable pull. I was drawn to him. It wasn't even a facet of our interactions that I was fully aware of. It just was.

He paced the floor, stomping over littered debris. It looked like he had thrown both the side table and antique vase which had sat in the hallway. Their pieces now littered the space, and an icy chill hung in the air.

I tried to send a flare of energy to the chandelier hanging above, but it was snuffed out before reaching the candles. It didn't matter. I preferred the light, but I didn't need it.

His voice was a growl from the shadows. "You were supposed to leave." I could see his hands clenching and flexing over and over again.

"I told you I wasn't," I replied.

He began to trudge towards me, pausing in between steps. I could feel the frenzied battle within. He was warring with himself. He did not want to come close to me, but he *needed* to.

I had lit fires in both hearths of the sitting room with a flick of my wrists as I had passed by in my haste for the suite door. The chandelier within was also ablaze. The light from my suite bled into the darkness of the hall. And as he crossed into its glow, I could see the black branching into the crystal blue of his irises. Those eyes were narrowed on me, and a muscle ticked in his jaw.

He made a grab for me. But I flung the spelled powder at him. It smattered across his face and drifted in a cloud around him.

It had worked. He had stopped in his tracks. Only . . . he didn't look *vanquished*.

I have been in many battles throughout my life. There is a certain look an opponent has once he knows he is defeated. It's always there if you know what to look for.

But there was no realization of defeat on his face. If anything, he looked confused and irritated. He did begin to cough on the powder though, and he wiped it from his eyes.

I took a step back into the anteroom. I wasn't entirely sure what was happening. However, as soon as I took the retreating step, he picked his head up, lasering his focus back onto me. He advanced, entering the suite.

"What was that?" His voice was a deadly growl.

"Something to stop you," I replied.

He lunged and grabbed my wrist pulling me into him. "It didn't work."

Being close to him, having my body pressed into his . . .

"You. Leave. Now," he gritted. And he began to pull me. I had no doubt he would drag me down all five flights of stairs if that was what it took to get rid of me.

I dug down to find the full effect of my power and I hurled a blast of Light straight into him. Instead of dropping my wrist or stumbling backwards, he stood his ground. Yet, he shuddered and then took a gasping breath as if he had been without air for far too long.

I braced myself, expecting his rage to redouble. But instead, he seemed slightly eased, as if a little of the chaos and frenzy had been subdued. He closed his eyes to take a more calming breath, and when he opened them, the black had been erased leaving behind untarnished crystal blue. Dropping my wrist, he took a step back from me.

Even with the space between us, I had to look up at him. Again he wore a black shirt, opened down the middle, and I inanely wondered if he ever wore anything else. The thought made me self-conscious.

I realized I was standing there in a flimsy nightgown with loose, disheveled hair. It made me feel too exposed. Too vulnerable.

He eyed me, and it was as though the sight of me alone maddened him. "Leave."

I marched over to the coffee table and seized the little black box that had been sitting there. I had yet to open it again. It had been inspected and deemed safe, free of any magics or spells, but I could not bring myself to wear the ring Barrister Corbett had presented.

I tossed the box at his feet. "Who extended this proposal?" I demanded.

He said nothing. He didn't even glance at the box. He just stared at me.

"It obviously wasn't you," I continued.

"Leave," he repeated. Even when angry, his voice had a deep silky caress to it, and I stifled a shudder.

My own irritation rose, and I crossed my arms over my chest. "I. Can't." I fought the urge to take a step closer to him. "I have asked to be taken to the Shadow Court—"

He clenched his jaw and looked away. As if fighting against better judgement he bit out one word. "*Don't.*"

"Well, I can't. I don't know where it is, and no one is responding to my request."

"Go somewhere else. Go *home.*"

I huffed. "How exactly do you propose I do that? I have requested a vehicle. That request has been denied. I have also been informed that there is a ward in place around here and the surrounding area. Even if I wanted to have one of the Angela pulse me out, they could not reach me.

"And on top of all that, no one's tried to kill me . . . no one's tried to announce this *marriage . . .*" This time I did take a step closer to him, and I drilled him with a look. Maybe if I stared hard enough into him, I could read his mind. "So why am I here?"

"It does not matter. You are not wanted here. Return to your home."

"You need me," I countered.

A sneer formed across his face, and even with condescension dripping from his every pore, he looked too gorgeous for words. "What could I possibly need you for?"

I made my way into the bedroom and retrieved the flyer from my clutch. When I returned to the sitting room, he was standing in the same spot, but the fires had banked down making the room less bright. I knew it had been his doing. Just to be difficult, I stoked them higher.

Careful not to touch his skin, I thrust the flyer at him. He didn't take it.

I shook it in front of him. "Your people are revolting. You have the beginnings of a revolution on your hands. Something needs to be done to ease dissent. I can help. That is supposed to be what this marriage is all about. Take me to the Shadow Court. Let me help."

I looked at the flyer again. It was the same as the first I had procured from the pub except Belcalis's copy looked like it had been held over a flame. The additional text on the second flyer provided a date, time, and location as well as a short blurb:

Those in power have failed us,
The decaying courts must die.
Our voices will be silenced no longer,

They will hear our battle cry.

I didn't understand why *courts* was plural. Perhaps the Shadows had several branches to their system. I needed to get inside and figure all this out. I had to find out where this unrest was stemming from and find a solution.

"It doesn't matter," came the low reply. "None of it does."

I looked back up and realized something . . . He didn't care.

"How can you say that?" I asked "This could turn violent. People could die."

"If they are too stupid to understand their place then they deserve to."

I don't know why I was surprised by his response. I shouldn't have been. It's exactly the disposition I should have expected from him.

I was angry at myself for forgetting about the monster that he was. I clenched the flyer in my fist. He had reminded me why I was here. Why it was so imperative that I stay.

I decided to try and employ the same tactics that Maxim was currently using on me. I would be agreeable . . . and stall.

"Fine," I snapped. "I'll leave. But I can't go tonight. I need to make some arrangements first." I turned my back on him and began to cross through the room, heading for my bedroom. "And the hallway better be cleaned up if you expect me to walk through there on my way out."

Then I did something that was probably inadvisable. But I didn't care. My attitude had gotten the better of me.

I walked out on the Dark Prince—sauntering the whole way with an extra swish of my hips. Just before I turned the corner of the hall though, I sent a flick of energy behind me, not bothering to glance back, and stoked the fires with a loud pop.

***

I grabbed my brush and sat on my bed. The windows to my room showed nothing but darkness now. I had the fire in the large hearth going and the chandelier was lit. If I couldn't have sunlight, then warm, cozy firelight was the next best thing.

I had made sure not to disrupt the circle of powder surrounding the bed. Belcalis's spell hadn't seemed to work, but I left the protective ring unbroken . . . just in case.

Having slept for the whole day, I was up for the evening, it seemed. There was a lot to accomplish and I began to make a mental list of what I would need to do.

I should check in with Killian. I needed to find a way to see Belcalis again. I also had to discover the location printed on the flyer. I would need to attend that rally. I desperately needed to visit the Shadow Court. I would have to find a way to get there.

And as much as I didn't want to, I needed to spend more time interacting with *him*. He had dodged my first attempt with such ease. There would come a second time when I would need to strike. And when that time came, I would have to land a killing blow.

I needed to uncover more about him. Find his faults, his weaknesses. Knowing as much as I could about him was my best chance for success. And if there was some minute way in which I could gain his trust and make him see me as an ally, it would be all the better.

179

I was going to call Killian first. I was. But sitting on the bed with the hypnotic firelight, I began to hear something.

Whispers. So faint. Not truly detectable. But there. They began to float all around me. Through my mind. Murmuring gossamer secrets and then drifting away in a little tendril of smoke. Having never been.

They told my chest to rise. To breathe deep and slow. They told my eyes to close. But they did not tell me to dream. This time they told me to rise. They beckoned me outside.

Come and see the brilliant night. Breathe the cool crisp air. Feel the damp earth on your toes. The moon shines for you, lovely girl.

I listened. I had no choice but to listen and heed their call. But before I reached the door, I stopped. *I need clothes*, I thought. *I wear a flimsy gown.*

Come. Come, they urged. *You need nothing but your open heart. Come. See how your skin sparkles in the moonlight.*

I hesitated. *The Dark One . . .*

He does not leave the manor. Come. We wait for you.

All the way through the dark halls and down the stairs they sighed and murmured. And once I was outside, I saw how right they were. I had never known the night as it was then. The peace and beauty of it glimmered as if enchanted.

This way, they called. And the large wrought iron gate swung open soundlessly. *Come.*

I crossed through the gate and entered the tree tunnel. It was black, and I could not see. But one by one the grand oaks lifted their branches revealing the night sky above. The twinkling light of stars glittered down and lit the path.

This way. Hurry!

I began to run. The night air streamed through my hair, and I could feel the delicate cotton of my nightgown envelope my figure.

Smile, lovely girl. You are free!

And I did smile then. I tilted my head up to the night sky and took in the beauty of it all. After I had run for an untold amount of time those whispers spoke to me again.

Here. Here, they told me. *In the clearing. Over here.*

I veered off the path and through some trees until I reached a clearing by a small stream. But the moment I emerged through the trees, the night shifted.

And I learned just how quickly a beautiful dream can become a nightmare.

CHAPTER 16

THE SPELL WAS BROKEN IN AN INSTANT. The magic, the dreamy quality, the twinkling light—it all disappeared, and I was plunged into the cold darkness of night.

They had been waiting for me. My only chance was to turn and outrun them. But one was right next to me. It grabbed my arm and flung me forward before I could change course.

I spun in a quick circle trying to assess. Trying to clear my mind. Trying to process what was happening.

There were three of them. They formed a triangle around me. I didn't have my dagger. I had no weapons. Without hesitating, I dug deep and sent the most powerful blast of energy I could summon all around me.

But instead of acting like a bomb, the pulse was simply absorbed. Gobbled up, like a star devoured by a black hole. It had been present one moment and sucked into nothingness the next.

It was all I had. I would need time to access my power again—to recharge. I now had no choice. I would have to fight.

What made me uneasy was not so much that I was weaponless in the dark wearing a nightgown. What made me uneasy was that I would have to battle an unknown enemy.

They were tall and sickly thin with gray ashen skin. They all had dark hair with lifeless eyes. Their eyes had a reflective quality, like an animal's, that made them seem to glow in the dark. And each one wore a black robe.

They were the Shadows from our reference books. What I had expected my first night at the Dark Manor. Their true form.

They did not brandish any weapons. And that alarmed me.

They began to close in on me. I charged the one closest. Just before it could make a grab for me, I sprang into a front flip, tumbling directly over it while twisting midair so that I landed behind it, facing its back. It had already begun to turn around. With a sweeping kick that pushed into the direction the Shadow was turning, I struck its sternum.

The strike continued the momentum of its turn causing it to fall to the ground on its chest. At the moment of contact with the ground, the Shadow's arms lay splayed out to each side. I leapt onto its back in a crouch and grabbed each arm. Then I sprang up, my feet digging into its spine, pinning its torso to the ground while wrenching its arms up. There was a sickening pop and crunch as I dislocated its arms and bones snapped.

I would have grabbed its head and given it a brutal twist as well, but the others were upon me.

I jumped from the back of the first one and sprang at one of the other two. I used the height and positioning of my jump to lock my arms around its head. Then employing the downward momentum of my vault, I yanked the back of its head down in a Muay Thai clinch.

The moment my feet slammed into the earth, I jerked to the side. I still had the Shadow by the head and my change in position caused it to move with me. I now had it situated between myself and the third Shadow acting as a shield.

It swung its fists and I took a few brutal blows to my abdomen. I wasn't certain, but I thought I felt a rib break. It didn't matter, I drove my knee up into its face and heard bones pulverize. I used the impact of that moment to swing my hands out to each side of the Shadow's face. With as much speed and strength as I was capable, I bashed my fists into its temples.

Instead of dropping to the ground in front of me though, the Shadow went flying across the clearing. I was caught off guard. The third Shadow had ripped its partner out of the way and flung its body aside as if useless garbage. A solid punch connected with my chest and I went hurling back landing flat on the ground.

There was not even a moment of time for me to right myself in a kick up. The instant the Shadow had landed the punch, it dove after me landing on top of my body. I was about to snap my head up in an attempt to butt its nose, but something happened.

It was what I had feared. It was why these things did not carry weapons. It was my undoing.

The Shadow had put its thin cracked lips together and began to blow. A black acrid brume billowed from its mouth. It grabbed my face with its skeletal hand and squeezed forcing my own lips to part.

Vile, burning smoke filled me. It swept its way through my airway and veins, corroding my organs with a putrid stench. I would have been sick, but my esophagus would not function. It had rotted the instant those fumes had slithered down my throat.

I could barely move now. The caustic poison had weakened me in an instant. Tears streamed from my eyes and my stomach heaved over and over again with no effect.

I began to hear a steady thump, thump, thump. Perhaps it was my heart taking its last beats.

Except I could feel vibrations shaking the earth under me. It was unhurried. Confident. And with each thump, the ground at my back grew colder and colder.

Despite everything that had happened up to that point, I became truly fearful. Something terrible was approaching. Something evil. Something from the very depths of hell. If the Shadow sensed whatever approached, it did not make any indication of it.

I needed to cough. I needed to breathe. I could do neither while that thing continued to release its black poison through my lips. The gray skin, the emaciated face, those reflective eyes . . . it would be the last thing I'd see.

And then black sludge splattered across my face. The tip of a sword protruded from the Shadow's mouth and instead of that brume, now a river of thick black liquid poured from between its lips spilling across my own.

I was horrified, but at least its grasp on my jaw had gone slack once the sword had entered through its head. I was able to clamp my mouth shut and turn my face to the side. However, we did not remain that way for long because with a swish, the sword was retracted from the Shadow's head, pulling its skull back at the motion. With incalculable speed and precision, that same sword arced from the side and while the Shadow's head was still in mid-air, the sword sliced through its neck coming a fraction of an inch away from my own.

The Shadow's head landed on the ground at the crook of my neck in a macabre nuzzle. I wanted to scramble out from under its body, but my organs had been cremated. I couldn't function. I was surprised I was still clinging to consciousness at that point.

As I lay there, staring up at the black night sky I heard the most gruesome sounds I ever would in my life. From time to time more of that black sludge would arc through the air covering me—*staining* me.

What would haunt me the most, though, until my dying day . . . were the squeals. God, how I wished I could tear off my ears.

The Shadow's body that was on top of me was finally pulled off. I thought that would be the end of it. But more sludge was splattered as those horrific sounds continued.

Although I was no longer being assaulted, the pain radiating through my body was more than any I had ever known. I wanted to scream out, but my insides were ash. I couldn't. That didn't stop me from doing so over and over again in my head though.

I can't begin to imagine how long I lay like that. But it had been a significant amount of time because I had begun to regain movement in my fingers and toes. It would be a long, grueling process, but perhaps my body would recover. However, I did not have the luxury of time on my side because finally . . . the darkness became quiet.

Thump. Thump. Thump. Those footsteps began again. Unhurried. Vibrating the ground beneath me. Frost crystallized over the grass around me, scuttling up my skin and freezing the tears which leaked from my eyes.

I was next.

An immense dark form loomed over me. I could not see more through the ice coating my eyes. That was when I was hoisted into the air, and my body disintegrated. I became smoke. There was nothing left to me.

But at least, there was no pain.

***

Unfortunately, I still had a body. One that resolidified instantly. One that was battered and bruised, but substantial just the same. I did not drift away into the peaceful quiet of the ether. I remained earthbound. And the punishment that came with persisting in this world was brutal. The pain that tore through me made me wish for the end.

In solidifying once again, the ice covering my eyes thawed leaving behind two pools of water. I blinked rapidly trying to clear my vision, and I realized I was being set down.

Dark. Cold. Bed. Cavernous room.

I recognized the blurry outlines of this place. It was one of the rooms within the manor. One I had spent time inspecting. It was a large bedroom with a floor to ceiling wall of dusty books. There was a crumbling fireplace and cobwebbed chandelier.

And then I looked up at *him*. His eyes were black. Wild. There was seething hatred in them. It was so prevalent, so all consuming. I had never before witnessed such a level of odium in another. It seemed I was facing death itself then. And I wished for a quick end.

If he had been wearing a shirt earlier, he wasn't now. Black sludge covered him. It was splattered across his face, his torso, his arms. It probably saturated the dark slacks he wore. But it could not camouflage the definition in his arms, shoulders, chest, and abdomen. With every billowing breath, each highly defined muscle flexed with latent power.

He was larger than he had been before. He took up more space. More air. And although all he did was stand there, his motions were so fluid, so lethal and precise—I understood why I should have feared him above all else.

He was also lost. He had entered a maze of such deep fury and violence. He could not find a way out.

I hated that I knew things about him. That I somehow understood his inner psyche. Because it made me fear him. Because it made me understand what he was capable of . . . and what he was not.

In a movement too fast for me to track, he shoved his hand behind my head and grabbed a fistful of my hair. He was about to say something but didn't get a chance to. Although my vocal chords were raw, I let out a moan.

He immediately let go pulling his hand back before flexing it repeatedly at his side. It took all the strength I had but I somehow managed to lift my own hand and grab his. Then I brought it to my throat which throbbed with unbearable pain.

The violence and rage churning through him turned sharply into confusion and . . . *fear.*

189

I couldn't fathom was happening. And I didn't care. When he had touched me, I had felt better. A surge of energy had pulsed there like a balm. But the moment he had withdrew his touch, I was plunged back into the pain.

I didn't care if he was an incubus. I didn't care if he was a Shadow. I didn't care that he was evil.

It didn't matter what he had done before and what he would do after. Just then, all I cared about was what he could give me. And for some inexplicable reason, his touch was curative.

Now his hand lay over my throat and I arched my back, my spine leaving the bed. And again, he drew away his hand.

"I don't want to touch you," he grated. The look of abhorrence would have made a lesser woman wilt and die.

But in that moment, I was a glutton. The relief I'd felt while his skin was on mine made me delirious for it again. "You have to," I told him. It was barely audible, but I had gotten the words out.

The rage and contempt returned. This time when he grabbed a fistful of my hair at the nape of my neck, he did speak. Leaning his cruel, perfect, sludge splattered face towards mine he seethed, "I'm one of those things."

He said it in a way that was supposed to frighten me. To disgust me. To repel me from ever asking for his touch again.

I laughed. "I don't care." I began to cough. The pain, the burning, it was continuing to eat away at my insides. "Abdomen," I choked out. "Ribs."

"No."

His reply was so stern and clipped, I would have laughed again if I was able. But I wasn't, I was suffering. I gasped for air. "Then leave."

I turned my head away from him. It was the closest thing to a dismissal I could manage. It was absurd to think he would willingly help me. He had probably been the one to direct the attack in the first place. Although why he would then come to my aid was beyond my comprehension.

I couldn't dwell on the details of it all. Nothing mattered but this misery. As I lay there, I began a chant in my mind. *This will pass. This will pass. This will pass.*

I didn't know if that was true, but I had to get through each agonizing moment somehow.

And then, I couldn't be sure, but I thought I felt a featherlight touch across my navel. I turned to look.

His hand was hovering over my midsection, making the barest hint of contact with the cotton of my stained nightgown. But there was no relief from the pain.

"On my skin," I told him.

A look of horror crossed his face. He withdrew his hand making a fist with it. And he paused like that for a long while.

I couldn't bear to simply lay there and watch him. I was in too much pain. I was about to turn away and resume my meditation, but then he released his index finger. Slowly, hesitantly, as if afraid of being bitten. He opened his fist—finger by finger—and reached for the hem of my nightgown.

His fingers brushed my thigh as he pinched the fabric and began to slide it up my legs. It felt as though a small beam of Light trailed my leg where his skin slid across mine. He was concentrating so intently on his actions, I didn't dare move or speak. I desperately wanted him to keep going.

And he did. He slipped the fabric over the cotton of my underwear all the way up to my ribs. He stopped there and released the nightgown letting it fall across my chest.

He swallowed, staring at my abdomen. Then he looked at his hand, at the black gunk staining it. And I knew he was about to plunge himself back into that wretched maze of loathing and darkness he lived in. I couldn't allow him to. I needed him.

I reached up and took his hand. He looked at me then, jarred from his internal struggle. I silently pleaded with him, and he placed his hand on me.

I closed my eyes and let my head tilt back.

I could breathe. I was warm. My skin tingled. Deep inside, my body mended. That dark, acrid smoke was chased away by tiny crackles of Light.

He moved his hand up to my ribs, and my chest heaved at his touch. I took breath after breath, filling my lungs with clean air.

And Light help me, I couldn't stop my body's response to him. My chest tightened. I rubbed my thighs together at the throbbing ache that started pulsing at my core. I tried so hard to stop myself, but the need I felt for him was a force beyond my control.

He grabbed my ribs with both hands then. Squeezing. The tops of his hands brushing the underside of my breasts.

I opened my eyes to look at him. His nostrils flared. And brilliant blue lines branched through the black of his irises.

He slid his hands down the sides of my stomach to either side of my hips. Squeezing again. Watching the path of his hands in fascination.

And somehow, in some way, we had stepped away from time. From rolls. From rules. From titles. And actions.

It was just us. Just now. Nothing more. Something simple and basic. Something that I had never experienced before. The time and space that we occupied stretched on. And became a moment that would last forever.

Yet in spite of all that, it was still a moment that would come to an end. And I wanted to know what he would do next . . . I still wonder sometimes. How it might have changed the arc of our story.

But I did not get to find out. Because with a long low creak, the door to the chamber began to open.

His eyes flashed to mine as if ripped from a trance. He snapped his hands back to his sides, those clenching fists forming again. The veins of crystal blue in his eyes were consumed by black once more. And a look of fury caused his jaw to clench and brows to slash.

"You will leave," he hissed. *"Tomorrow."*

And then in a wisp of shadows, he disappeared.

CHAPTER 17

THE CRONE ENTERED.

I stared up at the cracked ceiling and cursed the wretched sight of her. She shuffled into the dark room carrying a basin. It sploshed with each labored step she took.

When she finally reached the bed, she set the tub down next to my legs. Then without so much as a word, she turned and hobbled away.

I thought she was going to leave, but she stopped at the wall length bookshelf. She collected a few books in her arms and unceremoniously dumped them into the crumbling fireplace.

From inside her robe, she procured a long match and struck it on one of the hearth bricks. Then she tossed the flame onto the collection of books.

The academic side of me was horrified. I could only begin to imagine what ancient knowledge or art had been preserved there, tossed aside like garbage. I couldn't help it. I let out a gasp.

But the destroyed part of me, the part that was still in pain now that *he* was gone, was grateful for a little light and warmth, no matter how small.

She pulled a few more books from the shelves, attempting to fling them to the ground in the direction of the fire before feebly kicking them towards the flames—without much success. Then she made her way back to me. I don't know if it's possible to intuit another's irritation by the way they shuffle about, but if it is . . . she certainly didn't seem cheery.

And without any preamble, she grabbed the sopping cloth from the tub and sloshed it across my legs.

I was speechless. I didn't understand what was happening. Before I had time to react, she dunked the cloth and splattered my abdomen and chest. I raised my hands in an attempt to take the cloth from her. "I can do that," I told her, my throat hoarse and painful.

She paused and whipped her head in my direction. And although I could see nothing but darkness beneath her cowl, I knew she shot me a charged look. I could *feel* it. The flicker of faraway power made me lie still and say no more.

Once she was satisfied with my submission, she began assaulting me with water again. Over my arms, on my hair, and then a big fat smack right on my face. I spluttered, not expecting the mouth full of water. After more wet blows, she finally picked up the almost empty bin and tossed the remaining water over me.

Taking her bucket in one hand and the still dripping cloth in the other, she hobbled out just as unannounced as when she came in.

It seemed the baptism was over.

***

I could move. I could walk. I could breathe. It was all excruciating, but doable.

So I dragged myself to my quarters. The room *he* had brought me to was on the same floor as my own, just the opposite wing. I left a trail of water in my wake and was happy for it. I hoped the old bat slipped on it.

I didn't have enough energy to light the chandeliers and sconces along the hallway, so on top of being soaked, I was forced to trudge through the dark. *And* the hallway outside my suite door was still littered with debris.

But there were fires burning in the main room of my quarters, and for that I was grateful. The fire in my personal bedroom had died down. I grabbed a robe and my phone and returned to the sitting room.

I was about to throw my nightgown and underwear into the fire, but I was afraid of what the black stains might do when they came in contact with the flames. I didn't want any caustic smoke billowing through the room.

Instead, I stripped down and tossed the contaminated clothes out into the ravaged hall. After wrapping myself in my robe and a blanket from the settee, I called Killian.

I was stunned when I got his voicemail. In the entire history of our relationship, I don't think I ever once got his voicemail. He *always* answered my calls. I was afraid something was wrong.

Although I did not have any windows to the outside in the sitting room, I could feel that night was breaking. The sun was about to bloom from the horizon. I briefly thought of moving to another room, of trying to bask in whatever amount of light I could get. It would be good for me.

But the exhaustion was undeniable. And while I put my head down on one of the settee pillows, I told myself I would work up the energy to scour my skin clean and then move.

Instead, though, I passed out where I was.

***

I tried to convince myself it was better that I adjusted my schedule. That it made more sense to be active at night and rest during the day. That it would help me with my final goals to adopt the habits of those I hunted.

So I tried to brush off the unease that came with waking at dusk. I certainly didn't dwell on it long because the pain from the previous night's events was undeniable. It wasn't paralyzing, but it would be difficult to focus on other tasks with the misery my body was experiencing.

Something I had learned with my time in The Unit was to keep things simple. When presented with a problem, identify the core issue and find the most basic solution.

My problem at the moment was physical pain. It was preventing me from focusing, from doing, from carrying out my plan. My mission.

There was a basic solution to this problem: Stop the pain. Sunlight was always great for my kind. The warm restorative rays could charge and heal our souls—our life force. But I would have to wait another twelve hours for sunlight. Time I did not want to waste.

There was another solution . . . I could find *him*.

I didn't know why his touch had healed me. I didn't know if it somehow had to do with being an incubus or if because he was a Shadow, he could remove or cancel out the harm done by another Shadow.

It didn't matter. The moment I began trying to analyze it and deconstruct it, the solution was no longer basic. It became complicated and convoluted.

And besides, any interaction I had with him was a learning experience. The more I learned about him, the greater prepared I was to fight him.

Perhaps, even touching me and taking away my pain, was somehow detrimental to him. Maybe that was part of the reason why he did not want to touch me. Maybe it somehow caused him harm or weakened him. Which again, would be beneficial to me.

I bathed. I dressed in a t-shirt and leggings, not bothering with some frilly dress. And I left my quarters high on the top floor of the manor, ablaze with firelight, to descend into the darkness far below.

I was surprised to find the hallway outside my suite door was righted. The debris had been cleared and the chandelier and sconces were even lit.

But once I reached the grand stairway, the light and warmth ended. The subsequent floors were all quiet and dark. In a way, it felt wrong to pass through. It felt as though I was trespassing on the stillness of the manor.

I didn't let that feeling stop me though. I made my way to the boarded-up door down the long wing of the foyer. The last time I had opened it, I had needed to access a great deal of power. Power which I was currently lacking.

I tried giving the door a tentative push and snatched my hand back. It was so cold, so solid, I knew it was heavily barred. Even with the full extent of my Light, I am not certain I would have been able to open it.

It was childish, I know, but I was offended. My ire rose. And I began to pound on the door.

Although it hurt my throat, I shouted through the wood. "Hey, numbnuts! If you want me out of here I need to be able to function! Come fix what your nasty friends did!"

I paused, listening for any signs of movement below . . . There was nothing but silence.

I began pounding again. "Are you really going to make me go back up five fucking flights of stairs?!"

After a few more moments, I stopped pounding and gave the door a kick. "Fine! You have ten minutes! And I swear to the Light, if I have to come back down here, I will burn this door and your entire creepy wing to the ground!"

I took a deep breath, my throat killing me. "Don't think I won't do it!" I warned. "You're going to damn well touch me, whether you like it or not!"

I was about to make my way to the stairs but then I turned back to the door to amend, "Don't think *I* like it, though! I . . . I . . . I don't! I . . . I just need this poison gone . . . okay? Bozo!" I gave the door a final kick and began to drag myself down the long foyer.

I took my time, feeling spent. I would rest and wait for sunrise. It was probably my best option. I didn't expect that he would visit my quarters.

My wrist was grabbed, and I was spun around. I was about to let an angry expletive fly, but a large powerful hand clamped over my mouth. With my head craned back to look up, *he* gave a single shake of his head in negation.

Then he began walking us away from his wing. He kept his hand over my mouth the whole time, glaring at me. I cooperated, shuffling backwards.

Finally, my shoulders pressed against the back door that led to the rear veranda. We were behind the main stairway and moonlight poured in through the glass panes lining the wall, leaving slanted slabs of light on the floor at our feet.

He was shirtless again and as he removed his hand from my mouth, I couldn't help but notice his muscles bunch and flex with the movement. "She's meditating," he murmured. His voice low and deep.

"Who?" I whispered. "The . . ." I couldn't bring myself to say it out loud. I had been raised with some manners, and it felt wrong to call someone that, especially an elder.

He nodded.

"So what?" I countered.

"She is very tired after helping you," he supplied. And I could tell by his tone, by his calm demeanor and concern, that he . . . *cared*.

"Helping me?" Although I still whispered, I made it clear that I strongly disagreed with his assessment. "She attacked me with water!"

"It wasn't just any water," he growled. "It was special. Blessed. She helped cleanse you."

"It was nasty old bucket water," I countered. "I could have *cleansed* myself."

"You're too stupid to understand," he snapped. "You need to leave." He stood against me, towering over me, looking down at me—trying to intimidate me.

I refused to cower. I pressed myself into him, notching up my chin and staring right back at him. "No."

I had forgotten about my plan to appease and stall. I looked away. "I mean, I will. But there's something wrong with me." I met his eye again. "I need your help first. I need you to undo . . ." I didn't want to mention the previous night aloud. It was still too raw.

"I can't. No one can. Leave. Before it's too late."

"You were able to last night."

"That was your doing. You and your witchery. Find some other individual you can spell."

I found his comments interesting. He thought I was spelling him somehow. I decided not to correct him. I would let him keep believing so for the time being. Perhaps it could be helpful in some way.

I canted my head. "How did you know I was out there?"

He clenched his jaw and the muscle under his eye ticked, but he said nothing.

I let my weight fall back and leaned against the door behind me, crossing my arms over my chest. I had forgotten about the pain I was in. "What's your name?" I tried.

He crossed his own arms and leaned forward. "I don't have one."

I arched a brow. "Everyone has a name," I countered.

"I don't," he challenged.

"What does your family call you?" I tried again.

"I don't have a family."

"Everyone has—"

"I don't," he snapped while still keeping his voice low.

"We've only just heard of you. Where have you been all this time?"

"Here."

I shrugged, looking to the side and eyed the cobweb covered staircase. "Hmm. Hell of a job you've done with the place."

He uncrossed his arms and placed his hands on each side of my head, leaning down. "If you don't care for it, then you should *leave*."

"Oh, believe me, tiger. I plan to." I patted his pectoral, just over his heart, over the tattoo he had there. I meant the gesture to be patronizing, in line with my tone. But touching him had been a mistake. Because I found it difficult to take my hand back. Instead I found myself running my fingers over the black mark.

I was pulled to him, wrapped up in him. "Don't do that," I warned on a sigh.

He pinched my chin, forcing me to look at him. "You're the one touching *me*," he accused.

"Yes, but you're using your incubus power on me," I told him.

He narrowed his eyes, "I'm not an incubus. You're the one using your witchery on me," he accused.

203

"Hmm," I sighed. "You think so?" I licked my lips. I knew I shouldn't, but I just couldn't help it. I continued rubbing the tattoo. "You're strong. You can fight it."

He grabbed my hand in his, stopping me from running my finger over him. Then he let go of my chin to trail his own finger down my throat.

His touch left me feeling weak. It sent tingles down my spine directly to my center.

He stopped his hand at the base of my throat, lightly grasping. He looked at me with those crystal blue eyes and allowed the branching black veins to fork through his irises. "I'm one of those things," he warned. "Leave. Tomorrow. Find someone else to spell."

"Why do you wear a glamour?" I asked. "If you're one of those things, then take it off. Show me . . . Scare me away."

His grip on my throat tightened. "You mock me?" he growled. He was angered. I had struck a nerve.

"Not mocking," I corrected. "Just trying to simplify things. Why not show your true face?" He was so close to me, I nipped his chin with my teeth.

The air around us chilled. My skin, where he touched me, iced over. His eyes turned black.

Through clenched teeth he grated, "As though there could be a worse face than this one. Do you think I am ignorant to my appearance? Do you think I do not know the horror my visage evokes? I am the monster mothers warn their children of."

I began breathing heavily, my chest rising and falling under his hand. I had chills again, but this time they ran down my arms.

He *believed* what he was saying. I could feel the truth of it. He wore no glamour and he believed he was hideous.

I let out a breath on a quiet laugh. "Oh, dear sweet, Prince of Darkness." I reached up to take his hand in both of mine and moved it down a few inches over my own heart. "You could not be more wrong."

I wanted him to feel the truth of my words now. I shouldn't have wanted to ease him. But I could feel the contempt he had for himself. And it was so ill-founded. At least, in that aspect it was.

It worked. He could not deny the genuine nature of my words. He began to search back and forth between my eyes, unable to believe such a deep-seated truth he held about himself.

"More witchery," he concluded.

I shrugged again. "Believe what you will."

He grabbed my waist with each hand, pulling my hips into him. "Why are you here?" he growled.

"Because we're married, dear prince. And I was supposed to come to you. In a neat little package for you to unwrap." I was getting carried away. I couldn't stop myself. I had never wanted someone like this. Had never enjoyed the teasing power of drawing out such tension.

He ground his hips against mine and I clutched his arms at the motion. I wanted to cry out at the electricity that exploded with the contact, but I did not want to shatter the quiet darkness enveloping us. There was something seductive about it. An experience I wanted to savor.

It didn't matter, the floor began to shake, sending the chandeliers swaying and clinking.

He snapped his head, his focus traveling down the length of the foyer, towards the door to his wing. Something had happened.

Looking back at me, he clenched his jaw, his nostrils flaring. "You will leave," he insisted. "Tomorrow." Then he let go of me, taking two retreating steps back before turning to disappear into the darkness.

I stood there, in the moonlight, being held up by the door at my back for a long while before I eventually made my way up to the fifth floor where I spent the rest of the seemingly unending night . . . alone.

CHAPTER 18

I TRACED MY FINGER over the symbol on the flyer. Three intersecting crescent moons. The same symbol tattooed on *his* chest.

I had vacillated on whether or not to ask Maxim about it. Whether or not to show him the flyer. But in the end, I decided I had nothing to lose.

The dining area of the inn was quaint and charming. Fire and candle light flickered against the exposed wood beams. Various groups of people were gathered around the tables talking, drinking, and eating. Long skewers packed with whole vegetables and squashes sat over the crackling flame in the firepit while bread loaves baked on a rack, filling the inn with a wholesome aroma. Although, the look and feel of the medieval space had not been altered, there were clearly a few updated amenities noticeable throughout.

I sat in a high back booth. Rheneas and Stefan were at a free-standing table just a few feet away. And Maxim kept his eye on me the entire time he ordered at the bar.

When he offered to wait on me, I didn't object. I was tired. I had slept through the entire day again and had not seen the sun.

I was also still in pain. It had lessened, but I still ached. Being near *him*. Having him touch me, although only for a few moments, had helped. But was not enough to chase it away entirely.

And this had complicated my goals. Because now I feared I might need *him*. I was still committed to my plan, but I needed more time. There was too much I didn't understand about him. About what had happened.

Maxim took the seat opposite me and set down a carafe of wine with two glasses. He poured a glass for me and a glass for himself. But I had a feeling it was just for show. I did not expect that he was going to partake.

I slid the flyer over to him. "Have you seen this?" I asked.

He didn't look surprised. "Yes."

"The symbol. What is it?"

"It is the *tenebris*. The ancient symbol of the *Dark Light*."

"I'm not familiar with it. Can you tell me what it means?"

"Where did you get this?" Maxim countered.

"From the witch who runs the vegetable stand across the street," I told him.

His brows rose. "Honesty. How refreshing."

"You knew?" I asked.

209

"I had an inkling," he replied.

"You didn't say anything about it," I pointed out.

"You were unharmed. You must have had your reasons. And given your current living situation I, frankly, didn't blame you."

"You know what, Maxim? I like you."

He inclined his head. "The feeling is mutual, Violet."

I pointed to the flyer. "So this *tenebris*. The ancient symbol of the *Dark Light*. What is it?"

"Do you know anything of Shadow history? Of the stories of our origins?" he asked.

I shook my head.

Maxim took a deep breath and leaned towards me. "There is some debate surrounding the lore of our people. There are differing accounts, differing story lines.

"My mother was a scribe for the Shadow Court. She was tasked with organizing and updating the historical texts housed within the Central Library. And while she was instructed to preserve certain aspects of our history, she was forced to re-write or completely destroy others.

"So I would like for you to understand that it cannot be proven, but I believe the stories my mother recounted to me as a child are those most closely associated with the truth of our race."

When Maxim paused, I nodded.

He did drink from his glass then, taking a moment before beginning his story.

"Long ago, before any of us ever existed, was the *Tenebris Rex*. The Dark King. The original Shadow. The first son of the night. He wore the symbol of the *tenebris*. The three intersecting crescents in honor of his mother . . . the moon.

210

"The king ruled for eons. He was respected by his people. They found him to be just—worthy of his position. And they were honored to be his subjects, viewing their own status as ones of dignity and prestige.

"Eventually, though, the king grew tired of the ways of this world, and he decided to leave. Without notice or fanfare, he wisped away one night, stopping only to pay homage to his mother, the moon, and then departed this world never to be heard from again.

"Where he went and what he did, no one can say. There is no record of him for millennia. In fact, enough time passed that his people had no choice but to believe he had forsaken them.

"However, the king did not repudiate his people. Because one night . . . he returned. During the longest night of the year, when there was a blood moon, the king wisped back to our world for a fragment of time.

"He did not return to court. And he did not call upon his people. Instead, he took a walk through the forests of the world. It was that night when the ancient king met a young woman and left an heir for his people."

Maxim sat up then and gave a slight shrug. "It was how the Dark Prince was identified. He bears the mark. He is the offspring of the Dark King and the rightful heir to the Shadow Court.

"So while the tenebris had come to symbolize the honor and prestige of our race, it now also symbolizes the royal bloodline of the Shadows."

I held up my hand, interrupting Maxim. "But anyone could have that symbol tattooed on them. It proves nothing."

Maxim inclined his head. "True. But the mark which the Dark Prince bears is no tattoo. It is not something which can be placed upon him nor removed. The mark he bears is a part of him. If you try to cut it off, it will only grow back.

"It is how his identity was verified. Those at Court tried to cut, burn, scour, and mystically remove the symbol. They were not successful. His identity was undeniably confirmed."

I pulled the paper back and traced the symbol again. "So why is it being used to symbolize a revolution? It doesn't make sense. You have found your prince. He bears the mark. Why use his symbol when wishing to revolt against him?"

Maxim leaned across the table again. He took his wine glass in hand, holding it by the rim and swirled the liquid inside. He didn't look at me but instead watched the wine spinning within the glass.

In a low voice he said, "What I tell you now is off the record. Do you understand?"

I took a sip from my own glass while giving a slight nod, not wanting to call attention to our conversation.

"He does nothing. He does not leave that place. The Dark Prince has been found, but he does not lead. Through his inaction, he has truly forsaken his people in a way his sire never did.

"So the tenebris now symbolizes the hope for our future. The hope that someone or some people worthy of a royal status will once again lead us. And that our people may reclaim the honor and prestige that we once held."

"You don't seem to have a negative tone," I noted. "Are you in favor of the revolution?"

Maxim's posture straightened, and he nailed me with a look. "I take my position and my duty to the Shadow Court . . . to my *people*, very seriously."

I didn't bother to try and point out that he had not answered my question. Instead I leaned in, bowing my head. "Maxim. Who sent for me?"

His dark eyes were somber. "Those at Court."

"What do they want with me?"

He picked up his glass this time and took a healthy slug from it. "I don't know." He began swirling the remaining wine again. "I have been told to guard you. To keep you safe. To try to appease you and keep you happy—within reason. To keep you at the manor. Little visits into town are acceptable, but beyond this, you are not to leave."

"Barrister Corbett said they hoped this marriage between our two Courts would ease the tensions and dissent brewing among your people," I shared. "Do you think he was telling the truth?"

"I could see how a member of the Court, such as Barrister Corbett, might believe that to be true," Maxim acknowledged.

"But then why am I being sequestered here?"

"As far as I have been told, it is because the Court does not feel they have all the necessary facets in place."

"Do you believe that?"

"Whether it is true or not, I cannot say. What I do believe is that you should leave the manor and return home. You are residing with someone who is unhinged. He is not of sound mind. You are in danger here . . . with him."

I notched my chin and met Maxim's eye. "I can't."

Maxim pinned me with a look. "He is truly a monster. He is not a Shadow. There is no Dark Light within him. He is something else. He does not walk this world as the rest of us. He is a shell. And all that you will find within is darkness and depravity."

Maxim's expression turned grave. "I have seen much evil and darkness in my lifetime. None of it has ever compared with the things he is capable of." His eyes bored into mine, and they cinched slightly with conviction. "You should leave."

I was about to repeat that I couldn't. That I wouldn't. But instead I asked, "Does he have some kind of influence over others?"

"Of course," Maxim said simply.

I squirmed, pursing my lips together, not wanting to have to admit anything to Maxim. "What about attraction? Does he have some kind of influence over attraction? Like an incubus?"

Maxim looked sick. Closing his eyes and turning his head away for a moment. Then he did something very unexpected. He reached across and took my hands in his.

"I do not doubt that he is capable of a great many things. He is powerful. There is no telling what he is capable of. What kind of evil he has at his disposal.

"I was afraid of what might be done to you. Violet, please. Leave this place. Whatever you believe to be true. Whatever mission or agenda you pursue, this is not the way."

I pulled my hands back. "Nothing has happened," I replied.

"Your hands are very cold. Something chilling pumps through your veins. And your aura has dimmed since your first arrived."

"I just haven't been out in the sun for a while. That's all. After a few hours of sunlight, I'll be fine."

I didn't want to tell him what had happened. Instead I tried to shift the focus onto him. "Why are you sharing this with me?"

"Because I think you should know."

"You really don't wear glamours?" I asked.

Maxim shook his head.

"What about tall gaunt figures? Ones that have ashen skin and dark hair. Ones that have reflective eyes in the dark. Aren't those your people? Isn't that the true Shadow form?"

Maxim's eyes narrowed. "Absolutely not. What you describe are the *Umbra*."

I wrapped my arms around myself. "What are they?"

Maxim's tone sent chills down my spine. "Evil incarnate."

"Can you explain?" I asked, hugging myself tighter.

"Not really. No," he said simply. "How do you explain evil?" he asked. "I don't know what to say other than that they are malevolence personified."

He took another swig from his glass, draining it. "Imagine an ancient evil, seeping up from the earth and taking form . . . Deciding to walk among men. Wanting to infect and rule the night.

"The Umbra is an evil. A presence. It is not a being, but a collective spirit. Although it has taken physical form, it extends far beyond the nightmare figures. It is much more than individual beings."

I eyed my own glass, rolling it between my palms. "I don't understand why I was taught that the Umbra are the true form of the Shadows."

215

Maxim's shoulders bunched, and the dark slash of his brow intensified. "While we are unquestionably *not* the same . . . our histories are tied together."

I raised my brows.

Maxim held up a finger and I felt as though I was being scolded. "However, this does not justify generalizing the entire Shadow race as dark and evil."

I nodded. I didn't say anything hoping Maxim would explain.

It must have been obvious because with a heavy exhale, he continued. "The ancient evil awoke and crawled up from the bowels of this world. They took form, becoming the Umbra. How and why they were released, I do not know.

"They were truly dark beings. They were not welcomed in the Light. The day would not have them. They could exist only in the darkness of night . . . the muted light . . . the *Dark Light*.

"Knowing they had been freed, knowing they would roam the night, the Dark King did not shun them. Instead he decided to rule them. He somehow mastered them. And in doing so, the Umbra became a royal guard, of sorts, for the Shadow kingdom.

"It is said that when the Dark King left this world he commanded them back into the depths from which they sprang and imprisoned them there. For he knew how capable, how horrible, and how vile they were. They could not be allowed to roam unleashed.

"Some speculate that the Umbra were part of the reason for the king's departure. You see, as powerful and almighty as he was, he was not immune to the darkness of the Umbra. Over all the years spent under his command, their evil began to seep into the

216

king. And while he was powerful enough to contain it—to control it—it began to weigh upon him."

I interrupted Maxim again, desperate to understand. "If the Umbra harmed someone, could the Dark King undo it? You know, heal the individual who had been affected?"

Maxim looked suspicious. "What would prompt you to ask such a thing?"

I just shrugged.

After a moment's hesitation Maxim finally replied. "That is not something I can answer. I do not know."

It had been worth a shot to ask. But in the end, it really didn't matter. Whether the king had been able to or not . . . it seemed his son could.

"What about the *Dark Light*? What is that? You referred to the tenebris as the symbol for the *Dark Light*."

Maxim exhaled again. And whether he was weary of talking to me or felt he was sharing too much, I didn't know.

"Violet, you and your people, you consider yourself to be of the *Light*. Do you not? You are Radiants. You find strength and power in radiant energy, specifically visible light. The brighter and stronger, the better.

"And I could be mistaken, but it seems that you believe yourselves to be the only ones who are of the Light. You view yourselves as more powerful and more virtuous than the rest of us. You are Light. You are good.

"What you fail to understand is that your dark brothers and sisters are also of the Light. However, it is of a different ilk. We are not the same, that is true. While you are children of the sun, of the day—we are children of the moon, of the night. We are of the Dark Light.

"Shadows too gain a level of power and energy from Dark Light. From the moon and the heavenly celestial bodies which shine down upon us.

"And you must remember that the moon is not her own source of light. She basks and glows in the light from the Sun, just as you do, to then shine down and share it with her children. Those of us in the night.

"The moon is balance. It is the light in the dark. We are not dark people. Not evil. We are of the Light. The same as you. Except our light is that of the moon—the Dark Light. You see us as the Umbra, but nothing is further from the truth.

"We are all of the Light in some way or another. All who breathe, who exist, who truly live in this world hold within them a spark. The way this Light ebbs and flows through us all may differ, but at the most basic elemental state . . . it courses through us all.

"Yet, it seems, that you and your people have decided since you shine the brightest, since you rely the heaviest, and since you wield the most power in terms of Light—that only you possess its warmth . . . its goodness."

Maxim sat back, clearly done with his explanation. He gazed at me with those solemn gray eyes. There was conviction there, and I found my respect for him reaffirmed.

I could understand a little of his point. Because, like Killian, he had an apparent goodness. He had a certain strength of character that was admirable and undeniable. And if he was a Shadow who possessed this decency, then perhaps there was some validation to his point.

In spite of that acknowledgment though, I found Maxim's explanation confusing. Try as I might, it was difficult to believe that we shared a commonality between us.

"Why then," I asked him, "do your people feed from us? From our Light?"

Maxim closed his eyes and shook his head before looking at me with disappointment. "What nonsense about my race do you speak of now?"

I pinned him with a stare. I would not be made to feel foolish. It was his people who were attacking mine. "The attacks upon Radiants by Shadows. I have been out there in the night, fighting for years now. Innocent civilians, *children*, are dying at the hands of Shadows."

"And you believe it is because Shadows wish to feed from you? No. Violet, Shadows do not feed from Radiants."

At that his phone rang. When he looked down at the caller ID, his jaw clenched. Leaning towards me and placing his hand over my own, me he murmured, "I suggest you return home and have a long talk with the leaders at court about why those attacks occur."

Standing from the booth he said, "Please wait here. I will be just a moment." Then he gave a nod to Rheneas and Stefan before exiting the rear entry of the inn.

I didn't know what Maxim was insinuating with his last comment, and I exhaustedly filed it away as yet another detail I would have to look into.

And although I had come to like and even respect Maxim, I didn't wait for him to come back. Knowing that it would unfortunately piss him off and knowing that Rheneas and Stefan would follow me . . . I left the inn.

***

"I ain't done nutin' wrong." Belcalis pursed her lips and threw her hands up, showing her palms. "Just cause some of y'alls people need my services don't mean I'm doing anything wrong. And I'm registered with the Shadow Court, *and* I have my witch's permit up to date, so I ain't doing nutin' wrong."

Although Rheneas and Stefan had insisted on standing in front of me as a sort of shield, I could still see Belcalis over their shoulders at the door to her camper. Today she wore a black satin jumpsuit with a plunging neckline that placed her ample cleavage on display. Over the jumper was a white open sleeve jacket that had large black symbols painted on it. Her shoulder length hair was straight and had an ombre effect which started as black at the roots and ended in silver at the ends. Her long pointy nails were an ice blue.

And while it wasn't a look I would try to pull off myself, I had to hand it to Belcalis—the witch had style.

I pushed past Rheneas and Stefan. "It's fine," I told her. "They're with me."

Belcalis pursed her lips again and gave me a once over. "You?" she said with her Bronx accent, "I gave you some quality, grade A shit the other night."

She looked at Rheneas and Stefan and added, "All totally legal." Then she turned back to me, "You ain't got no reason to bring the authorities."

"I'm not," I groused. "They're following me."

As I had suspected, Maxim's underlings had been right on my heels. The instant I had set foot outside the inn, one of them—I wasn't quite sure which was which—had grabbed my elbow to stop me.

I had immediately wanted to claw out his eyes, just to make a point, but instead I stared at his hand on my arm as if it were a maggot I was about to squish.

To his credit he didn't let go, and while his grasp was firm, he was in no way aggressive. He looked at me in all earnest. "You're not safe out here," he said. "You need to go back inside. Wait for the master-at-arms. And allow him to escort you home. Your *actual* home."

There was what seemed like genuine concern in his tone. So I tried to show some consideration in return. "Look, I just want to visit the witch at the vegetable stand across the street. I won't spend more than five minutes there. Then I will go straight back to the manor. Okay?"

I looked back at the inn. "I really don't want to make Maxim's life more difficult. I'm not trying to run out on him, or anything like that. I just need five minutes with the witch."

So naturally, they had insisted on coming with me. In all honesty I was surprised they had been so accommodating. I had been certain I would have to knock them both out or make a run for it.

"Just ignore them," I told Belcalis. "I'd like to talk to you for a minute."

She looked like she was about to say no, so I added, "I'll compensate you for your time, of course."

Just then I heard sniffling behind Belcalis. When she turned back to look at the sound, I was able to see through the camper door that a young woman was sitting at the small dining table, crying.

Belcalis stepped out of the camper and shut the door behind her. "I'm with somebody right now."

"Fine," I told her. "Can I make an appointment?"

She eyed Rheneas and Stefan before glancing at my clutch. She seemed to be contemplating something for a moment before turning back to the closed door of her camper.

"I know that!" she snapped. "But this ain't worth it!" Then she turned fully around to face the camper and put her hands on her hips. "Fine. But don't say I didn't warn you. You're the one who is always sayin' you can't fix stupid! And there ain't no fixin' this."

Belcalis jerked her thumb over her shoulder in my direction as she made her last statement. She was obviously talking about me with her ghost granny—and it rankled. Couldn't they save their conversations about how dumb I was for after I left? I cleared my throat.

Belcalis turned back towards us bringing her hands together in a peaceful prayer gesture and a smile plastered across her face. Her voice was all sweetness. "I can fit you in tomorrow right at dusk." In her best receptionist voice, she added, "Cash only. Large bills preferred."

She turned to reach for the camper door. "Wait," I said, "One more thing." Belcalis turned back and I held up the flyer. "Where is this taking place?"

I could feel Rheneas and Stefan shift behind me, and I had a feeling they were trying to decide if they should intervene at that moment. But to my surprise, they didn't stop Belcalis when she replied, "The old part of town. At the other end of the main street." Belcalis didn't wait for a response. Without a farewell, she entered her camper and shut the door behind her.

CHAPTER 19

SHE WAS BEAUTIFUL. She was chilling. She was an exquisite nightmare.

There was no glow, no hue, to her alabaster skin, and yet her black hair shined in the firelight. Even pinned up, it was obvious it would tumble down her back in a thick luster if left free. Her black lips, black nails, and the black lining of her eyes amplified the stark contrast of paper white skin. And the black gown she wore was so dark it seemed to absorb any light the moment it came near.

But the most strangely beautiful part of her, were her gray crystalline eyes. They looked as though they had frozen over one day and never thawed.

Her air of confidence and authority were unquestionable. Unforced. She was not powerful. She *was* power. She would rule all and any within her reach.

She entered my suite as if expected, as if it were her own space. There had been no knock, no hesitant greeting. I had merely been a squatter in her domain.

But none of that bothered me. What made my instincts immediately begin a steady pump of adrenaline through my system, were those strange beautiful eyes . . . They were soulless. Lifeless. There was no light in her eyes. Nothing but a deep pit of darkness lay within.

And behind her trailed two of those *things*. The Umbra, Maxim had called them. I would not have thought it possible, but they were even more harrowing then I had remembered.

All three of them simply walked in.

I did nothing at first. It embarrasses me to admit, but I did nothing. I was confused. I could not connect what was happening with the concept of security I had constructed within my quarters.

She looked around the sitting room with distaste before settling her lifeless gaze upon me. There was nothing but contempt in her expression. And it was enough to finally set me into action.

I jumped up from the settee, grabbing the dagger of Light strapped to my thigh. But before I could do anything with it, she gave a bored flick of her hand and the dagger went flying into the fireplace on its own accord.

"Don't bother," she said. She spoke with a sophisticated British accent that was silky and dark. It was void of any brightness or vitality and it sent chills down my spine.

"Come with me," she commanded. And as if I would undoubtedly follow, she turned for the door.

"Who are you?" I demanded.

She spun around, crossing to me, and backhanded me. The motion had been so fast I hadn't been able to block her blow.

She grabbed my face in her hand, her nails digging into my skin like claws. "Do not test me, girl," she hissed. "There is nothing I would like more than to let my little pets have their way with you. They put on a wonderful show when they are granted a treat. I do ever so enjoy watching them play."

I believed I understood her meaning and I had to hold back a gag. I wanted to fight her, to strike her . . . but I *couldn't*. There was something around her, some kind of field or energy. And although she could touch me, and I could feel her, I could not initiate any contact with her.

Those dead crystallized eyes of hers searched my own. Then a smile spread across her black lips, and she reached up to hold my face in both her hands. She tilted my head up a notch and kissed me.

I tried to pull away from her. I didn't want her anywhere near me. But I was powerless. She had a hold on me.

She traced my lips with her tongue and then bit my bottom lip—*hard*. She sucked on the blood that welled there making an *umm* sound.

Then she pulled back from me, smiling, with my blood staining her white teeth. "But," she whispered, petting my cheek, "if you are a good little girl . . . *you will be rewarded.*"

I cringed. Disturbed by her.

I gathered all of my will, all of my strength, and I tried to hit her. But my hand wouldn't move. Whatever shield she had in place was too powerful.

I could try to make a run for it. I would have to get around her and those two *things*, but if I made it to the door . . . perhaps I'd have a chance.

A black smoky shadow began to expand around her. It arched and grew like a cobra's flaps, making her appear larger and more dangerous. The firelight in the room fought to remain, gasping as if the oxygen suddenly became sparse. The world became cold and black—so bleak and hopeless.

And with an eerie stillness, those two things behind her lost their physical form. Their bodies shifted, and they seemed to dissolve. I realized what I had seen—the physical shape they had maintained—was merely a shell. It was a vessel for what they truly were.

They became actual shadows. They were dark space, nothing more. Yet the evil they carried was somehow intensified, freed of the constraints of the bodies they walked around in.

When she spoke next, her voice became layered and amplified, underscored by screeches and wails as if monsters from the grave had possessed her. "You stupid girl! Attempt to defy me one moment more and you will know suffering unlike any you could have ever imagined."

She held up both palms, curling and flexing them as if contemplating doing something. In the end, though, the shadows wavering around her began to settle and vanish. And as they did, the two Umbra behind her solidified once again.

"Seize her," she commanded. And she turned away to exit the suite without waiting for them to collect me.

I tried to dig deep for a blast of energy, but I just didn't have any to release. I was empty.

Really, it didn't matter.

One of the things made a low whispering gurgle sound and I felt a faint stir in my chest. I cringed at the feeling . . . at the horror . . . at the realization.

I was *connected* to them.

It was a paltry thread. One that I knew I could break. I knew if I could just purge more of the dark and cold from my body—if *he* would take it away again, completely—this connection would be destroyed. But none of that was comforting. None of it could cushion the shock of my newfound understanding.

And they grabbed me.

I didn't fight them. I didn't want them to release any of that black acrid smoke. I couldn't bear the thought of inhaling more of it. Of having it take up residence within my body. Of having a piece of them inside me.

They grabbed me. Swaths of evil, like long cold skeletal fingers, enveloped me. And as if I had never been, they turned me into smoke.

***

It was the ruins of an ancient castle. Remnants of stone walls were all that remained. We entered through a massive archway which at one time would have housed the portcullis. Above us was the night sky, full of heavenly bodies. The large expanse of the bailey was covered in grass and littered with piles of fallen rock. Pieces of the walls had crumbled and collapsed giving an uneven and odd shape to what was left of the structure.

Perhaps Rheneas had known something. He had tried so hard to convince me to listen to Maxim and return home. Yet he had not warned me of this.

After our visit with Belcalis, Rheneas and Stefan had driven me back to the manor. Apparently, Maxim had been called away on something urgent. I had found out that Rheneas was the one with dark brown hair and Stefan the dark blond.

Both had been very reserved and detached in their interactions with me, but one thing had been clear; they both held a deep respect for Maxim.

Just as he had done outside the inn, Rheneas had urged me to return home. He had told me they could take me that night. At the time, I had a feeling it had to do with the uprising that was brewing, and the fliers for the rally. However, as I was led into the castle remains, I wondered if they had known this woman would come for me. Only a few hours had passed since they had dropped me off, and now I was being bound.

The woman had one of the Umbra secure my wrists. The other slipped a hook through the bindings and then my arms were raised by a pulley hanging from a beam which had been rigged to one of the walls.

The Umbra pulled until my bound hands were directly overhead. Then it gave an extra yank so that my feet were no longer flat on the ground. My toes just skimmed the earth and I was left hanging there.

But being restrained and held captive was not the worst offense in the darkness of the castle ruins. What turned my stomach, was the oozing mess gurgling on the grass.

I almost vomited when I realized what I was looking at.

It was the third Umbra. I knew it was. It was the one that had breathed into me. The one that had poisoned me. The one that had forced itself into me. I could feel the connection to it.

It was in its physical form, yet much of its midsection had liquefied, turning into a congealed mess of body parts. Organs and skin floated in black greasy oil.

And because of the flicker of connection I felt with the thing, I knew it suffered in untold agony—the likes of which most would never be able to comprehend.

Following my gaze, the woman gave a wicked smile. "You see," she said crossing to me. She began to circle around me, skimming her fingers along my body as she did. "You don't want to defy me princess. I will make you pray for your end. It is ever so much better if we get along."

I had changed into leggings and a t-shirt after Rheneas and Stefan had dropped me off. Now hanging from my bound wrists, my shirt had ridden up, exposing my midriff. The woman stopped to rake her black fingernail over the exposed section of my waist. Then she trailed the nail up from my navel to my chin, curling her finger there. I felt compelled to look at her, and those iced eyes chilled me.

"What?" she asked. "Don't tell me you have pity for it." Rage contorted her face and she leaned into me. A sickly-sweet scent filled my nose.

"Do you know how difficult it is to manipulate dreams? Have you any idea the level of power it takes to manifest a waking fantasy? To influence another from a great distance with nothing but a single strand of hair?"

She reminded me of the Shadow Prince then. There was a madness in her eyes—the same as that which I had seen in him. And I couldn't stop the shiver that spasmed over my skin.

I tried to appease her, wanting to buy myself time. "I can't imagine," I murmured.

"No," she snapped, pulling her finger back with a flick. "Of course you can't. Your puny mind is nothing. You have lived but for a speck of time in the unending drudgery of existence. You are not capable of understanding.

"I have spent thousands of lifetimes waiting for this. Planning and sacrificing for this. And this cur thinks to ruin it all in an instant?!"

She crossed to the Umbra lying on the floor, and reached down to stroke its matted, gurgling head. "But I am a forgiving mistress, am I not?" she cooed. "I have shown leniency."

The thing looked up at her with black ooze dribbling out of its mouth and moved its lips wordlessly.

"I know," the woman reassured, patting the Umbra. "You are forgiven." Then she gave its head a shove and walked away from it. "Only three more days of sunlight for you," she called over her shoulder.

The woman looked at me then, shrugging a shoulder. "You see the mercy I show?"

I glanced at the sweeping view of the open sky above. Although it was night now, it seemed obvious that the Umbra was being tortured by the exposure to the daylight.

"What did it do?" I asked.

"It disobeyed me, my dear. They were not to kiss you. Only to fetch you." She threw up her hands. "And yet here I am, forced to do the work myself. Such banality."

"What do you want with me?"

The woman crossed to me again and began to pet my cheek. She put her lips next to my ear. "Oh, fair princess," she murmured, "I've come for your Light, of course."

My reply was calm and firm. "I don't have any. I used the last of it to try and stave off your minions. And I haven't seen the sun in days."

She laughed then. It was a cackle unlike anything I had heard before. The crazed, demented sound bounced across the stone walls and assailed the quiet night sky. When she had calmed, she stood in front of me and played with the strands of my hair that tumbled down the front of my shoulders, gently pulling and tugging, twisting tendrils around her finger before letting them fall.

Her black lips parted in a smile. "You don't know, do you?"

I said nothing.

"Although," she chastised, disregarding her own question, "I am very unhappy with you." She continued to caress my hair, letting her nails claw over my neck and collar bone as she did. "I sent you all kinds of wonderful dreams and fantasies. I gave you your deepest desires. And I know my pet must be frothing at the mouth for you."

She yanked on my hair. "And you two do *nothing*. You waste my time!"

Taking a deep breath, she released her hold and began to fix my hair into place. "Still, I have you here now. And I know my pet will join us shortly—he will not be able to stay away from you."

She smirked. "I am so delighted that you accepted my proposal. It has made everything I've worked so hard for begin to fall into place. I'm so close now, I can *feel* it."

"Your proposal?" I asked.

"Of course," she replied. "You didn't really think my little pet had anything to do with it, did you?"

"I thought it had been the decision of the Shadow Court," I replied, hoping she would keep talking.

Her eyes slitted and the air around us froze. "I *am* the Shadow Court," she hissed. "Those twits in parliament are there to serve *me*. They do *my* bidding. I am *The Contessa*."

She reveled at her own title and it seemed to soothe her. She took a breath and notched her chin, calming. "It matters not. What we need now is my pet." She began stroking my hair again.

"The Shadow Prince," I established.

"It has been ever so long since I paid him a visit. He must miss me terribly," she huffed. "But I've been rather busy, haven't I? Tell me, does he talk of me? Does he regale you with tales of our time together?"

I gave a crooked smile and replied. "Not at all." She was too vague with information, and I was beginning to get annoyed. I wanted to piss her off.

She took a step back from me and hissed, "You insolent girl. You *will* be punished." She looked at one of the Umbra in a silent command.

It came towards me. I tried to kick at it, but it clutched my legs and yanked them apart before stepping between them. As it put its face into mine, I ticked my neck back to head-butt it.

Except as the thing opened its black hole of a mouth, The Contessa grabbed its head, yanking it in her direction and put her lips over the Umbra's. After their gruesome kiss, she pushed the thing away. "Leave us!"

Vestiges of black smoke whorled around her lips. She licked and sucked at them, staring at me. The caustic stench of burning rubber permeated from her, assaulting my nose with each breath I took. I openly cringed.

And I could immediately see a difference in her. Those dead gray eyes became newly crystallized. Her hair became shinier. Her lips and the lining around her eyes, blacker. Her deathly white skin paled even more. And the air of malevolence around her amplified.

She also seemed revived, in a sense. She raised an eyebrow at me. "I think I'd like to have a little fun while we're waiting. What about you?"

I didn't answer, though. Because it was then that I sensed a presence just outside the ruins.

And the very tips of my toes iced. The ground below frosted over. And a large frame filled the archway of the crumbling castle.

He paused, taking in the scene before him. Time seemed to still and then a heinous roar erupted from his chest and blackness swirled in his eyes. He began to stalk towards me.

The Contessa's voice was quiet but lethal. "That's enough, mutt."

He stopped but didn't take his eyes off me.

"You can have her as a treat. If you behave." The Contessa skimmed her fingers across the swell of my breasts and up the column of my neck where she started to squeeze, slowly cutting off my air supply. "I might even let you keep her as a plaything after I've drained her."

Something within him snapped and he charged The Contessa throwing her into the stone wall where she crumpled to the ground. She looked up at him, stunned and disheveled.

"What are you doing?" she screeched. She staggered to her feet, menace rolling off her in icy blasts. She reached him and backhanded him across his face. "Kneel before me," she commanded.

He grabbed her by the throat and hefted her into the air. Her hands came up around his and her toes dangled two feet above the ground. He was breathing so heavily that his words came out between gulps of air, like an animal's growl. "If you . . . touch . . . her . . . I will end you."

A wave of blackness pulsed from The Contessa sending shadows screaming through the open air all around us. They obstructed all the light from the night sky, and I could see nothing for a moment. Then in a whomp of vibrating space, they were sucked away as if through a tear in the fabric of this world.

The Contessa and the Umbra were gone.

He stood there with his back to me, his shoulders heaving. After what seemed like a small eternity, he turned to face me. I gasped at the unadulterated hatred consuming his black eyes.

His dark hair was disheveled and wild with the gusts of arctic air blasting around him. Again, he wore only dark slacks. Each rigid muscle along his chest and abdomen flexed with the erratic breathes he took. And the black mark over his heart seemed to shimmer under the moonlight. It was enough to make me want to believe Maxim's tale.

He began to take one halting step after another towards me until he stood just an inch away. And in that inch of space I had no choice but to breath him in as he stared down at me.

I swallowed, looking up at him. I couldn't think about the ache in my arms restrained above or the icy chill on my exposed skin. I was trapped, bound in place, and he was too close. All I could do was breathe. And with each inhale, there he was.

I began to lift my legs up inch by inch, dragging out the motion, careful not to startle him in the state he was in. Until finally, I wrapped my legs around his hips. I closed my eyes for a moment and let out a breath. Then I felt his hands envelope my waist.

He lifted me up and I was granted enough slack that I could slip my bound wrists from the hook. I didn't dare lace my arms around his neck. Instead I brought them down between us, to let them cover my chest, feeling the sharp sting as blood rushed back into them.

And leaving behind the deserted ruins to bask in the quiet moonlit peace once again, we slipped away.

CHAPTER 20

"W*HAT. THE. FUCK.*" I shouted at him.

The instant we had slammed back into the Dark Manor—into that same room again, he had thrown me out of his arms and retreated from me.

"What the ever-loving fuck?!" I repeated.

There was no reply, and I snapped. "Oh, that's it." I began to make my way to the door, fuming, muttering to myself the whole way. "That is it. I am sick of this *boll*-shit."

I flung the chamber door open and stormed out into the dark hallway. "Someone is getting murdered tonight. I don't care if it's him or me, but someone is getting killed. And this time I mean it!"

I gave the bindings around my wrists a snap. I could feel him following behind me, and I was glad I wouldn't have to come back looking for him. It would make stabbing him that much easier.

I had put this all off for too long, and look where it had gotten me. It was time I stopped waiting for answers and *did* something.

"I'm getting my dagger and I'm running it straight through his heart or I'm gonna die trying." I raised my voice and called over my shoulder," Fair warning, Shadow Boy! You'd better make peace and prepare yourself for your ending."

Having done the honorable thing, I returned to my muttering and I made the long trek through the darkened hall on my way to my suite.

"And right after I stab him, I'm going back to that god forsaken place and I'll wait for that psycho-bitch and stab her too. Right in her black shriveled heart. Then I'm going to hunt down whoever is leading this resistance and personally shake their hand while contacting the Radiant Court and sending reinforcements.

"And finally, I'm going to make Maxim take me to his mother to learn how Shadow Boy's, here, fucking father locked away the Umbra, so I can bury them. Which should be his goddamn job— not mine. But it seems that he's too fucking lazy to put on some goddamn clothes and take care of his own fucking business.

"And then I'm taking a goddamn vacation. And I'm going to lay out in the sun all day every day. I'm going to go to the Caribbean with Kil. I'll figure out whatever incubus type bullshit has been going on here and I'll figure out how to use it in my personal life. And I can finally have a normal *adult* relationship with someone."

When I reached my suite, I flung the doors open and marched straight to my music player. I cued up one of the songs I liked to play before I went out hunting with Killian, Watts, and the other guys from The Unit. *Going to Hell* by The Pretty Reckless began blasting from the speakers.

Then I went to dig through the ashes in the fireplace to find my dagger of Light. I only had the one since they were so rare. It was easy enough to find. It was still lying where it had landed when The Contessa had flung it away.

I retrieved it and wiped it off on my leggings. I didn't bother with trying to ignite fires in the suite. My power was lower than it had ever been. I just didn't have enough Light to expend. And besides, *he* had followed me into the suite. He would probably just extinguish the flames once I had gotten them started anyway.

It was fine. I was perfectly capable of hunting in the dark.

But I was so annoyed by him. He just stood there—lurking. I wanted him to make a move. Try and attack me. Do something so I could lash out at him. It's hard to go bat-shit crazy on someone who's just standing there.

And come to think of it, who has just rescued you . . . twice.

I threw the dagger down and then rushed him. Maybe my conscience wouldn't let me kill him, but I deserved some answers. And I would get them one way or another.

Just before I reached him, I crouched down and swung my leg, intending to kick his legs out from under him. Except, he was no longer there. Instead, when I spun back into a standing stance, he was behind me, caging his arms around me.

However, this time I had been prepared for just such an instance, and I was properly aligned to shift forward and use his own mass to flip him over. He landed with a thunk on the floor. I pivoted as I landed on top of him, and straddling his waist with my knees, I gave his face a jab immediately followed with a cross.

241

Without a moment's pause, I gave his windpipe a chop and followed with another cross hook.

He didn't fight back but instead grabbed each of my wrists in his large hands. "I told you to go home," he growled at me.

"You did, but you didn't tell me about the Umbra or your lovely girlfriend." I was breathing heavily, not only from exertion but from so much frustration.

An icy blast hit me, and his voice deepened in anger while he squeezed my wrists. "Do not call her that."

"You're hurting me!" I snarled. He loosened his grip and with a snap, I twisted my wrists free, muttering what an idiot he was. I was about to jump to my feet, but he grabbed my waist and threw me to the ground, rolling on top of me.

I instantly tried to slide my knee against his hip to push my body out from under his, but he settled the full force of his weight across my pelvis, pinning me in place, and grabbed my wrists once again.

"Even if I had told you about them, you wouldn't have left."

I silently agreed with him.

I squirmed under him, trying to find a chance to throw him.

"You beheaded one the other night. And from what it sounded like, you played doctor with the others. How are they still alive?"

He grimaced. "They're not—*alive*. It doesn't matter what you do to them. They take form again once they're able."

"How do I stop them?"

"You don't." He made the statement sound like I was the dumbest person he had ever come across.

"Okay," I gritted, trying to tamp down my annoyance. "How do *you* stop them?"

That blatant hatred simmered in his eyes again and his voice turned lethal. "If I could, I would have by now."

I altered my tone as if talking to a five-year-old. "Well, how did your father do it?"

It was incredibly subtle, but there was a shift in his breathing. He didn't answer, and a hint of confusion crossed his face. His focus also turned inward. I took the moment to try and twist my hips out from under him.

The motion seemed to jar him from his thoughts, and he clamped down on me harder. "Contessa is the one who controls them."

I raised a brow. "Oh, isn't that sweet. Not *The Contessa,* just plain ol' *Contessa* for you. You two are certainly chummy."

Another icy blast slammed into me, and his control slipped. I could feel those turbulent emotions of his begin to surface. I needed him to focus. I couldn't let him slide away into that madness.

I freed my legs from under him and wrapped them in a triangle choke around his neck, pulling him closer. And then I cursed myself for turning on the music player. It had been on shuffle and Marian Hill's *Got It* began pulsing through the room.

Worst still, he barked, "Enough!" and pushed himself through my choke hold, forcing my legs open and to the side before laying on top of me and pinning my arms against the floor next to each shoulder.

The full weight of his body covered my own and his chest pressed into mine. "I can't breathe," I whispered.

"Then suffocate!" he replied, his black eyes narrowing.

"Fine," I huffed, abandoning the helpless girl routine. It had been worth a shot. After all, I had benefited from it just a moment ago.

He gave my wrists a squeeze. "Are you done?"

I shrugged. "Let me go and we'll see."

A growl was his only reply.

I smiled at him.

And he looked at me as though he absolutely hated me for it. I couldn't help it. I laughed out loud.

His breathing became deeper and his chest pushed into mine with each inhalation. And with the pressure, I felt a warmth under my ribs. Deep inside my bones. With a creeping slowness, it began to spread outward.

The music stopped abruptly, and I knew it had been his doing. I reminded myself that I wanted answers.

"Who is she?" I demanded.

"She controls everything," he replied. "The Umbra, the Shadow Court . . . everything."

"Not you," I countered.

"I don't know what happened tonight. I have never been able to stop her before."

I realized my breathing was in sync with his as I asked, "How many times have you met her?"

His eyes became unfocused and he was somewhere else when he answered. "She raised me."

Ice tore through my veins. But this time it was not an icy blast from him. This time it was of my own volition. "Is she your mother?" I gasped.

"No." The single word was a conviction. A victory.

I could not begin to imagine the childhood he had had. If that woman had been his surrogate . . . The horror of it, of an innocent little one raised by her—exposed to her. Oh god, if she had had the Umbra by her side during all those years . . .

Looking back now, I realize that in that moment a certain admiration for him began. He was a rabid animal deep within. He was maddened at his core. Yet he somehow controlled it. Although his demons were not tamed . . . they were leashed.

"How old are you?" I asked quietly, wanting to know how long he had been under her influence.

"I don't know."

I arched under him, my body pressing into his. I couldn't help myself. I knew it was inappropriate, but there were things happening between us that I couldn't stop.

His jaw clenched, and his nostrils flared. He squeezed his eyes shut and gripped my wrists tighter. He was grappling for control.

"What does she want with me?"

He opened his eyes and there was a single streak of blue breaking through the black in one of his irises. "I don't know," he repeated.

"She and the Umbra just walked into my suite." I couldn't help but notice there was a tinge of accusation in my voice. I tried to remind myself that it wasn't his job to protect me. He had never made any such pledge.

"I told you to leave," he snapped back. There was anger and frustration in the way he spoke, but I also thought there was an undertone of guilt.

I won't lie. I did think about leaving then. About disregarding any sense of obligation or duty I felt and running off somewhere on my own. I could leave everything and everyone behind. Let others take care of the messes within our two courts. And just find a beach somewhere.

But that wasn't who I was, and I knew it. I would never be happy sitting back and letting others see to my obligations. I was capable. I was a fighter. And I would continue to fight.

"Have you been supporting the rogue attacks upon Radiants? Are the Shadows who are killing our people doing so by your order?"

"What do I care for Radiants or Shadows?" came his reply.

"Answer me! Has it been your doing?"

He responded with an uninterested shake of his head.

I struggled against him, wanting to keep him focused, in the here and now. He shuddered against me at the contact.

"You have no involvement with the Umbra or the Shadow Court?"

He squeezed his eyes shut, clearly unhappy about this line of questioning, clearly wanting nothing more than to slip away into the shadows of the manor and become one himself.

"No," he gritted.

He was telling the truth. I could *feel* it. And I knew what I had to do. What my role now was. I knew it the instant I learned he had been raised by The Contessa and that she controlled the Umbra as well as the Shadow Court.

It all became clear.

I now knew that I *needed* him. That the peace and security of our two courts depended on him. I had to see to it that he claimed his rightful place as the Shadow Court ruler.

My main objective was the safety of my people. It was my birthright, and I would not shy away from it. And I finally understood that the true threat to the Radiant Court was not the Shadow Prince, but The Contessa. If there was any chance in defeating her, he would have to be a part of it.

If Maxim's story about the Shadow King held any credence, then I believed there was a chance that the king's heir could master the Umbra and lock them away once more. It was in his bloodline. Just as I had my own, this was *his* birthright.

He had saved me from the Umbra and I had witnessed him drive away The Contessa. I believed he was capable of claiming his place in the Shadow Court, if he just cared enough to.

On the surface it was impossible to understand why The Contessa would willingly raise a child. But it made sense why she would want to raise *this* child. To control him. To have power over him. It had been a calculated move to secure her position in the Shadow Court.

If I could get him to his rightful place on the throne, I could ensure peace within the Shadow nation. I was certain now that it was The Contessa who was behind the rogue attacks on my people. If she had extended the proposal in the name of the Shadow Prince, she was probably behind everything else done in his name. The reputation that had recently arose, attributed to the Dark Prince, was likely all because of her.

With the attacks upon my people ceased, there would be no need for opposition between the Radiants and the Shadows. And with the Umbra and The Contessa defeated, there would be no need for a revolt among the Shadows. The prince could work to make his people happy. Our two courts could find an understanding and move forward in a way that was beneficial for all. We could have peace.

Pulling me from my thoughts, he squeezed my wrists again. "You will leave—"

"Yeah. Yeah. I know," I answered. "Tomorrow."

I took another deep breath, savoring the feeling of my chest pressing into his. "How can I protect myself here? How can I bar her entry?"

"You don't!" He jumped off of me then and crossed to the door. "Between the two of us, *you* are the one who is insane," he growled. "Are you determined to die here? Why do you insist on staying?! I don't want you here. The Shadow people don't care about you or want a Radiant princess to save them. And The Contessa will feed you to the Umbra after she has tortured and broken you."

He grabbed the door handle and flung it open. "You will leave! Tomorrow!"

"No," I insisted. I couldn't let him walk out. I needed him. He had to help me. I sent a pulse of energy, slamming the door closed.

I looked down at my myself, taken aback. A little of my energy had recharged. A little warmth and Light had returned. Not much. Not enough. But *something*. And it had been while lying under him. While being touched by him.

He reached to open the door again.

I ran up to him and grabbed his arm, hoping he would turn around. I no longer wanted to try and hurt him. I wanted to try and talk to him. Actually talk to him.

He had the ability to rule or possibly lock away the Umbra, at least there was a chance he did. And I had witnessed him drive away The Contessa. I had experienced glimpses of the chaos that he had churning inside. There was incredible power there. It was feral and untamed, but there just the same.

"You have to stop her. You need to lead the resistance movement and take back your kingdom. Your people are waiting for you."

"I can't."

"Okay." I let out a heavy breath, grappling for patience. He was still facing the door. I let go of him and took a step back.

The first thing I needed to do was secure my place here. "I can't leave just now," I told him. "I am grateful for your help tonight. But The Contessa wants me. She believes she *needs* me for some agenda that I don't understand and know nothing about. She made it sound like it's been her life's mission. She's not going to simply give up.

"If I return home, she could come for me there. And I want to keep her and the Umbra far away from the people I care about.

"Yes, I could leave here. But I have no doubt she will track me. She is capable of dark magics. She has already been using them against me. She said she had been shaping my dreams. She was the one who lured me out to the Umbra.

"I think she suggested that she has a strand of my hair. She was also touching my hair tonight, and she drank a few drops of my blood. With those things at her disposal, I doubt there is anywhere I can go that she won't find me.

"There is no point in running from her. I need to stand my ground and fight. If there is any chance for me, I need to defeat her. *Please.* Is there any way I can secure the manor against her?"

He didn't respond, but he also didn't walk away. After I could take his silence no longer, I walked to stand in front of him. I had to crane my head back to look up at him. More blue streaks had broken through the black in his eyes.

"You can't pretend to be a ghost in this manor forever," I told him. "You can't hide from who you are."

His face was grim.

I cocked my head to the side. Trying to assess the firm set of his lips, the pinched quality of his angled features, the tick in his jaw. "Are you in pain?" I asked.

"Always," was his reply. It was a quiet and simple confirmation.

I opened my mouth, unsure what I would say in response. But he cut me off.

"I can ask the Crone if there is anything we can do to keep The Contessa from entry and from influencing you. She . . . *knows* certain things."

"Who *is* she?" I asked.

And as he had done in the past and would do in the future, the Shadow Prince answered my question without really doing so.

"I don't know."

CHAPTER 21

"STAY HERE."

"Why can't I just—"

"Stay here!"

"Okay, fine!" I huffed and leaned against the wall. He passed through the boarded-up hole with the wood plank slamming behind him. It was as though neither he nor the abandoned wing of the manor cared for my presence.

I slid down and sat on the floor. I figured I would be waiting for quite a while. But after a moment of inaction, I decided I should run back up to my quarters and fetch my phone. I needed to check in at court and update Killian.

I stood to leave and began making my way down the dark, silent corridor when I slammed into him. "Stop doing that!" I hissed.

"Stop running off," he growled back.

I glossed over his comment. "*How* are you doing that anyway? I thought it was just the Angela who could pulse."

"It's different from that," he grumbled. "Come on."

"Wait, where are we going?" I began running along behind him. He had a quick gait, but it wasn't tense. The way he moved was lethal and precise. He cut right through the darkness without disrupting the air around him.

"To the master chamber. The Crone will meet us there." His deep dark voice came floating back to me.

"Why?" I asked. I knew he meant the room we kept returning to. Of all the rooms in the manor, that one had the most *masterly* feel to it.

It was cavernous. The bed in there was larger than any I'd ever seen. The floor to ceiling wall of books certainly created an air of authority, and I had even noticed a wide tub in front of one of the multiple oversized hearths. If I remembered correctly, the chamber also had four towering windows along the outer wall that were buried under layers of heavy drapes.

There was something about the air in that room. Something ancient and *big*.

We had reached the stairs without a response to my question. I decided to try another. "How long have you known the . . . the Crone?" I had a difficult time calling her that. It seemed disrespectful to call an elder such a rude term. "Does she have a name at least?"

His voice was quiet as he spoke. "I have only ever known her as the *Crone*. And I have known her for as long as I can remember. She has always been here tending to the manor."

I eyed the dust laden banister, the cobwebs coating the chandeliers, the blackened stone walls . . . and decided not to say anything.

I thought about how that added to the picture of him I was now forming. I tried to imagine a small child living in this dark and dreary place, being raised by a mad woman who was flanked by the Umbra, with a hooded and hunched hag *tending* to things.

"Which room is yours?" I had caught up to him and we were now side by side as we ascended the stairs. I looked up at his profile and was struck anew with the perfect angles of his face. There was also a way the darkness settled around him that was . . . *right*. It somehow drew out his features in a way that I had never seen before in another.

But in answering my question, there was a tightness in his jaw. And again, there was that pained way in which he spoke. "It is downstairs."

I had thoroughly searched the manor, and I knew there were no bedrooms on the first floor. There was the massive foyer, dining rooms, sitting rooms, two ballrooms, libraries, dens, the kitchen and butler's pantry, but no bedrooms.

And as always seemed to be the case lately, a shiver ran down my back. "You mean," I clarified, "down in that abandoned wing? Underground?"

He gave an imperceptive nod in response.

"Why don't you move—"

He whipped his head in my direction stopping where he was. "You speak about things of which you have no knowledge."

I bit my lip, having stopped with him. And after a moment's pause, I nodded. His eyes were that electric blue now and they sparked in the darkness.

I was about to comment on them. To ask him about them. But he began to climb the stairs once again, walking right into the shadows ahead and disappearing into them. I hustled after him, determined not to lose him. And we walked the rest of the way to the chamber in silence.

As we neared, I saw that the doors were already open and the light of a small fire flickered and swayed across the wall in the hallway. I could hear shuffling within.

I followed him into the chamber, and the first thing I saw were the books burning in the collapsed fireplace. I inwardly cringed. I made a note to collect some firewood from outside. At this rate the tomes and journals in this room would be gone by the end of the month.

There was a little pot sitting on one of the old bricks among the fire, and the Crone was standing above in her ragged robe with the cowl drawn. She was stirring the contents of the pot with great difficulty.

In a brittle and ancient voice, she wheezed something in the Dark Tongue. *He* turned to me. "She says you need to stir the pot."

"Okay, sure," I replied, crossing to the Crone. Before I reached her, she let the spoon drop with a thunk against the pot. Then she turned to rummage through a little burlap sack.

When I went to pick up the spoon and resume stirring the pot, I noticed two things. The pot was empty, and the spoon was not

255

a spoon at all but a stick. Still, I grabbed the end of the stick and began to stir. Only, it wouldn't budge.

"It's stuck," I said.

The Crone swiveled in my direction. She released her pinched fingers over the pot, as if adding an ingredient, but her fingers were empty. She said something again in the Dark Tongue.

"She said to stop being so weak and stir it. She said if you want the ward, you must stir the ingredients."

"It's *stuck*," I repeated, looking up at him. "And there's nothing in here."

Instead of a reply, he stared at me, unimpressed. I couldn't take the clenched jaw and narrowed eyes, so I redoubled my efforts. I used both hands and the full force of my weight to try and lean into it. But still nothing.

I was about to write off the Crone as completely senile, when one of the burning books caught my eye. It was open, and as the fire burned the page, I noticed gold script within the book begin to shine and shimmer.

I was mesmerized. I couldn't look away. The pages did not continue to disintegrate. Instead, it was as though the fire had cleansed the dust and dirt. It had burned away all that was unnecessary until these inner pages were revealed.

I couldn't understand the script, but as I stared, I felt warmed. The darkness surrounding us, hanging heavy in the room, encompassing the manor, settling all around the property grounds—was gone. It was no longer a looming presence. All that remained was the bright, golden, shining Light in front of me. And I felt that same bright Light flare somewhere deep within my chest.

I was vaguely aware that the flames before me began to take on a violet hue. Somewhere in the recess of my mind, I realized that my eyes must be glowing. And while I was standing there, transfixed, the old bat attacked me.

"Ow!" I yowled in pain, holding my eye. She had jabbed her knotted finger straight into it. I turned to ward off any other advances from her, but she simply flicked her fingers over the pot as best she could with arthritic movement.

"What was that for?!" I screeched. But as I still had my other eye open, I could see that the bottom of the pot now held a violet glow.

The Crone mumbled something, and *he* supplied, "She needed a tear."

"Well maybe next time she can ask first," I grumbled.

The Crone continued with her labored mumbles, pointing the same bent and bony finger at his chest.

There was a flicker of something across his face at her words, but he gave a slight nod. The Crone shuffled over to stand in front of him. The hood of her cowl just reached his midsection. She raised her hand and placed one gnarled finger over his heart.

I gave a gasp when she began to push into his flesh, stabbing her finger through skin and muscle all the way up to her knuckle. She turned her hand as she went, reaching as far into him as possible.

I was about to take a step to stop her, but he noticed my movement. "She needs a drop of blood from my heart," he explained through gritted teeth. And then with a sickening squelch, she pulled her blood-soaked finger out.

257

Wine red blood poured from the hole in his chest in a stream down his abdomen. Yet he had remained stoic throughout, with nothing more than the clenched jaw and blackened eyes that he seemed to always emote.

The Crone hobbled back to the pot and flicked her fingers over it once again. A single drop of his blood fell to join the violet glow. She grumbled something at me again, and I didn't need him to translate this time. I grabbed the stick and I found that I was able to move it. I began to stir the pot.

The violet hue slowly became streaked with white, until an intense bright Light began to flare from the pot. Then from within the folds of her robe, the Crone procured a handful of rocks. She held her open palm containing the rocks above the pot. However, I noticed—with my good eye—that among the small rocks, was the ring I had been presented. My ring for this marriage.

The Crone dumped the handful of rocks into the pot and with the sound of the stones pinging upon the metal, the Light was extinguished, and the burning fire snuffed out. The room was cast into blackness. Yet, after a moment's pause, the faintest bit of Light began to glow from within the pot. I leaned over, peering in. Each stone pulsed with a tiny flicker.

The Crone scooped up the rocks from the pot and placed them into her robe. She mumbled something and began to shuffle to the door. Before she exited, she swiveled her head in my direction. I could still see nothing but blackness beneath her hood, but I knew she stared at me. And although she said nothing, I felt as though she was demanding in some way that I not let her down. That flicker of faraway power sparked from her, and then she left.

"What now?" I asked.

"She's taking the stones to place around the manor. They will bar entry for The Contessa and the Umbra."

I looked back into the pot, noticing that a tiny glow of Light remained. It was the ring. The Crone had not taken it with her but left it in the pot. From the shadows he said, "You are to wear it. Do not take it off. It will act as a shield from certain dark magics. The Contessa will be unable to reach you through dream casting. However, be warned. It cannot protect against the Umbra."

"Can I trust her?" I asked, uncertain as to what to think in regard to the Crone.

"Yes."

I hesitated to pick up the ring. "It's from The Contessa," I said, cringing at the thought.

"Not really," he countered.

I looked over at him. He had come closer without my notice. The hole in his chest had closed.

"She told me earlier that it was she who extended the proposal."

"Yes," he agreed, "but the ring is not hers to give. She found it here at the manor."

"Who's is it?" I asked.

He shrugged.

"Was it your father's?"

"I don't have any family," he replied.

"Was it the Shadow King's?" I amended.

He didn't answer, and I took his silence as a *yes*. If it had been his father's then by right, it would be his. It also made sense for The Contessa to offer it with the proposal. It had made the gesture all the more authentic.

"Seems a little awkward to take it." I commented.

He exhaled, and I could hear the heft of irritation in it. "You are difficult. You insist on staying here. You beg for help in concerns to The Contessa. And when you are provided with a means for your desires, you suddenly hesitate to accept."

"Fine!" I reached down and grabbed the illuminated ring, which had been mixed with my Light and his blood. Then I shoved it on my finger. "There. Okay?"

But I was silenced as I locked eyes with him. There was something. Something amplified. It was as though something muddy and murky had just been made a little clearer. As though it had been pulled closer to the surface.

Goosebumps broke out over my skin. I was now certain there were much larger forces at play here. Whatever I had thought, whatever I had believed, I now knew I had been utterly naive.

And I did something then that I had never done in my life. I did something that I thought only weak people did. Something I had thought I would always be too strong for. Too bright for.

With my eyes locked on his and a certain clarity beginning to surface . . . I honest to god fainted.

CHAPTER 22

A NOTE HAD BEEN LEFT on the pillow next to my head. Sloppy, uneven writing had been painstakingly scratched onto a piece of paper. It simply read:

Do not take ring off. Do not leave.

I crossed to one of the towering windows in my room and drew back the curtain. The sun was setting. I had slept away another day.

I slid down the window casing and sat on the floor wrapping my arms around my knees. Leaning my forehead against the glass, I watched the evening shadows blanket the grounds. The darkness of night was coming.

I indulged for a moment. I imagined that my mother had not been terrified for my safety as a child. I imagined that I never took a fighting lesson, never picked up a weapon. I imagined what my life would be like if I had only pursued ballet, and music, and art.

I even took the fantasy a step further and pictured a life for myself without the obligation of my lineage. I created a simple childhood for myself. One that involved running barefoot through fields and having friends and siblings.

Perhaps I wouldn't have had these *intimacy issues*, as Killian had called them. Perhaps I would have met a simple farm boy. Maybe we would have fallen in love, tumbling through the fields under a clear blue sky. We would have been married and had little babies.

I would have been soft and sweet. He would have had rough hands and tanned shoulders. We would have had a simple life, not wanting more than one more day with each other.

But it was a futile exercise . . . I let the thoughts go. There was no point in wondering what my life could have been like under different circumstances. I was here now. What mattered was what came next, not some false illusion of what I wished had come before.

I picked myself up. I was still wearing the same leggings and t-shirt from the night before. They felt dirty and tainted. I made my way into the bathroom and found that I had enough power for a fire. Warmth and light illuminated the space.

I ran hot water, turned on my music player, and stripped down. I looked down at the ring. It felt odd to keep it on, but I would do whatever was necessary to keep The Contessa at bay.

I didn't sit and luxuriate in the hot water, though. As soon as I was cleaned up, I dressed in a fresh pair of leggings and one of the cropped tees I had folded in the closet. I brushed out my wet hair, leaving it loose to dry.

As I passed through the main living space of my quarters, I noticed a tray had been set out on the dining table. However, I hurried right by without eating and exited the suite.

I passed down the long hall and made my way into the master chamber. With the little power I had I began two more fires in both hearths.

I started pulling books out, wiping them off and stacking them up. After last night, I was convinced they held important secrets, ancient knowledge, great power. I was going to go over them and see what I could find.

"What are you doing?"

I jumped to a fighting stance, startled by the silky deep voice floating from the shadows. When he stepped forward, I relaxed, releasing a slow breath. "Don't do that," I scolded, and I began to dig through the books again.

"Go back to your room," he directed.

"No."

"Why are you in here?"

"I have to start somewhere."

"Meaning?"

I huffed and stopped rummaging through the books to glance at him over my shoulder. "Meaning I think there's something to these tomes. Something significant about them." I tried to shoot my best scowl in his direction.

In all honesty it wasn't his questioning that irritated me. It was his *presence*. The pull, the awareness—they were so much clearer now. I understood things I hadn't before.

After last night, now wearing his ring, I knew we were connected. Bonded. It was a fact I could no longer deny.

The need to be closer to him made my breathing faster and my skin hotter. Everything was amplified around him. Every little movement I made ignited sensations that would ripple to my very center.

I slammed shut the book I had been flipping through. A whomp reverberated through the quiet dark of the cavernous room and the fire in both hearths flickered. I stacked up as many books as I could in a hurry and began to make my way to the chamber door.

I had to get out of there. I needed more time to figure things out.

I made it past him. Past where he lurked in the shadows. I had just enough control to get back to my quarters.

But he grabbed my arm. And I let the books I was holding tumble to the floor. He spun me around, keeping the firm grip on my arm with one hand and shoved his other hand through my hair, fisting a handful of it at the base of my neck, forcing me to look up at him.

His nostrils flared. His jaw ticked. The perfect angles of his face were tight with anger. And his eyes crackled with electric blue sparks while branching with black veins.

"You need to leave," he hissed.

I glared at him. Trying to hate him. Trying to blame him for all the conflicted emotions I was experiencing. Angry that he made me feel things I had always wanted but had given up on. Angry that he never wore a damn shirt.

I tried to shake my head. But his grip on me tightened.

"Why are you doing this to me?" he seethed. "Have I not suffered enough? Why do you torment me?"

My chest was rising and falling in a hectic pace. Pressed against his. Meeting him breath for breath.

"I'm not doing anything to you," I replied, pouring all the defiance and vehemence that I could into each word.

"No?!" he challenged. "Each day I lie in bed, stiff and aching, thinking of you. Wanting you. Constantly haunted by you. The smell of you, the sight of you, the sound of your voice—it all *covers* me. Unrelentingly. Without cease."

He tightened his grip on me. Pressing his body into mine. Forcing me to feel all the hard planes and angles of him. Overwhelming my body with his. Surrounding me.

"No matter where I go. No matter what I do. I cannot escape you. How much more am I to take? You win. I will do whatever you want. Just release me of this."

He brought his face closer to mine. "Because if you do not. You will pay. You are strong. You are capable. You are skilled . . . But you are no match for me. If you continue to do this to me. I will lose control. And you will not like it."

At his words something inside me exploded. I pushed myself into him even harder, bringing my face right up to his. "I *win*?" I gritted. "I *win*?"

I pushed against him. He took a step back but didn't let go of me. "Are you really so thick?" I gave another push and he took another step back. "I don't want this either!" I gave another push against him and he backed into a large sitting chair.

I gave a final shove against him and pushed him down into the chair. With his grasp still on me, I had no choice but to follow him down. Then I was straddling him, with my knees bent on each side of him.

I was hot and wet and throbbing, and I didn't even pause. I did what I wanted. I took what I wanted.

Whatever force was pushing us together, it was too powerful to fight. We were two meteors colliding, and we could not change course. It had been foolish to ever even try. We had been set on this trajectory from the start, and I was finally willing to accept that.

I grinded against him, feeling how bruisingly hard he was. Shockwaves exploded, radiating from my core. I threw my head back with a cry. And his large hand wrapped around my throat.

There was so much strength, so much power in his grip. But he didn't squeeze. Instead he tilted my head to the side. And then his mouth was over my pulse point—an energy center. He sucked, and I cried out again at the explosion of pleasure it caused.

I could feel him draw on my power, on the very little energy I had at the moment. But instead of draining what I had, the act caused a little of my Light to recharge. I felt a warmth spread through my chest.

I ground my hips against him again and again. Unable to stop myself. A slave to my impulses. Giving in to the need and the want.

And I felt the chaos he housed envelop me. But it didn't become my own. I was too swept up in lust and desire to care about the dark forces which haunted him.

The darkness, the despair, the longing, it all swirled around us. But we were somewhere in the center of it. Somehow untouched by it.

He tore his lips from my throat. "Can't stop it," he gritted, bucking against me, bouncing me on his lap.

"Then don't," I begged, grinding against him again.

He bucked against me a second time, clamping his hands over my ass to pin me in place.

"Oh, god, yes. Please don't stop." I had no shame in pleading with him. I wanted this. I had been denied this my entire life. I would not let him slink away this time. If there was to be a battle between me and his demons, I would win this round.

I squeezed my thighs around him, digging my hands into his hair. Then I leaned forward to bite his neck where his tendons strained. Tasting his skin and doing all that I could to keep him there with me. Present. In this moment only.

With a roar he gave one more agonizing thrust against me. It was the last push to send me over the edge. It caused an eruption of energy which sent waves of pleasure spasming from my center.

Then with a burst, the flames from the burning fires exploded in each hearth before settling into embers. Some of the surrounding books and drapes ignited, though, causing small fires to break out in the chamber. One of us, I'm not certain who, must have sent a subconscious pulse of energy to smother the flames, because they were snuffed out before they could grow any larger.

And after the ignition, while small ripples of energy continued to wash over me, we were immersed in the quiet dark.

I was hyper aware of everything about him. Something about his presence. How solid he was under me. How big he was. How even though I was on top of him, he still managed to overwhelm me. The smell of him. The taste of him. How silky his hair felt between my fingers. The way his chest heaved with heavy slowing breaths, and he languidly continued to thrust against me.

There was a kind of magic in being so close to another. So consumed by them. And I didn't think this kind of magic was the fabricated kind. I had a strong suspicion that it was a very basic, primal kind of magic. It was separate from whatever intervening force was driving us together.

I was certain that it must be what other people experienced. That this was why people pursued one another. I was finally privy to the secret of it all. And I found it incredible.

I leaned my head against his shoulder. Resting it there. Letting my breath fan across his neck. The dark forces that had expanded around us, those that haunted him, began to settle. To calm. Even if they hadn't though, it would not have mattered. The space we occupied was untouchable in that moment. There was only enough room for the two of us on that chair.

I let my fingers knead and pull on his hair. I rubbed my face against his neck and jaw. And when I felt him begin to stiffen again under me, I started to subtly shift around on top of him.

I would have stayed with him all night in that chamber. But his hands moved up my back, into my hair, pulling my head back so I was forced to look at him. The electric blue of his eyes sparked. And I knew my own violet eyes must have glittered because there was a glow of light on his face.

For just a moment, just a fraction of a second, he looked at me with something like wonder. The tense angles of his face were relaxed, his firm lips parted, the dark hair swept back from his forehead.

And I think my own lips parted on a silent *oh*, because I was so thrown by how gorgeous he was. But whatever he saw, whatever he read on my face, was something else entirely. Because instantly, his features hardened, his jaw clenched, and those black veins branched through his eyes.

"I warned you! I told you to leave! Why would you do this to yourself?"

I grabbed his face in both my hands. "Wait! Just wait! Stop for a minute. Wherever you're going in your head right now, whatever's happening—just stop!"

He pushed my hands away. And picking me up, he stood before turning to toss me onto the chair.

Then he headed straight for the door. With his back to me he growled, "You will leave! Tomorrow!"

"No." It was a calm defiance. "We've already discussed this. I can't leave."

His voice was a cold murmur in the dark. "If you stay, I will not be able to stop myself."

I took a few silent steps towards him, talking to his back. "From what?" I asked.

"From attacking you."

I drew in a startled breath. "Is that what you think just happened? That you attacked me?"

He didn't answer. And I didn't know what to say. I stood there watching his hands clench into fists.

Finally, I broke the silence. "What if I told you that I don't want you to go. That I want to be with you again."

"Then I would say you're pathetic." His words were iced, and chills ran up my spine.

270

"What is wrong with you?!" I cried.

His voice was a pained hiss in the dark. "*Everything.*"

And at that, he didn't even bother with the door. He simply wisped away like the shadow that he was.

***

But I couldn't just let him disappear into the night. I wasn't done with him. It was selfish and desperate of me, but I couldn't allow him to leave. I was still wrapped up in him. I still wanted to be near him. To feel his presence.

And I had found a small thrill in being able to affect him. It sounds too maniacal to confess, but somewhere deep down inside, I *liked* that I drove him wild.

It took me a good ten minutes, but I eventually got the boarded-up plank open. Enough of my power had been restored after being with him. I tried to brace myself for the drowning sensation I would encounter once I crossed into the abandoned wing of the manor, but it just wasn't something I could prepare for.

The desolation, the despair, the darkness, it all pressed upon me, until I felt as though I was suffocating, as though I would never know joy again. I tried to keep a steady glow of Light around me, and it was barely enough to keep my feet moving.

I knew I would find him down here, in his pit of darkness and despair. I could feel him down here.

I forced my feet down the dark hall to the one room with the door slightly ajar. I pushed open the old rotting wood, feeling the dampness of it. And just as I imagined, he sat at the piano with his head bowed. Instead of manipulating the keys though, his hands rested on the bench at his sides.

Red embers glowed in the fireplace, but nothing more. I wrapped my arms around myself, standing just inside the door. I fought the urge to start a fire, knowing it would be rude. Knowing I was intruding here.

It wasn't close enough. I wanted to be next to him. To feel him again, as I had just moments before. But I knew I had to grab on to some semblance of self-respect. I would not allow myself to completely unravel.

I stood there for a long time staring at the stark muscles and planes of his shoulders and back. He was so strong. So powerful. And yet, so broken. I wanted to understand why.

After an indefinite amount of time passed, I began to think perhaps we would both remain just as we were for the rest of eternity. Buried down here, like two statues. Him at his piano. Me standing on, watching, forever longing for another moment together.

But finally he spoke, his quiet voice seeping through the cold dark air. "One day, a long time after she brought me here, I ventured beyond the confines of my room. I found the piano. It was covered in dust and cobwebs. I would come and sit at the bench but not touch the keys.

"Finally, after hundreds of times, I struck a dust covered key. The flat note was too loud in the quiet room. It hung here in the space surrounding me, vibrating in the air for what seemed like too long, before floating away.

"It was a release. I never wept. Although I was a child, no matter what she did or made me do, I never wept.

"But the piano could. All I had to do was tell it every unshed tear and it would take them from me. Releasing them into the air where they would be carried away."

He paused, and I believed he was done with his admission. I didn't say anything at first, knowing there was nothing to say. Knowing it had been a statement only. A sharing of a fact. I believed he would despise a reply of sympathy or comfort. And instead I simply accepted what he offered.

But then he continued with a heavy exhale. "Why are you here, Violet?"

Hearing my name on his lips sent a shiver down my spine. I suddenly felt very exposed. As though I had been stripped down in front of him. It was too intimate.

"You know my name?" I asked.

"Of course," he supplied.

"Of course," I repeated. I took a small step closer to him. "Why do you never face me?"

He shuddered. "You know very well why I spare you."

"No, I don't."

His tone was harsh. "I have already told you I know of the monster I am. Of the horror of my appearance."

"Stop," I gritted through my teeth.

Still he remained sitting at the piano with his back to me. "Don't do this, Violet. Don't do this to yourself. You are so much better than all of this. Go back to your home full of light and beauty. That is where you belong."

I straightened. "Perhaps I will if you keep pushing me away, but you should know something first. You are not a monster. You are the most gorgeous being I have ever seen. There is good

273

and Light in you. I know it. I've seen it. I saw it a long time ago. And I know it's still there.

There was something about him saying my name, that made me want to say his.

"I want you to touch me again. I want you to kiss me again. I want to feel your skin on mine. Most of all, I want you to turn around and look at me, Zagan."

His shoulders stiffened. I silently pleaded for him to face me. I knew he would feel the compulsion of it. We were connected. And I had been so stupid not to realize the extent of it. The power of it.

He did rise then and crossed to me. He was breathing heavy, and an aching confusion contorted his face. "What did you call me?" he whispered.

"You know that's your name," I told him.

The room began to shake. The keys on the piano rattled and dust and debris began to sprinkle from the ceiling. Dark energy vibrated in the air around us and the temperature in the already cold room plummeted. His voice was a deadly hiss. "I do not have a name."

I notched my chin staring into the turbulent storm brewing in his black eyes where whorls of madness spiraled. "Is that what she told you?"

Shadows began to bleed from his skin and swirl around him. His voice was monstrous. Guttural. "Don't ever speak that name again."

He took a predatory step toward me, leaving only an inch of space between us, forcing me to crane my head up to his gaze. The misery and torment twisting around him caused my skin to

274

freeze. I could feel my inner Light flicker as the cold and dark he possessed tried to embrace me.

I stood my ground. "I'm not afraid of you, Zagan." I reached up and touched his chest, placing my hand over the frigid black mark there. I let my Light flow through my touch, trying my best to thaw his dark heart.

He clutched his head and dropped to his knees letting out a roar that rattled the piano keys, which gave off a matching shout. The ground shook violently and the debris from the ceiling now rained down on us.

I kneeled with him trying to hold him, trying to keep him with me. I would force my Light into him. But it was no use. My offering was too weak in comparison to his power and was unwelcome.

I lost.

He slipped away, and I was left with nothing. The dark energy, the coldness, the shaking, it all disappeared as if he had never been. I was left alone in the silence of his decayed sanctuary.

It was just as it had been all those years ago when we were children. He had vanished without a trace. And I was left abandoned.

A red-hot guilt flushed my skin. I had driven him away. I had forced him into a truth he did not want to face. And now the ghosts which haunted his wing demanded I pay for my trespasses. The misery and despair began to descend upon me. I would be trapped in this space, buried alive, if I didn't get out of there.

And as I had done before . . . I fled.

CHAPTER 23

SEVERAL NIGHTS PASSED. I did not see Zagan again. I did not feel his presence.

I was afraid of what I had done.

I tried to sift through memories, searching for answers. But I had been so young.

I did not remember him arriving at court. And I did not remember much of our time together. I did recall a time when my mother had warned me that we would soon be separated.

She had let me know that Zagan would eventually move to another residence. The immense mansion was the heart of the Radiant Court. It was where official business took place. But there was a whole city of homes, shops, and buildings which sprawled from the entry gates down at the bottom of the vast grounds. And Zagan would not continue to live with me.

My mother had told me that Zagan and I both needed to spend time with other friends. We were about to start the next level of schooling and it was important for us to have some distance as we grew older. I would be tutored with the girls around my age while Zagan would study with the boys.

I was assured he would still be a part of my life. But my mother tried to press upon me the importance of us finding our own identities. She said we would be better friends as adults if we took some time to grow separately.

I wondered then if she had known the extent of our connection, of what it would one day turn into . . . She must have. Why else insist on breaking us apart?

But had she known he was the son of the Shadow King? I didn't recall any defining marks on his chest. Had my mother known he was the heir to an abandoned throne? I had always been under the impression he was a Radiant, like the rest of us.

And I could understand why The Contessa wanted him. She must have been behind his disappearance. She had turned Zagan into a shadow of a man, and in doing so had secured her place as master of the Dark Court.

But why did she want me?

She had said it was for my Light. So why not just kill me? Why draw it out? Why take me somewhere to wait for Zagan?

With her psychotic ramblings, she had indicated there were plans in place, something she had worked long and hard for—yet I could not begin to fathom what that was.

It was all too convoluted. It was as though I was standing in front of a painting in a dark room with pinpricks of light beaming upon the image. I could see certain things, tiny blips, but I had no idea what the big picture was.

And desperate times call for desperate measures. So I had decided it was time. I did the unthinkable . . . I called my mother.

We had initially agreed that Killian would be my point of contact. It could become too messy if I was reporting back to various people. Errors in communication occur that way, and in this situation we couldn't afford any misunderstandings. However, since I doubted Killian could answer questions as to whether or not my mother knowingly fostered the Prince of Shadows, I decided it was time to make an exception.

I was surprised when my mother answered.

"Everything's fine," I said right away, not wanting to cause her panic. "I just haven't been able to contact Killian," I explained.

"What a warm greeting. Thank you, Violet," came her reply.

"I'm sorry," I told her. "I just didn't want you to think something was wrong."

"Even under the most stressing of times, there is no need to forget your manners," she chastised. "However, I am ever so glad to hear that my only child still lives, after days of not knowing." Her tone was mockingly cheery.

"Mom—"

"Violet, I am entitled to handle this in my own manner," she snapped. "Light forbid you one day have a child who pulls a stunt like this, but maybe then you could possibly begin to understand what you are putting me through! I have had no idea whether you were dead or alive since Killian's last update. So you will forgive me if I am less than pleased with this entire situation, and if a phone conversation with me is somewhat tense at the moment."

I took a deep breath. "Yes. I'm sorry for all this."

There was a pause, and then my mother asked, "Are you in danger?"

I looked down at the ring on my finger. "No. No I'm not. Things are . . . *complicated*. But I'm safe."

My mother sounded disbelieving and perhaps a little hopeful. "It was a genuine proposal, then?"

I still didn't know what The Contessa wanted with me. And considering it had been her proposal, I wasn't sure how to answer. Although, as far as I knew, the documents I had signed had been legitimate. But none of that mattered because more than anything, I just wanted to give my mother peace of mind.

"Yes," I told her. "There are still some details to work out. But all in all, it's looking good."

She made a dignified sigh and I knew it was her way of releasing some anxiety. "In that case, I will be planning a ball here at Court to announce the marriage. I will expect you and the prince to attend. I have decided this may be a positive situation after all. We should use it to calm some of the fears and concerns of our people." She was jumping right into business and I wasn't surprised. It was usually how she handled nerve-racking situations.

"That sounds wonderful," I told her. But there was no way in hell it was going to happen. "Except hold off on any specific dates for now. The prince is incredibly busy, and I will have to reference his schedule." And before she could continue, I tried to get to the reason for my call. "Mom, I want to ask you—"

There was shuffling in the main room of my quarters. And I was afraid The Contessa had returned with the Umbra. I snatched my dagger from the dresser and mentally chastised myself for not having it on me. I had become lazy about it. I needed to be sure I had it strapped to my body at all times.

I pressed the phone against my waist, and then I silently ran down the hall to peek around the corner into the main room. The Crone was leading Maxim into my suite.

"Violet? Violet!"

"Yes, I'm here. And I am sorry to cut things short, but I must go," I told my mother.

"Honestly, Violet. What has happened to your consideration. This is no way to treat your mother—"

"It's . . . uh . . . time for tea! You know, I don't want to be late. I'm still trying to make a good impression and all. I'm just not used to the schedule yet."

"Fine, fine," came my mother's begrudging agreement. "But, Violet, please be safe. And don't wait so long to call and check in."

"Okay! I will call you back. I need to ask you some things. Bye!"

I felt awful ending the call so abruptly, but I couldn't imagine what the Crone and Maxim were doing in my quarters.

I didn't wait to find out. I tucked the dagger into the waistband at my lower back. And as soon as I entered the room, Maxim gave a formal bow.

"Good evening, Violet," he greeted.

"Hi, Maxim. What are you doing here?"

"Your request to visit the Shadow Court has been granted. I am to take you directly."

"Now?" I asked.

"Yes," he confirmed.

The Crone had been silently standing in the corner, unmoving. Just then, though, I saw her make a motion. It was almost imperceptible, but I saw her cowl move a fraction of an inch to the side. And I knew she was telling me not to go.

If she had followed through with it, the Crone had placed those stones around the manor to bar entry from The Contessa. And if it was to be believed, I was apparently safe from The Contessa and her Umbra, here in the manor. I wondered if The Contessa knew about it and if it was why I was being summoned to court. I also wondered how much—if any—Maxim knew about the situation.

"I can't," I said. And to emphasize my point, I flopped down on the settee. I gestured to the wingback chair, but Maxim remained standing. He looked confused.

"But you were quite upset about being denied an invitation before," he pointed out.

"Yes, but," I rubbed my forehead, "I haven't seen the sun in too long and am becoming ill. It will have to wait."

I thought that would be the end of it, but then I realized there was an opening here. I had a chance to make progress of some kind. I couldn't pass it up. I would be going into the situation blind, but maybe there was something to be gained. And I had my mother to thank for the inspiration.

I straightened. "However, Maxim, I would like to extend an invitation to the Court members for a dinner party here. This Saturday."

"I'm sorry. What?" Maxim was thrown.

The Crone also seemed ruffled, shifting in her corner. However, I pretended not to notice.

"Yes," I confirmed, standing. The idea began to take shape in my mind. I knew I couldn't leave the manor. And a counter offer would help distract from the fact that I was blatantly rejecting the summons to Court. This could turn out to be a key step in overthrowing The Contessa.

I had no idea how involved she was with those at Court. All I knew was that she claimed to have absolute power there. Whether the other members of Court knew of her influence or would agree with her claim, I didn't know.

What I did know was that if there was any chance to drive The Contessa out and help find a peaceful resolution to the revolt that was brewing, I would need to convince those of the Court to accept me as their new monarch.

"Yes," I repeated. "I understand that the Shadow Court was moved to London long ago. But the Dark Manor was the original seat of the king, was it not? It is where the current prince and his new bride reside. It is a place of high honor and prestige. It should be treated as such. And in my attempt to demonstrate the respect I wish to show, I find it quite appropriate to host a dinner party here to honor my new prince, his Court, and his people."

I nodded then, deciding that the reasoning sounded good to me. I believed it should pass as an acceptable explanation for my invitation. And I hoped Maxim did a proper job in passing on the highfalutin sentiment.

"I will, of course," I continued, "need you to find the appropriate individuals to handle the preparation of both the manor as well as the food and service. I would think that should be a reasonable enough request for the Court to approve."

"Violet, I—"

"I can't begin to imagine how difficult it is to act as my babysitter, Maxim." I said as I crossed to him. I took both his hands in my own and gave him my warmest, most trusting smile. "And I am ever so sorry to put you in the middle of all this. But there is really no need for us to have a discussion about it."

I squeezed his hands in mine. "Will you do this for me, please?"

Something I had learned through my years at Court is that it is more difficult for someone to say no to you when you're touching them. And as I hoped, Maxim face contorted into an expression of defeated acceptance.

"Yes," he confirmed. "But Violet, please do not be surprised if your invitation is not acknowledged."

I nodded. "I won't," I reassured.

"It is also very possible," Maxim continued, "that they will be unhappy at your refusal this night. I may be sent again tomorrow night to bring you to Court with a more forceful insistence."

"I understand," I told him. But I had a strong suspicion my invitation would be accepted. The Dark Manor held too much intrigue.

"I'll expect the first level of the manor to be sparkling and an exquisite menu for the evening." I told him as I crossed to open the door to the suite. I gestured for him to exit with a warm smile. "Thank you ever so much, Maxim. I do appreciate it."

He didn't look happy with the direction I had taken things, but he also didn't try and argue. He gave another formal bow and began to leave.

"Oh, Maxim," I called, realizing I had forgotten an important detail. "I'll need a dress too. Thanks!" And I shut the door before he could respond.

When I turned back into the room, the Crone was already shuffling towards me. I could sense her agitation, but she said nothing. She simply opened the door and hobbled out.

***

Two nights later, I was getting what I asked for.

Maxim had arrived the previous night to inform me that my invitation had been accepted. He also let me know that he would be returning with a witch to perform a few cleaning spells the following evening. I thanked the Light for the serendipitous timing. I now had a solution to a problem.

Ever reliable, he followed through with his promise and the two arrived at dusk. After greeting and thanking them both down in the foyer, I excused myself. I let Maxim know that I was tired after being up for most of the day and that I was retiring to my quarters for the evening.

I went straight to my room and changed. I selected a full-length black dress. It had long sleeves and buttoned all the way up the front. Two strips of lace detailing ran from shoulder to ankle. The garment had a wonderful vintage look to it that I felt would be appropriate.

For footwear I chose a pair of black boots which laced up to the knee and had a wedged sole. And then I draped my cape over my shoulders making sure it was inside out so that the black fabric of the lining was on display and the red material was tucked away. In my pockets, I stashed my dagger and several large bills.

Finally, I pinned my hair into a loose bun at the nape of my neck and drew my cowl. It had taken ten minutes, and I was ready.

Silently slipping down the staircase, I listened for Maxim and the witch. They were in a room down at the other end of the manor. I made my way to the rear door and did not hesitate. I exited onto the veranda.

However, once I shut the door behind me, I did pause. I knew I was taking a significant risk, but I believed it was a calculated one.

I supposed I had a good chance of avoiding The Contessa and her Umbra. She had tried to collect me on her own terms the times I had encountered her. And if she had known or felt the wards go into place, which now barred her, I doubted she would have spent more than a night or two waiting to see if I exited the manor. I believed she would feel something like that to be beneath her.

Still, I was wary . . . wary and troubled.

I had not seen Zagan since our confrontation. I had not felt his presence anywhere in the manor. Sorrowful notes from a piano far below did not sound. And no one had insisted I leave. I was afraid I had pushed him too far.

I could not think about him. I ached each time I did. And instead of mulling over our circumstances, I took action. I made my way over the manor grounds trying to blend in with the shadows. Then I waited.

Thankfully it seemed the witch Maxim had employed was adept. It was not long before the two were climbing into Maxim's vehicle. As the SUV approached the tree tunnel, the towering gate swung open, granting passage. And as I watched the tail lights fade, I slipped through.

I began a brisk pace. I had until midnight.

CHAPTER 24

A STOP LIGHT SWAYED with the staccatoed gusts of wind. It had come unhinged at some point and now hung at a limp, crooked angle over the dusty lane. Yet there was no intersecting street. And although it was one continuous road—the only road—I felt as though I had entered another world.

I paused before the light and looked up. It blinked with a muted click, the red neon flashing in the dark. I watched the steady pulse and waited. For what, I don't know.

Behind it, shops lined the street. However, there was no life, no activity here. Each structure had been abandoned. They sagged in their places, doors and windows boarded. Graffiti covered the facade of most.

The wind whipped, sending dirt and dust flying into my face. I bowed my head and held my cloak shut tighter.

I had traveled over the cobblestone at the other end of the main street. I had passed the inn, Belcalis's vegetable stand, and the various small businesses. Until it all stopped.

The shops, the cobblestone, and the gas lamps had ended in a neat line as though sliced with a knife. With one step I had been on the main street, and with the next, I was shuffling through a dirt road, leaving the lights and sounds of the village behind. The darkness closed in on me and I was exposed to the wind and skittering grime with nothing but empty fields buffering my sides.

But now that I had reached the old part of town, as Belcalis had called it, I didn't know where to go. It was abandoned.

I passed beneath the swaying stoplight and through the ramshackled structures. I continued to glance over my shoulder and to the sides, trying to inspect the shadows surrounding the decrepit buildings. Searching for reflective eyes. But there was nothing.

As I continued though, I eventually began to hear a low rhythmic sound. Chanting. I picked up my pace and reached a section of the street which sloped downward. And a scene unfolded before me.

The street dipped into a little valley. At the bottom, a crowd of possibly five hundred had gathered. A large bonfire lit the dark sky and a rickety looking, impromptu stage had been arranged. I had found the rally.

The gathering had been scheduled for midnight. I guessed the time was drawing near. I was thankful Maxim had arrived at the manor just after dusk and had not stayed late. I had needed those long hours to make the walk here.

I descended upon the crowd with the cowl to my cloak drawn, slipping through the others. Those who had gathered all wore the same type of apparel I had noticed in town. The women mostly wore long dresses, the men in trousers and tunics, some in cloaks, some not. But what I could see now—what I had not cared to see before—was the general *weariness* they wore.

It was apparent in the patched holes and mended rips of their clothes. Unkempt strands wisped from the women's long braids and pinned buns, while the men were generally unshaven with hair that had gone too long without a trim.

These were people who worked. Who worked hard. They were struggling to get through each day. But they held on to their pride and dignity. It was clear in the way each and every one stood tall with shoulders back.

Welcome to the new age.
Welcome to the new age.
Welcome to the new age.

The chant rose and fell through the air. I could feel the vibrations of so many voices spoken at once beat within my chest.

A young man in simple clothes and shaggy hair stood upon the stage. He was raising his hands with the rise and fall of the mantra, encouraging those who had gathered. After a few minutes a cloaked figure joined the man. The crowd instantly ceased their chanting and began a deafening cheer of shouts and claps.

The figure took to a podium, arms raised for silence. While the whoops of support died down, a group of men took up buckets around the bonfire and simultaneously emptied them upon the flames. With a hiss, darkness enveloped the little valley. The crowd was silent.

Finally, the man spoke, his voice ringing across the lowland. "We honor our mother. The moon." And he turned his back to face the sky behind him.

The Shadows began a chant in the Dark Tongue. It started as a murmur, a heartfelt pledge each one spoke to themselves. But as it continued, the magic of the words grew and with it so did their voices. Louder and louder the incantation became, until finally, a silver light broke the midnight blue horizon. And the moon, larger than I had ever seen, rose.

It hung behind the speaker, glimmering upon the people in the valley. And once it paused in its ascent, the chanting ceased. A reverent silence hushed across the crowd. Even the babies which had been carried in slings by their mothers quieted their cries and coos.

Everyone present bowed in deference, taking a moment to honor the heavenly body.

It was enough to make me believe Maxim's tale.

When the speaker straightened, so too, did those in the crowd. They seemed at peace in the silver light. Revived.

The speaker turned to address the assembly. I could see a face beneath the cowl, but I could not make out any defining features. Too much was hidden within the fabric.

"My brothers and sisters," he began. "Welcome to the new age!"

The crowd cheered.

The speaker continued. "For too long we have been forgotten. Our leaders have abandoned us. They claim sovereignty over us. Demand our allegiance. All the while they lead from the safety of their high-rise among the mortals.

"They have left us to die. To fend for ourselves against the attacks upon our people. They take their taxes from us and give nothing back.

"It is time we reclaim what is rightfully ours. It is time we reclaim our honor and prestige. It is time for a new age!"

And again, the crowd demonstrated their support, wildly cheering.

When the shouts died down, the speaker took up his rhetoric again. "The Courts must fall! They are corrupt. Those in power care only for themselves.

"We have tried diplomacy. We have tried to establish a dialogue with those in London. We have tried to establish a dialogue with those in Maine. Both Courts have refused us."

At his words, I was confused. The Shadows did not have a court in Maine. We would have known about it. That was Radiant territory.

"And where is our prince? Why has he forsaken us? We have been told he was found. Yet, we await salvation.

"And while we have been cast aside by our very own Shadow government, the Lady of Light has done far worse. She has murdered. Taken countless, innocent lives. Shadow blood stains her hands. The Radiant Court must pay for their crimes against our people!"

At his words, the air had charged and then out of nowhere, a bolt of lightning struck the earth behind the stage. The crowd let out startled gasps and flinched at the surge of electricity. The speaker paused at the crack power which lit the sky. And in that brief flash of light, I was certain I could see his eyes on mine. He *knew* it had been because of me.

However, as soon as the outburst of power dissipated, his attention was back upon the crowd. He pointed behind him and shouted, "The moon displays her anger!"

Then he raised his hands and cried, "Welcome to the new age!"

The chant tour through the crowd once more. But not everyone had resumed their focus upon the stage. A few of the people around me had begun to look my way.

I drew my cowl farther over my face and averted my gaze, looking down at the ground. I closed my eyes, forcing myself to calm. I had been caught off guard and a wave of anger had shot through me. In addition to the outburst of power, my eyes had begun to glow.

I turned and started to retreat, pushing through the crowd, trying to make my way to the back of the gathering, keeping my eyes cast downward. But as I reached the outer limits of the audience, I felt each of my arms grabbed from behind.

I attempted to look behind me, to see who had apprehended me, but the generous fabric of my cowl, blocked my vision. I could feel two sets of strong hands.

I did not lash out. Not yet. There were too many people. I waited to see the direction I would be taken. If it was towards the stage, I would fight here and free myself. However, if I was taken somewhere more isolated, I could prevent outing myself to the entire crowd.

The two assailants began to march me forward, away from the assembly. I cooperated, hoping for a more private setting. When we reached a large tent, they did not take me inside, but around the back.

I didn't wait any longer. I let myself go limp. As I did, both attackers strengthened their grip, holding me up. With that, I sprang from my crouch into a backward flip, allowing the hold on my arms to act as leverage.

I landed behind the two cloaked individuals. They hadn't let go, but each now held on to my wrists. I brought my arms together while leaning back with all my weight. The act was supposed to cause the attackers to crash into each other. Instead, one sidestepped the other, ducking under my arm. They each continued around me, so that my arms were pinned. I was hugging myself now as each pulled a wrist towards my back.

They were talented. I smiled. It had been too long since I sparred with my group in the Unit, and I was glad for a challenge. I would take them down in the end, I could tell. But I would have to put up a fight.

I was about to twist free when one yelled, "Violet. Stop!"

I froze. I knew that voice. I was let go, and I spun around.

The two men threw back their hoods to reveal themselves.

"What are you doing here?" I gasped.

"It's our job to be here," shot Rheneas. "What are *you* doing here?"

I pointed behind me. "That man is spreading vicious lies."

Rheneas didn't address my concern about the speaker. "You are not to leave the manor without Master Steel. Have you any

295

idea the danger you are putting yourself in? You are lucky we spied you."

"Who is he?" I demanded. I would not let this drop. Something had to be done about this zealot. Even now I could hear the cadence of his voice rise and fall as he continued with his speech. "We have to stop him. He is making false claims against the Radiant Court, blaming us for unfounded atrocities!"

Rheneas placed his hand against my shoulder blades. "Come. We are taking you back to the manor."

"No." I pivoted away from him.

Rheneas and Stefan both glanced around, as if checking for something out in the dark. Stefan answered in an angry whisper. "You have no idea the dangers. If you remain here, it will not end well. We must leave. Now."

It was the first time he had spoken to me. And there was something in the timbre of his voice that sent a chill down my spine. I pressed my lips together and gave a single nod.

They were clearly unsettled. There was no point in trying to have a discussion with them here and now. "Okay," I agreed.

They had been here. And that said something. After all, they were members of the Shadow Court. They were probably already working to smoother this uprising. I took some comfort in that.

"Is Maxim here? Does he know about this?"

Rheneas and Stefan exchanged a look. And it made me uneasy. Something was going on. Something big. I could *feel* it.

Neither replied to my question. They drew their hoods once more. "Stay between us," instructed Rheneas. "Don't make a sound."

We traveled for about a mile down the dirt road until we reached one of the old street front structures. The two grabbed a large wood plank, that boarded up a section of the graffitied shop, and slid it to the side. Their SUV was parked within.

They had me climb in immediately, and as Rheneas pulled the vehicle out of the makeshift garage, Stefan slid the huge board back into place. Then we sped down the street without the aid of headlights, scattering dust in our wake.

After I had had enough of the charged silence, I asked, "Did you know someone was coming for me? That night you dropped me off at the manor. Did you know?"

They would tell me nothing. I tried to ask them questions. I tried to engage in conversation. They would have none of it.

I sat back and let it be. After a while, the two began to converse with each other in the Dark Tongue. I couldn't understand a word of it.

However, when we passed through the tree tunnel, I sat forward in my seat. I tried to listen for the word which would open the gate. I needed to learn the command. But Rheneas uttered the four syllables so quietly, I could not make it out.

Back in my room, I changed. I traded the dress and boots for leggings and bare feet. Unpinning my hair, I ran my fingers through the dark waves. I tried to call both Killian and my mother.

Neither answered.

My concern increased.

Things were out of control. The situation here was so much worse than we could have imagined. Something had to be done about not only the Shadow Court, but it's people as well.

Pacing through my suite, I began to feel my agitation rising. My breathing deepening. My hands clenching. I rolled my head around my neck, feeling heat spread through my chest.

My anger began to have a visceral effect upon me. My emotions spiraled chaotically. I took a deep breath.

I needed to calm the rage. I needed to tame the demons. And I realized I could find relief. I was pulled from my suite to descend far below. It became clear that the emotions coursing through me were not entirely my own . . .

Zagan had returned.

CHAPTER 25

THE RAGE. THE AGITATION. I knew there were deeper issues, but at the surface, a hot fury welled. I could feel it all.

And I ached. His torment was my own. The compulsion to soothe him, to put him at ease, was too great a force to ignore.

Descending flight after flight of stairs, I felt his dark power grow. As I hit the final landing, standing above the main foyer, I was met with tortured shadows and icy air.

I had not bothered with attempting to light chandeliers and sconces on my way down. It seemed I no longer cared to these days. I had come to find a certain allure in the darkness. I had come to realize the dark could hold things which were too fragile for the harsh exposure of light. There are some types of touches and breaths which do not exist in the light of day.

There is a seductive quality to the dark. You are unable to see all and are forced to *feel* more.

But down in the foyer, the light from the night sky seeped through the windows. And throughout the meager swaths, shadows silently wailed and swayed.

Yet, I was allowed passage. I slipped through the dark and cold of the foyer with a firm grasp on my own power. I began to make my way down the long hall, expecting to find him near the entry to his wing. However, I did not make it that far.

I was suddenly pushed against the wall. My body pressed against the stone and my hands cinched behind my back.

He covered me, pushing into me while holding my wrists in his iron grip. I didn't fight him, and I let my chest rise and fall against the cold stone, my cheek pressed to side. I couldn't see him, but I didn't need to. I could feel him against me and a small thrill rushed through my veins.

He let his head hang at my neck. His hectic breaths fanned across my skin, and I felt a tremor shake his big body. He was grappling for control. Angry and confused, he was utterly lost. And he wanted to punish me for it. He warred with himself trying to fight the need.

It had been too long. We *needed* each other. A facet that I had begun to understand, yet he continued to deny.

I was willing to bet that was what he had been doing down here. Pacing the long hall fighting the compulsion to come to me . . . But I had come to him.

I rolled my hips against him, feeling how hard he was, knowing he was in agony. He yanked my wrists in response, wanting to demand I stop. Again, I rolled my hips, feeling his erection against my ass, causing my already wet and aching center to throb.

This time he pressed into me and I let out a breath. I wanted to tell him *yes*, to tell him *more*, but I couldn't break the silence between us with words. They didn't belong here. They would shatter this moment—this moment that was only about touch and breathing and need.

If I spoke, the moment would become too real, too exposed, and he would wisp away to bury himself where I could not reach him.

He splayed his free hand across my stomach, just above the waistband of my leggings. I hitched in a breath, waiting, not wanting him to stop. I tried to rise up on my toes to force his hand lower. I didn't need to though. He slipped his hand inside my panties.

He began gliding his fingers over me, back and forth, at such a slow pace that I was certain it was a particular kind of torture.

My chest and cheek were pressed against the cool stone. My hands pinned behind my back. And my hips were tilted away from the wall, shoved into his pelvis. His touch had me ready to explode.

I could feel his tension. His ache. His want and need.

But I could also feel the guilt and self-loathing. He believed he was a dark monster. He believed I was a thing of light and beauty. He would taint me if he succumbed to the overwhelming instinct he felt to take me.

When he abruptly removed his hand, I was certain he would disappear once again. And I was momentarily shattered. But then he was slipping the waistband of my leggings down around my thighs and releasing himself from his trousers.

I panted, another agonized breath, when I felt him rock his shaft against me, slipping between my thighs to slide along my center. He was so large, so impossible to fit, I had to shift my legs wider.

Then his arm snaked across my hips, his hand landing over my exposed skin. He palmed me with a possessive squeeze and pushed me back into him. Still he bound my hands.

The pressure of his palm over my clit paired with the sliding of his shaft along my channel resulted in a strike of lightning just outside. It lit the hall in a flash of light. Then another and another, each stronger and brighter than the last.

But he would not penetrate me. And although he didn't make a sound, I could feel his massive body shudder over mine as I drenched his erection with my arousal. Every slick thrust was driving him mad, sending him closer and closer to the brink of agony. I squeezed my thighs together, and he hissed.

When he leaned in to bite my neck at my pulse point and suck, I exploded. Multiple streams of lightning lit the night sky. I came for him over and over, loving every radiating pulse of pleasure, while hating how empty I felt inside.

I needed him completely. The connection I had with him demanded it. This wasn't enough.

But he had me pinned. He had full control over me. And I could not direct what was happening between us.

Even if I had been able to angle my hips or turn around, it didn't matter. He had reached his limit. My climax ignited his own. It was the final strike. And he buried his head in my neck as he slipped over the edge. He shuddered behind me until I thought it would never end.

When he finally stilled, he slipped the waistband of my leggings back up, and the bruising grip on my wrists lessened. I took the opportunity to break my hands away and turn to face him. Grabbing the back of his neck, I pressed my chest into his. I would refuse him the chance to vanish.

I was rewarded because for a moment I saw that same gorgeous face from the other night. And before he could say anything, before he could spew hatred about himself or insult me, I placed my index finger over his lips ensuring he remained silent.

He looked at me then. He didn't embrace me. His hands remained at his sides. But his eyes were clear and electric in the dark. They met my own with fascination.

After he didn't move, and he didn't speak, I dropped my finger to trace his lips. They were firm and full. Relaxed.

And it made me realize that it had not been enough. I wanted more. I wanted to kiss him, I wanted to lie in bed with him and whisper secrets in the dark. I wanted to be with him for the entire night. To hold nothing back. I wanted to *know* him. I wanted him to know me.

I realized the shadows which haunted the hall had settled along the periphery—pacified.

I whispered, "Come to my room with me."

His eyes narrowed, the tension returning to his face. He gave a slow shake of his head. I clutched him tighter. "Nothing has to happen. Just talk to me," I pleaded.

He was slipping away. That wall was going up between us. I had to hold on to him. "Zagan, you have to know how much we all loved you. We still do. I don't know what happened. You just disappeared. We searched everywhere for you.

304

"Please. Just talk with me. Nothing has to happen. We can just talk. There is something going on between us. Don't you want to figure out what this is—what's happening? You have people who still care about you. People who still love you. Don't push that away."

"*Love?*" he scoffed. "Do you think I know anything of *love?*" The sneer he wore on his face cut deeper than his words. "This is all I am, Violet," he gestured to the hall. "Dark, empty shadows. Whoever you think I am—you're wrong. You mistake me for some child you knew twenty years ago. You mistake me for a memory. You envision the man that boy would have become, and you try to tell yourself that you will find him here somewhere within this darkness."

When I inhaled a breath, about to interrupt him, he grabbed my face in one large hand and forced my head back to look up at him. "Stop looking for Light here. Stop looking for a spark in the shadows. You won't find any."

With each word, he squeezed harder until he held me in a bruising grip. My eyes began to burn, so I closed them. I brought my hands up to grasp Zagan's wrist. I opened my eyes.

Slowly and with barely any pressure, I let my touch travel up to the hand that was viced around my chin. I gently began to pry his fingers from the sides of my face. I moved his hand down to my neck and then lower until it rested on my chest. He didn't pull away and hope flared beneath my ribs.

His hand moved up and down with each deep breath I took.

I saw confusion in his eyes. He had been rough with me, both with his words and his actions. I knew his intent was to drive me away. But he discounted the connection I had to him.

As much as he would deny his past, it was still a part of him. No matter how much darkness now filled him, we were still connected as we once were. Mere threads remained, but it was enough for me to know that he craved to touch me, and he ached to be close to me.

We stayed like that for moments. Neither of us speaking, neither of us moving.

But she came then, and chills ran down my spine. Through the windows lining the back wall, two pinpricks of bright light beamed from the woods. And they were directed at the manor.

There was no reason for it, no explanation, but I felt that I needed to somehow shield Zagan.

"You're right," I told him. "I shouldn't be bothering you like this. You should go." I leaned away from him, pressing my back into the wall, wanting to severe our contact.

And for as much as I wanted him to listen to me, to leave immediately so I could protect him from what was outside, a large part of me wanted him to refuse. In the romanticized version of my life, he would stay with me. He would grab onto me and we would spend the night together.

But that was not my reality. He turned and left without another word. I knew he believed he was sparing me. He thought he could somehow absolve me from darkness, from evil and misery . . . from him.

Little did he know, my time was coming, and there was nothing anyone could do to stop it.

I opened the back door and exited onto the veranda. Over the unkempt gardens and past the sagging structures upon the grounds, I could see the little girl standing at the edge of the forest, black wolf by her side. She simply stood there, watching, those two beams of light directed at me.

We stared at each other for a long moment, and then a strong breeze rushed past me and the little girl turned and left. I had been granted more time. For what, I didn't know.

But words the little girl had spoken now came back to me . . . *It's coming closer.*

I turned back into the manor and shut the door behind me. I went up to my quarters and did not look outside again.

CHAPTER 26

I LET OUT A GASP. I had just finished dressing. I turned around in front of the mirror, wanting to check the fit from every angle.

I would meet the members of the Shadow Court in just a few hours, and I was expecting the chef for the evening even sooner. I had been sure to wake before dusk. I wanted to be certain that everything was in order, including myself.

And while I would be ready and present for the evening's events, I believed I would be the only host. Zagan had buried himself down in his dark haunted wing. I had tried repeatedly to force my way in. When that hadn't worked, I tried shouting threats through the door. I whispered seductive promises. It was all to no avail. He would not answer my calls, and I could not budge the door.

Again, I had tried to call my mother as well as Killian, but neither answered their phones. Something was wrong.

I also tried to phone Maxim, but it was Rheneas who picked up. He would tell me nothing except to say that Maxim had delivered a box to my suite sometime during the day. And I had a feeling Maxim had deliberately avoided me.

However, what I found in the box was enough to make me forgive his evasion. Maxim had procured the most gorgeous gown I had ever seen. I had been expecting something acceptable, something predictable. And instead I had received something *extraordinary*.

The blood red gown had a simple corset bodice with one angled strap across the open back. There was a V down the center of the neckline that was bold and striking, without being inappropriate for the occasion. And while the dress was backless, the thick angled strap which ran from my shoulder to my hip provided enough material to create a visual break of all the skin I had on display.

Although the bodice of the gown was beautiful in its own right, it was the skirt of the gown which made this garment unlike any I had ever seen. It was full and floor length, swelling out around me. However, it was not forced into a certain cut or shape. The fabric of the skirt was free. It ebbed and flowed, floating around me as if the force of gravity was ever so slightly lessened for it. It reminded me of drops of ink in water.

But what had me breathless and stunned was a very special feature which had been added to the fabric. The material of the gown had been spelled, and rose petals continuously bloomed all across the skirt with the slightest shift in movement. Any motion I made resulted in delicate petals fluttering around me, as they drifted to the floor.

I kept spinning just to watch the petals lightly dance through the air. Then I would stop and take a deep breath, savoring the perfume they released. The floor in my room quickly became covered in crimson.

My lips were glossy red and my eyes dramatically lined. I was just about to pin up the loose waves of my hair when I heard someone shouting from outside.

I was jarred by the noise. I had become so accustomed to the quiet of the manor—to the lifelessness of it, that I believed I had to have imagined the sound.

I was absolutely convinced there had been no shout. I crossed to the center window in my room, just to prove to myself that it was nothing. But when I stepped up to the towering glass, I couldn't quite believe what I saw.

Killian was out on the lawn, calling for me amidst the long shadows cast by the setting sun.

I knocked on the window, and he spotted me. He looked desperate, and in his hand was a dagger of Light. I could hear him, muffled, through the glass. "You have to get out of here! You're in danger! Come now!"

His presence was so unexpected, it took me a moment to react.

"Princess of Light, hurry! Come to me!"

I found it strange that he was using my title. I couldn't remember a time, in all our years together, when he had ever called me that. Or told me to *come to him*. I believed he had to be incredibly rattled.

"It's okay!" I tried to call back. I smiled and waved my hands as though nothing was wrong. "I'll be right down!"

A dark form sliced through the air and knocked Killian to the ground. Then it rose.

Zagan was looming above Killian. Dark shadows coiled and slinked around him. There was an unhinged rage in his eyes.

"No," I tried to shout through the window. "It's okay! He's a friend!" When there was no recognition to my words, I banged on the glass.

But neither of the two men below, looked up at me. Killian had scrambled to his feet, holding out the dagger. And the shadows surrounding Zagan screeched and swayed.

A certain horror swept over me when I realized what was going to happen.

Killian dove, leading with the dagger, trying to make contact. But Zagan sidestepped the attack.

I banged on the glass again. "Stop! Killian don't!"

I needed to get between them, but I was on the fifth floor. It would take too long to get down there. I also foolishly thought if I could keep my eyes on them, then I could somehow prevent things from escalating.

Killian lunged for Zagan. But Zagan delivered a solid punch to Killian's nose before flashing out of the arc of the dagger.

Killian didn't stand a chance. Zagan had seemed to grow in size. Taking up more space, his very presence demanding it. The immeasurable power he housed, which he kept so tightly bottled, was expanding. And it was as though Killian was fighting a phantom.

I thanked the Light that Zagan did not have a sword. It was the only reason Killian was still alive. It was the only reason Killian had a chance of living.

However, Killian was still in grave danger. Blood had exploded from his broken nose. His head had whipped back, and he had landed on the dirt ten feet away.

"Stop!" I screamed. "Don't hurt him!" I banged on the glass again. "Stay down!" I tried to direct Killian. But he was rolling onto his side and attempting to stand. He looked up at me then and desperately beckoned for me.

"*You will never touch her.*" Even through the distance and glass, I could hear Zagan's cold, controlled words. The ice in his tone terrified me. He began to stalk forward.

I had to save Killian.

I punched the glass and a small cracked formed. I took a step back and kicked it with my bare foot. The crack lengthened, but the glass did not break. I ran to the other side of the room, putting as much distance between myself and the glass as possible. Then I charged for the window at full speed, leading with my shoulder.

Glass rained around me in thousands of tiny pieces. I had shattered the window. I would jump the five stories to land between them and explain everything. Killian would be okay.

Yet, as I felt myself break the plane of the window, I did not tumble through. Instead a pulse of energy threw me back.

And in the fraction of the second I broke the glass, I had just a snapshot of the tableau below.

Zagan had been about to strike. But he had diverted his attention from his advance on Killian to stop me. He had sent a pulse of energy to throw me back and prevent me from jumping. That one act had left him vulnerable, though, and Killian was in the perfect position to strike.

I was hurtled to the other side of the room, slamming to the floor. The instant my body made contact on the hardwood, I rolled onto my hands and knees. I scrambled to the window with broken glass digging into my palms. Once I looked below, I felt my heart stop. I could not believe what I saw.

The hilt of the dagger was sticking out of Zagan's chest. And I felt a pang in my own. He roared, and determination saturated the air. With his last breath he would end Killian. I could feel it.

Killian was trying to dodge away after landing the strike, but Zagan was too fast. He grabbed Killian's head in his hands and gave a vicious twist.

He didn't stop there, though. He continued to twist and yank, until in a rip of flesh and tendon, he had torn Killian's head from his body.

I heard a blood curdling scream. A woman's scream. It tore through the night. It filled my ears.

I covered my own mouth with my bloody palms. And the woman stopped.

I stared at *him*. I let my hands drop. I knew my eyes were filled with hatred.

He stared back. Taking it. Accepting it. Taking it *from* me. And in doing so, he knowingly accepted his death.

Then he fell to his knees, and grabbing the hilt of the dagger, yanked it out of his chest. A small stream of blood escaped his lips and a torrent of it gushed from his heart.

He collapsed to the ground.

Dead. They were both dead. Killian beheaded and Zagan stabbed in the heart with a dagger of Light.

I turned, stumbling out of the room. I didn't know what I was doing or where I was going. I didn't believe what I had just witnessed. It wasn't true. It hadn't happened.

I wasn't aware of what occurred next. All I knew was that at some point I collapsed at the base of a tree in the woods behind the manor. Without realizing it, I had made my way into the forest.

I hugged my knees and rocked back and forth. Over and over again, I told myself it wasn't true. I was going to pick myself up and go back to the manor. I would see that it wasn't true. I would go in just a minute. Over and over again I told myself Killian was fine.

A small eternity later, a twig cracked nearby. Leaves crunched. And I heard labored breathing. I whipped my head up and saw the hooded figure of the Crone approaching through the dark woods. Night had fully descended.

"Leave me," I told her.

"Not safe," she wheezed. "Inside."

"Never," I swore. I would never step foot back in that god forsaken place. I no longer cared about my safety.

But the Crone didn't reply. Instead, from the folds of her robe she threw something at my feet. It took a moment to process what I was looking at. What was now laying on the ground in front of me.

I was going to scream. I was going to be sick. I was going to black-out.

But more than anything, I was going to kill the Crone for what she had just done. I would do that first and then follow through with the others.

I rose. I could feel the vengeance and wrath punch through the air from every inch of my skin. But before I could have my retaliation, the Crone spoke.

"Look," her ancient voice hissed.

I would not. I *could* not. If I looked down at Killian's detached head on the forest floor, I would never know sanity again.

"*Look!*" she commanded, this time with the force of far off power. "It is not he."

And at her words, I did the unthinkable . . . I looked down.

I wanted so desperately for her to be right. I wanted so desperately to not have just witnessed Killian's brutal death. So I looked.

I stumbled back, sick and dizzy. I let out a low moan, squeezing my eyes shut. "Why are you doing this to me?" I cried.

"Look again," she rasped. "Closer. Look . . . *harder.*"

"Leave me alone! I am going to kill you, you old hag!"

"See through the lie," her wheezy voice persisted.

There was something in her words. A certainness. An authority.

It was a gruesome torture, but I looked again, glancing at him before turning my head away. It was Killian's perfect, yet bloody face. Only . . . it wasn't.

Something was *off*. I slowly opened my eyes, daring another glimpse.

It was Killian's features on the surface. But there was no open honesty, no nobility, no goodness.

My eyes flashed to the Crone. "What—?"

"See the truth," she demanded.

I looked again, determined now. I looked for my friend. For the person I loved. And I did not find him there. With that certainty, the lie began to melt away.

It was one of those *things*. Gray, ashen skin. Lifeless, reflective eyes. The Umbra.

I looked at the Crone, needing confirmation. I needed to know that my mind was not playing tricks on me, showing me things that I wanted to see.

"A glamour," she confirmed. "Court. Not. Coming."

The events began to replay in my mind. And I saw everything unfold in a new light.

One of those *things* had come for me, trying to lure me out. Zagan had seen it for what it was and had tried to protect me from it. When I had jumped to its defense, he had sacrificed himself, to keep me safe.

Oh god—the hatred I had unleashed upon him . . . *What had I done?*

If I had only trusted him. If I had seen this monster for what it truly was. I was going to collapse.

"He lives," the Crone whispered. "Dying, but lives."

At her words, the breeze stirred, rustling through the trees and whipping across the forest floor, rushing past us towards the manor.

And with it, I ran.

I began to run through the darkness of the forest with the moonlight filtering through the trees. My bare feet trampled the fallen leaves and twigs scattered upon the dirt. My heart pounded beneath my ribs, in time with each step of my feet, a drum in my ears.

317

As I ran, rose petals rained down upon me before the breeze caught them, sending them floating in a whirlwind around me.

Across the back lawn, I ran unerringly for that old rotted door within the manor. Through the back entrance, down the hall of the cavernous foyer, and around the corner into that little alcove.

This time when I came to the door, I did not pause. I flung open the barrier, smashing it into the wall–pulverizing the ancient wood—destroying it. I would be shut out no longer.

The rush of hectic breaths filled my ears, but I thought I heard a faint keening wail as the door was obliterated into dust. I descended the cold stone stairs to the buried corridor.

I sent a blast of energy through the dark hall with such a fervor that nothing remained in my way. No darkness. No shadows.

And I knew which dilapidated door I would find him behind. I could feel him there. But just barely. The Crone was right. He was fading.

I pushed open the festering wood and stilled for a moment trying to catch my breath, backlit by the dying burst of energy in the hall. I allowed my eyes to adjust to the darkness of the room.

He had been lying on the bed and sat up the moment I entered. With a pained effort, he swung his legs over the side of the mattress sitting on the edge to face me. Each hand was braced at his sides, holding himself upright.

And I knew this was his room. It probably had been from the very start. So dark. So sorrowful. There was no hope, no Light, to be found anywhere.

My heart shattered.

This was why he wanted to push me away. This was what he wanted to save me from.

The bed was the only piece of furniture within. The mattress was fitted with a black sheet and there was nothing else. No blankets. No pillows. The floor was dirt and the stone walls were crumbling. It was the dark pit where he had buried himself away. Even with free reign of the manor, he clearly did not feel he deserved to leave this place.

A bandage, soaked with blood, was taped to his chest, just over his heart. He still wore his black pants, and although it didn't' show, I knew they too were drenched in his blood. I couldn't understand how he was still alive. A dagger of Light through the heart of any of the Shadows we had ever encountered had killed them immediately.

His eyes were clear of darkness. His lips relaxed. The tightness in his features was gone. In its place was a calm acceptance.

The corners of his mouth were tilted ever so slightly. It was the closest thing to a smile I had seen on him. He believed I was the angel—he did not deserve—come to grant him final peace. Come to grant him death.

And in that moment, I was never more certain of anything in my life.

I ran for him and he caught me. Placing my knees on either side of his thighs and straddling his lap, I took his face in my hands and found his mouth with mine.

He kissed me. He did not wrap his arms around me. They remained at his sides. But he kissed me back.

He gave me everything he had in that kiss. It was a dying man's kiss. If this was to be the end, he would stop holding back. He would allow himself this one thing before leaving this world.

Even though he believed he did not deserve it, he would take what he wanted this one time.

The control, the tight leash he held on his wants and needs, was finally released.

He believed he was damning me—and perhaps he was. But it was I who had sought out the dark. It had been that way from the very start.

He rolled me onto the mattress and petals rained down around us. He looked at me, splayed out beneath him. The calm was replaced by need. By instinct. Even dying, he was a lethal, powerful male who could no longer deny what he wanted.

I had been granted enough chances to flee. I had had my opportunity to leave. He was going to take me now whether I wanted him to or not.

I could probably never convince him that my need matched his own. So I didn't bother to try. I climbed up him, wrapping my arms around his neck, and straddled his lap once again. More petals drifted through the air.

It had to be now. Before anything else could come between us. In another life, if we had had more time, if this wasn't the end . . . I could have moved slowly. But I was done waiting.

I reached through all the petals to rip open his trousers. I shoved my panties to the side and placed myself over him. He let out a hiss at the contact.

I tried to rock down on him, but he was so large, and despite how drenched I had become, I was too tight. He grabbed my hips and pushed me down, forcing me to open for him, to accept him. I let out a moan, just taking the head of his cock.

He tried to shove me down deeper, but I knew I wouldn't be able to take any more. I was pushed to my limit. Yet he demanded it from me. And with a brutal thrust, he encased himself fully. I let out a cry. I was about to come.

He looked at me and it would have been easy to assume it was with rage. He wore that unhinged, maddened expression I knew so well. But we were bound in a way I would have never thought possible. And I knew it was not anger which tightened his features but a fierce possession.

He was claiming me. He was finally admitting that I was his.

He began to thrust into me, over and over again. He was not gentle. He was crazed. His bruising grip on my hips pinned me into place. He plunged into me unable to stop himself, driven by a relentless hunger he had ignored for too long. Rose petals fluttered around us in the dark dismal room.

My lips were parted with each panting breathe I took. My head was tossed back. I reveled in the unbelievable ecstasy I never imagined I'd know. I was lost. Completely awash in what he was doing to me. In how it made me feel. My skin had ignited. I had never been so swollen. So hot. So wet.

He released a hand to hold my chin, forcing me to look at him. I turned my head to suck on his thumb.

He pulled his hand away with a hiss before letting it drop to my neck. He grabbed my hair there and held it back. Opening his mouth, he leaned forward to bite me. Then he sucked at my pulse point and I erupted. I came in a wet rush.

Light glimmered around us. Petals flew through the room. My energy recharged in a swell of power.

As my muscles clenched around him, squeezing him, he gave a roar. I could feel his hot release. He was shattering, breaking apart. We both were. On and on for far too long.

At some point, his head finally collapsed on my shoulder. I ran my hands through his hair, disbelieving I had the chance to be so close to him. I buried my own face in his neck. I breathed him in. The smell of him drove me wild. I rubbed my face over his skin with a featherlight touch.

Then I hitched in a breath. I had finally looked up.

In the small sorrowful room, rose petals drifted and spun through the air, held aloft by currents of energy. Swaths of darkness ebbed and flowed like inky cirrus clouds. And winking among them were tiny fragments of Light.

Zagan sensed my awe and drew his head back to look up. But his gaze held for only a moment. He was not as interested in the beauty and magic floating above us. He was not through with me.

He still throbbed with an aching need, and he pulled back his hips. Feeling the friction of his retreat caused me to moan. I needed him to thrust again, to fill me again. After a torturous pause, he did, but slowly, languidly, drawing out the pleasure, forcing me to wait for it.

Again, another agonizing pump. "I need this dress off of you." It wasn't a command, it was a necessity.

I arched my chest into him. "Zipper. In the back," I breathed.

He reached to free me from the dress, and then gathered it in his hands to slip over my head. He tossed it aside and I shivered as silky petals flitted across my bare skin. Then he tore away the panties which were still encasing my hips.

He pushed me back to lie atop me. My breasts pressed against the hard ridges of his chest. His mouth found mine and the sweeps of his tongue matched the slow thrusts of his hips.

He tormented me. He would bring me to the brink only to back off, to withdraw almost completely, making me desperate to be filled again. And when I thought I could bear no more, he would finally slide into me.

He needed my submission. He needed to master me. And I could only come when he allowed it.

I don't know how much time passed, but what felt like an eternity later, he freed me. And I burst into a million little pieces, tumbling over the edge, taking him with me. He filled me with his hot release, and I squeezed my thighs around him.

We remained in his bed for a long time. There was no satiating him. It was only when the sun inevitably rose outside, that he finally granted me mercy. We could not see its rays buried below the earth as we were, but I could sense its rise.

He lay on his back, and I sprawled across his chest. We finally slept. But just before we did . . . I felt his large strong hand grasp mine.

CHAPTER 27

H E WAS HEALED. I traced the symbol on his chest. The black mark now had a slight glimmer to it. I could feel his energy. It was not only restored, but there was a new element to it. There was now a spark of Light somewhere deep inside that had been stoked.

I had lifted the bandage over his chest to check his wound. It was gone as if it had never been. The three intersecting crescents restored.

I looked above us. While the currents floating through the air had begun to dissipate, a few lazy petals remained as well as some fragments of Light and veils of shadows. I sighed at the peace and rubbed my face against the skin on Zagan's chest.

I felt his large strong hand pet my hair. I rolled on top of him, feeling his erection between my thighs. I nipped at his lip. I was instantly wet and ready for him.

I wanted to talk with him. I needed to. And I would. Just not yet.

Instead of pushing into me, though, he placed his hand on my hips and stilled me. I looked at him with uncertainty. He shook his head.

"No." He said the word quietly.

I was confused. "What's wrong?"

"We can't do this," he told me.

"Last night—"

"I thought last night was the end. I didn't realize..." he searched to put into words what had happened between us. What had happened to him.

I sat up on him. Pinning him with my gaze. "You can't take it back Zagan. You don't get to do that."

He didn't look at me though. His eyes had traveled down to my chest. A look of horror crossed his face.

I looked down myself. Uncertain what was happening. And I saw it there.

It was imperceptible. I probably wouldn't have even noticed it on my own. It was not really something you could see directly. But he knew the symbol all too well, and it had not escaped his view.

A faint gray outline of three intertwined crescents sat above my heart.

He set me onto the bed and scrambled off the mattress, backing away from me. His hair was mussed, and his eyes turned wild.

"Do you see? Do you see what I will do to you?"

I sat on my knees and covered my chest with my discarded dress. I didn't want him to look at the mark which was clearly setting him off.

"Last night—" I began.

"Last night was supposed to be the end," he countered. "You were going to be free from me. I didn't know any of this would happen. I was supposed to die. I thought I would no longer be able to ruin you. To drag you down into the dark."

His fists clenched at his sides and the muscles in his chest and abdomen flexed and bunched with heavy breathing. "What will it take to make you understand? What will it take to drive you away? Have you no self-respect? Look at where you are." He gestured to the dirt floor and crumbling walls. Then he pointed at my chest. "Look at yourself!"

His eyes slitted and his jaw tightened. "All because you have some idea that this is love."

The anger I felt at his words, the hurt, sent a hot fury scorching through my veins. "This!" I flung my hand back and forth between us. "This isn't love! Love is something that can be broken. Something that you can walk away from."

"This," I flung my hand between us again. "This is a curse. The gods have cursed me."

I sat up on my knees, clutching the dress to my body. "And curses are fucking hard to break. They're stronger than love. They last. They don't end. They follow you across this universe and the next.

"I will be cursed by you for eternity. I don't know how or why. But I can *feel* it. And I hate you for it. I hate that I somehow know, without a doubt, that I will want you for the entirety of this immortal life."

I shifted to the edge of the bed, closer to him and my voice dropped. "I know you feel it too Zagan Black. I know that I will always be under your skin. You will always itch for me. There will never be a night when you don't reach for me. Every tick of the clock will drive you closer to the brink of madness."

I stepped onto the floor and looked up at him. I gave a shuddering exhale. "Well maybe it will make you happy knowing I will always be in the same god forsaken hell hole."

I stood there, breathing heavily, pinning him with my gaze. I silently prayed for him to want me. To reach out to me. To hold onto me.

But instead, black veins branched through his eyes. And in a deep, pained whisper, he said, "Go."

I did not run. I did not flee. There was no need to. I was leaving.

If last night wasn't enough to get through to him, nothing would be. He had told me when I first arrived that I couldn't save him. And I realized he had been right.

Zagan had been taken from me long ago, and he wasn't coming back.

I didn't know what was between us. It was something powerful, something impossible to deny. I would be bound to him forever, and I didn't understand why. But perhaps I didn't need to. Perhaps all I needed to understand was that I couldn't reach him.

I decided to stop trying.

I didn't bathe. I wanted to keep the smell of Zagan's skin covering my own for as long as I could. But I did change.

I hung the rose petal dress in the very back of my closet, knowing that I would want it sent along with all my other garments. It would be one of those things. A thing I would never let go of, but a thing which would remain tucked away and hidden. Too painful to revisit.

It was a tad dramatic, but I had chosen to wear the same dress I had worn upon my arrival to the manor. I clasped my cloak and pocketed my dagger. The only other items I carried were some bills and my phone.

I left everything else as it was. I hoped that Maxim would assist me with one final favor and see to it that my things were collected and sent home.

I was going to walk to town, and call Killian there. I would ask him if one of the Angela could retrieve me. If not, I would keep walking until they could.

I knew it was a risk to leave. But I had ventured out safely once before. I believed I could do it again. I doubted The Contessa would simply be waiting for me somewhere. Instead, I suspected she would come for me whenever she had the necessary means.

I couldn't stay at the manor. Not any longer. I also did not want to lead The Contessa back to the Radiant Court. So I would take Killian up on his offer. I would stay at his penthouse while I figured some things out.

I needed to talk with my mother. I had to find out how much she knew about Zagan. How much she knew about this entire situation and what was going on between us.

I descended through the dark silence of the manor for a final time. The air did not stir around me. I did not disturb the shadows which inhabited the place. And I wondered why that was. Perhaps he had been right. Perhaps I was becoming one myself.

I reached the towering doors at the grand entrance. I raised my hand about to push open the door and free myself of the Dark Manor.

Far off power crackled behind me.

I turned.

She stood at the center of the main hall. At the very heart of the manor. Her tattered cowl drawn, backed by the moonlight which poured in from the rear windows.

The Crone's ancient voice broke the silence of the night. "You leave." It was a statement and not a question.

"Yes," I answered.

She folded her hands inside the sleeves of her robe. "Cannot."

"Look, the prince doesn't want me here. And frankly I don't want to be here anymore. I think it would be best for everyone if I just go."

"Cannot," she repeated.

I began to get frustrated. "There's no point in me staying here."

She removed a hand and beckoned me with one long gnarled finger. I took a few steps closer to her. In a barely audible whisper she said, "Needs you."

When I began to protest she held out a hand. There was power in the command and I was silenced. "Must help him. Find the Light. Lost so long ago."

I sucked in a breath. "You know?"

She waved her hand in impatience. "Silly child. Think I a fool? Has a role to play. Destiny to fulfill. Cannot without you."

"Honestly, I don't give a damn about any of it. Find someone else to be his punching bag." I turned from the Crone and headed for the door.

The Crone took a deep wheezing breath, drawing on that far off power, and in a loud voice she called after me. "He's dying." The words rang through the hall, an unwelcome intrusion upon the quiet space, and the shadows lingering there shifted and swayed before settling back down.

I turned around to stare at her. She was a still hunched figure barely visible in the darkness. "He's healed now," I countered.

The whisper of her ancient voice floated through the air. "Not enough," she insisted. "Know you not the tortures he has endured. She of great darkness did everything in her power to snuff the Light of the Halfling. It has been a slow death. Strong he is to have lasted for so long, but the end nears."

"Halfling?" I murmured.

"He is both. Of the Light and the Shadows. The only of his kind. As the ancients were. There is no one more powerful. It is why she wants him. Yet he is weak without the Light. He cannot survive without it. Know you the way of your kind. Know you what you are to him. What he is to you."

"What are you talking about?" I demanded.

She laughed then, an eerie sound, and my skin chilled. "Ah, how they keep their children ignorant." She shuffled towards me. She came right up to me. Still I could see nothing under her cowl.

"Every thousand years. One male. One female. Each for the other. Wove a spell, your council did, into the fabric of your world. Only that male for that female. Only that female for that male. None other will do. None other will spark interest. All others dry sand in mouth."

She began to shuffle away, her voice floating behind her. "You leave, his not the only death. His of the body. Yours of the soul. Desolate, forsaken life without him."

I called after her to wait, but she disappeared into the darkness. I took a few steps after her. It was no use, though. She was gone, having vanished like an apparition.

I didn't know what she spoke of. I wanted to brush it off as senile nonsense, but I knew better—It was the connection we shared.

Yet, her words did not convince me to stay. More than ever, I needed answers. I needed to return to the Radiant Court.

There was nothing I could do here at the manor. I couldn't save someone who didn't want to be saved. And I had already known my life was forsaken. I had realized it down in that dark, empty bedroom.

Although I did wonder with a sad and heartbreaking curiosity what had happened to Zagan. What had he been through . . . Something told me, I didn't truly want to know.

But I had tried. What more could I do? It was time for me to go. I would try another avenue to find a resolution for all that was at stake. I opened the manor door and a bitter gust of wind whipped past me, blowing back my hair and cloak.

Somewhere, an animal bayed.

I dashed down the front drive and made my way straight for the wrought iron gate. I didn't know the command to open it, but as I reached the imposing structure, it began to swing inward.

I turned to survey the Dark Manor and surrounding grounds. On the cliff above the manor stood a figure outlined by the full moon. He had opened the gate for me. I had been granted passage. It was further confirmation that he did not want me here. And I crossed into the tree tunnel.

CHAPTER 28

THEY WERE WAITING FOR ME about halfway through. The reflection of their lifeless eyes made me stop in my tracks. I turned and ran for the gate. I was fast. And I had almost made it back. My arm outstretched for the iron.

But they had a way of moving, of chasing after me, of shedding their physical bodies which hindered them so that they were upon me. I tried to lash out at them with my dagger, but it passed through them. They were not solid.

The dagger turned cold. The Light within extinguished. A chill began to creep up my arm and against all my better instincts, I threw the blade away. The skin over my chest turned so cold, it burned.

I tried to release a bomb blast of energy, I wanted to scorch them with Light. But my power was shoved back down, as though I was forced to swallow it.

I still don't know how they were able to take me. They did not breathe into me and I did not go willingly, but somehow the two Umbra resumed their physical form and dragged me up the cliff that overlooked the manor.

She waited there. In her long black gown and paper white skin. Her crystallized eyes twinkled. I darted my gaze around the cliff. There was no Zagan. I had mistaken The Contessa for him. It was she who had commanded the gate to open and allow me passage.

The Umbra held me in place. I could not break their hold. Behind me was the edge of the cliff. In front of me the terrain sloped down. Zagan appeared at the bottom of the slope. He had known something was wrong.

He saw me, saw the Umbra, and his rage was so great, the earth shook. But before he could act, The Contessa flicked a whip she held. And it encircled his neck. The leather remained wrapped around his throat, and it was clear this was no ordinary whip. It was drenched in dark magic.

As Zagan's hands flew to his neck in an attempt to free himself from the binding, The Contessa launched two consecutive kicks to his knees. Her speed and power were unparalleled. I only knew that was what she had done because Zagan's bones were completely fractured. The anatomy there had been pulverized.

He collapsed to the ground, unable to stand. Yet he remained as upright as possible, kneeling on his shattered knees and trying to break the whip encircling his neck.

While the Umbra held me in place, The Contessa stood next to Zagan. She cradled his head at her waist. As I had been, he seemed unable to lash out at her.

336

"My pet," she purred. "Have you missed me? Tell me you have. I am ever so happy you have come. I was hoping you would."

The whip made it difficult for Zagan to speak. But he fought against the magic of the binding. And with the tendons in his neck straining, he stared at me.

His words were deep. Guttural. Strained. "I will always come for her."

I felt it was an atonement of sorts . . .

To this day, I believe if The Contessa and her Umbra had not been there, Zagan would have wisped into the tree tunnel just before I had reached the end of it—because it had been too late. We had passed the point of no return. I do not suppose he would have physically been able to stop himself from coming after me.

We were now linked, unequivocally, in a way that went beyond our control. And Perhaps I wouldn't have been able to travel any farther than the tree tunnel, myself. Perhaps I would have been forced to turn back. Unable to escape the hold he had on me.

Perhaps the two of us would have remained locked away forever in the large silent manor, full of ghosts and shadows. But maybe there would have been Light too. Maybe little by little, I would have brightened the darkness that consumed his heart.

I would never know.

Because The Contessa and her Umbra had, in fact, come for us. And she took delight in taunting Zagan. She licked his cheek and I shut my eyes, unable to bear the sight of her touching him. "Did you show our guest some of the things I've taught you?"

She eyed me then. "No probably not. She's just a little girl. She would have run from you screaming." She let out a bone chilling laugh. "But *finally*, you have effectuated the *Vinculum*. You have done well. I am pleased. Like a good little pet, you have served your purpose."

Her voice dropped, and The Contessa seemed to hum with anticipation. *"The girl is ready."*

I did not know what the *Vinculum* was, but I had a feeling it had to do with the supernatural connection Zagan and I had to one another. After being together, something had shifted. And for whatever reason, it seemed The Contessa had wanted the bond between us solidified.

I hitched in a breath, realizing it was why she had arranged everything as she had. Why I had been extended the proposal. Why I was to reside at the Dark Manor. It was why she had spelled my dreams. This entire time, she had been pushing us closer and closer.

I swore in that moment—if I ever had the chance again—I would listen to the Crone.

The Contessa skimmed a black nail over Zagan's bare collarbone. And I wanted to claw her eyes out. The possession I felt towards Zagan was unlike anything I could have imagined. A very primal part of my being seethed . . . She should not touch what is mine.

The navy blue of the night sky turned black as roiling dark clouds swept across the sky. A torrent of rain began to pound down on us.

One hand remained on the handle of the whip while The Contessa caressed Zagan's cheek with the other. "I was not very happy with your behavior recently. I think you need to relearn how to obey. And my, how my underlings are excited. They have missed you too."

The Contessa's razor-sharp nails were digging into Zagan's skin leaving behind inky welts. "But now that we're all here, I think it's time to initiate your little princess. Shall we show her what our playthings can do?"

She whipped her head towards the Umbra. "Strip her!" she commanded.

Whatever she was doing to Zagan prevented him from making a sound, but I could see a roar become trapped in his throat. His entire body was shaking, spasming. It seemed as though his body wanted to expand, to grow larger. It also looked like shadows were trying to push their way out from his skin but were trapped. Every raw muscle flexed and bunched with the struggle.

The Umbras' claws slashed through my clothes with no regard for my skin. The shredded cloth fell away leaving me in only the panties I wore. Gashes marred my shoulders, chest, abdomen and thighs. Blood welled at the incisions and began to stream down my body as it mixed with the rain.

The pain of the slashes in my skin was nothing. The true agony was the icy ache of dark evil that permeated my flesh from the Umbras' claws. I shuddered, but I did not scream out. For Zagan's sake I swallowed the wail my soul cried.

However, it was no use. Because of the connection we had, I could not hide my experience from him. He knew the pain I felt, and anguish fell across his beautiful face. A bolt of angry red lightning struck the clearing.

"Take her," the Black Queen instructed. "Do with her as you will. She is your reward." Her eyes were fevered with excitement.

Although her words and stance were those of someone coolly in control, her eyes belied her. She was a shark frenzied by the scent of blood.

At her words, Zagan began to stand on his broken legs through determined will alone. The Contessa yanked on the whip which remained coiled around his neck in an unrelenting hold. Unable to remain upright with the pressure she exerted, he collapsed again to his knees.

Every muscle in his big body swelled and shook with the ferocity of his rage. His tenuous grasp on sanity was slipping, and the violence of his fury was visible as the tendons in his neck stood in stark relief against his skin.

The Contessa made a tsking noise. "Look at what you're doing to my pet, princess." She toed Zagan with her boot. "He's going to be completely broken. I won't get to have any fun with him."

I found my voice. "Please. Please, you can do anything to me, just don't hurt him anymore. Take him away from here and let him be."

The Contessa turned serious, her words a hiss. "Give me your Light. Release it to me."

My head swam from the pain, from the nearness of the Umbra, from the agony of seeing Zagan breaking before my eyes, but somehow the impossibility of what she was asking slammed into me.

How does one person simply hand over their soul, their very self, to another. That was what she wanted. To give her my Light, was not even possible.

Why did she not simply kill me? My Light would be released then. She could have it. Why was she asking it of me? It was not something I could do!

When nothing happened, The Contessa's temper rose. "Take her," she screamed at the Umbra. Then she pointed at me. "If you move, I will have his head."

Again, Zagan fought the magic coiled around him, and a roar shook the night. Bolts of red lightning erupted in a cataclysm of energy.

Tears slid down my cheeks. I was drowning in his emotions. I didn't want this for him. Then and there I vowed I would destroy The Contessa. She could have chosen no greater torture for him. She was breaking him, taking him to a place from which he would never return.

I tried to will my Light free, but nothing happened. "You can have it! It's yours! Just don't do this to him!" I was desperate to free Zagan. I would have given her anything. But I didn't know how to give her what she asked.

She said nothing, and the Umbra dropped the black robes they wore. It was clear that there would be no negotiating. She would accept no promises. Either I released my Light to her, or the Umbra would have their way with me and Zagan would be forced to watch.

I looked away from him. Not wanting him to see the fear in my eyes.

From behind, I felt two icy fingers slip between the lace of my panties and the flesh of my hips. It was a deliberately slow, lascivious act as the Umbra slid the cotton down my thighs. I cringed at the touch, feeling more defiled and filthier than I ever

341

had or ever would. All the while, the one in front of me wrapped my hair around his fist, forcing my face up to him.

I was going to be sick. Again, a scream built in my solar plexus, and again I swallowed it, refusing to make this any worse for Zagan.

When I look back at that moment, I realize that it wouldn't have made a difference had I pierced the night with my cries. Zagan had reached his limit. He made one final attempt, successfully standing and loosening the binding encircling his neck. But The Contessa gave another yank on the whip handle causing him to fall to his knees once more and the binding tightened.

I felt Zagan's emotions hit a mind shattering crescendo before blanking into nothing.

A different kind of fear and panic surged through my veins. It was the kind you experience when you realize . . . *it's too late.*

I searched for Zagan. Sitting there in the muddy earth under a black sky that wept rain, he was lost.

And finally, the binding around his neck dropped. It was no longer needed. Dark shadows engulfed him. His eyes were fully black, and inky glyphs had appeared on his skin. They slithered across his flesh like live tattoos, like an evil lover's caress.

But what completely broke me. What finally made me understand what I had to do, was the defeat I found in his heart.

Up until that point he had fought. He had raged and roared. He had tried to get to me. His large body had been bulging with violence. Now he sagged where he sat, taking in shallow breaths, consumed by darkness and a black heart.

He was lost to me. The Contessa had broken him. *I* had broken him. And he had slipped away from this world.

In losing him, I lost any will I had possessed. The moment he was gone. Destroyed. I stopped trying to fight.

And that was how I did it. I simply let go. I sacrificed my Light, and in doing so, I sacrificed myself.

A silent explosion lit the night. The very earth rocked and shook. Invisible energy pulsed through the clearing in a tsunami of force. The two Umbra about to violate me were sent flying as if struck in the gut. Their dark forms became airborne—arms, legs, and heads flung forward while their midsections hurtled into the sky. The surrounding trees were blown away in concentric rings, like matchsticks being scattered.

All of my Light, my strength, my power, my soul—coursed in a direct pulse towards Zagan. The amount of Light that erupted from him was like that of a nuclear blast. His upper body was lifted from the ground as the power hit his chest. His back bowed.

I was blinded for a moment, my pupils shot. And the shock of raw Light engulfed The Contessa. I could not hear her in the silence—as all sound was being sucked into the vortex of power that was funneling into Zagan—but I knew she screamed in untold agony before she vanished in a swirl of shadows.

It was the end for me. I could not live without my Light. It was my essential self. And I hoped it had been enough to save Zagan. I hoped it had been enough to bring him back.

I closed my eyes and surrendered.

Once the energy transfer was complete, the intense light was extinguished, and blackness tore through the sky once again. There was no moon, no stars. Just the battering rain.

I sagged, collapsing to the ground. From where I lay, I could see that Zagan too had collapsed. The swirling shadows which had surrounded him began to drift my way. I realized that without my Light, they would infect me. I knew I was to die at any moment. I hoped I did before the shadows reached me.

But I was not so lucky. I felt the dark caress of malevolence as the shadows traced over my bare skin. They slid in with such ease. There was no resistance and I became consumed with darkness.

Except . . .

In complete darkness, the tiniest of light is powerful. A single ember does not shine amidst the brilliance of the sun. But in the darkest of nights, it will blaze, setting your world afire.

Somewhere deep inside, a tiny spark flared. There was a pull. The spark was connected to another. This shared energy was a tether that kept me grounded. It kept me from disappearing completely. But I needed more.

On its own, this energy was not enough to ward off the invading shadows. I had to find the source of this Light. The ember was directing me to relief . . . to reprieve.

I clung to the tiny spark with all the will I possessed. The need to tend to the small bit of light was the only direction I could follow.

I picked myself up. And I left Zagan. I left myself there on the cliff . . . to seek salvation.

ANNOTATION

How I ended up at Elijah's cabin, I didn't know. That time was lost to me. The details were something I would learn somewhere down the road.

Besides, the time I spent lost, was not what would matter. Not what would haunt me for the rest of my days . . . It was what came next.

I was about to do things. Things that would hurt others. Unforgivable acts. Cardinal sins.

And I would have to pay. There would be no absolution for me. At least not until I lost everything.

Oh, yes. I still had more to lose. So much more than I ever thought possible.

But that . . . is another story.

For book releases, follow along on Facebook at

TMHartShadowSeries

Or on Instagram at

TMHartAuthor

***

Made in the USA
Middletown, DE
08 August 2020

14755097R00208